QUEEN'S
GAMBIT

QUEEN'S GAMBIT

A Mystery Featuring
MARGARET HARKNESS

BRADLEY
HARPER

SEVENTH
STREET
BOOKS®

To Derek,
There would have been no book two, without book one.
There would have been no book one, without you.

AUTHOR'S NOTE

In Europe, the "first" floor is the first floor above ground level. As the story takes place in Europe, that naming convention will be used throughout.

St. Paul's Cathedral, Main Entrance and Surrounding Area

1. Queen's Carriage   2. Boarding School, Second-Floor Window

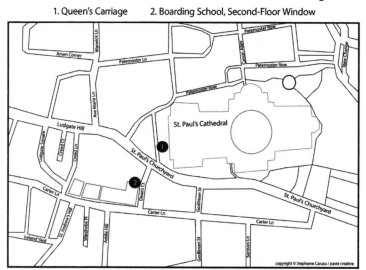

PROLOGUE

St. Petersburg, Russia, Tuesday, March 1, 1881, midafternoon

Viktor shivered in the afternoon sunlight both from the cold and his mounting excitement. Although the sky was cloudless so close to the Arctic Circle the steady north wind prevented the sun's feeble rays from having much effect. The snow was nearly a meter high along the sides of the road as he and Sofia walked up and down the sidewalk beside the Catherine Canal, stomping their feet and huddling deep within their thick woolen coats, as they waited for their chance to change the world.

The three bomb throwers were a hundred meters down the road, doing their best to look purposeful. Sofia had berated one for washing his salami and bread down with wine that morning. He'd shrugged and said if this were his final meal, she should be content he was drinking wine and not vodka.

Suddenly the royal carriage and Cossack bodyguards came rushing toward them, barely giving Sofia enough time to signal the bombers with her raised handkerchief.

The first assassin misjudged the speed of the carriage, and his nitroglycerin bomb fell among the following Cossacks, exploding with a flash which was accompanied by the screams of the wounded horses and men.

Viktor cursed and feared the tsar would escape. The *Narodnaya Volya*, or "People's Will," had tried twice before and it appeared their "propaganda by deed" would fail again.

But at a barked order from inside, the bulletproof carriage slid to a halt. Alexander stepped out wrapped in a thick fur coat. He approached the wounded men to console them while looking about for his attackers. The police chief of St. Petersburg in the following sleigh cried out, "Thank God!" when he saw his monarch emerge unharmed.

Viktor gritted his teeth as their target stood out in the open, unscathed. As he and Sofia drew nearer however, he saw a young boy writhing beside the road, blood staining the front of his clothes, and suddenly Viktor wanted to vomit.

The second assassin raised his hand from within the gathering crowd and cried out, "It is too early to thank God!" and dashed his bomb onto the ground at the tsar's feet. The second explosion knocked Viktor down from forty feet away, and when he rose, he saw the Russian monarch lying upon the packed snow, his entrails splayed between his legs. Viktor's nausea finally overcame him and he knelt retching into a ditch while the guards lifted the shattered man onto a sleigh and sped to the palace. In vain.

Within the hour, Alexander II was dead. Alexander III quickly set about to find his father's killers and crush their organization forever.

In the general confusion, Sofia and Viktor slipped away to her apartment and prepared for the aftermath. "Pack your bag, Viktor, our time is short," Sofia said. "The *Okhrana* will be unleashed like hunting dogs and sent everywhere to find us. Your age will be no defense, so I'm sending you where they cannot find you. We leave in five minutes."

Five minutes was ample time. A simple cloth sack with his spare shirt, pants, a pocketknife, two flannel foot wraps, and his father's pocket watch, and he was done. The watch had been given to his brother Andrei as the oldest son when their father died, but Andrei had given it to Viktor "for safekeeping" when they arrived in St. Petersburg. Now it was his, safe or not.

At the train station, Sofia pressed a thick wad of rubles and a false passport into his hand. Then hugging him fiercely, she gave him a note. "Memorize this name and address, then destroy it and come up with a new name for yourself. If I get captured, I don't want to know it. I have too much to forget already. Now go!"

Sofia disappeared within the crowd, and Viktor looked down at the creased paper and passport in his hand. The passport identified him as Vanna Petkovic and the paper read:

HERR THOMAS VOGEL, 471 INVALIDENSTRASSE, BERLIN. PASSWORD: PARIS

Viktor spoke no German, some English, and a little French, so the name and address were difficult to remember and impossible to pronounce. *Time enough for that later,* he thought.

The pale boy with the quiet gray eyes knew the shortest route to Berlin was through Poland. He also knew this would be common knowledge to the *Okhrana*, should Sofia break, so he bought a train ticket to nearby Helsinki. From there he could book passage on a ferry to Kiel on the north German coast, then a train south to Berlin. He was grateful for his brother's insistence that he learn geography.

Viktor worried about his brother, Andrei, a prisoner of the *Okhrana* for the past week. The fact that the assassins hadn't been arrested before today proved Andrei hadn't broken under interrogation, but now with the tsar dead he would be shown no restraint. Viktor shivered at what this meant, but there was nothing he could do. As much as he loved his brother, he knew the only way he would ever see him again would be if he joined him, first in prison, then on the gallows.

Alone on the train, Viktor looked again at the scrap of paper with the address in Berlin and wondered who or what awaited him there. He watched as his motherland, the *Rodina*, passed by his window while the train bore on for Finland. The next day he would take a boat to Germany and an uncertain future.

Two days later, a thin, exhausted young man approached the address on Invaliden Strasse and the gun shop of Herr Thomas Vogel. When he entered, a young girl with long blonde hair, slightly older than Viktor, was oiling a fowling piece with a rich mahogany stock and Damascus steel barrels. When she asked if she could help him, he could only say her father's name, and "*bitte.*" Puzzled, she motioned for him to wait. When she brought her father out from his lathe in the back room, he asked "*Ja? Was darf es sein?*" Viktor had no idea what he was being asked, but looked down at his feet and mumbled, "Paris."

Herr Vogel pursed his lips for a moment. "Astrid, make him a bed in the loft over the workshop. He will be my new apprentice."

Astrid threw back her hair and gave the young man another look. Thin, almost to the point of starvation, he had nevertheless been growing briskly the past year given the wrists and ankles protruding from his clothes. His hands were not rough. A student. Or he had been.

She was about to turn and lead him to the loft when his eyes rose, and the cool grayness of them caused her heart to pause. She imagined the color of the winter sky just before the snow fell, yet his gaze warmed her in ways she had never felt before. His eyelashes were a thick brown, the contrast making his eyes glimmer deep underneath. Astrid led him to his new home and found it difficult to sleep that night, imagining those eyes shining by candlelight in the workshop next door.

Herr Vogel took no notice of this. He could calculate the trajectory of a bullet at two hundred meters; the arc of Cupid's arrow was invisible to him.

That night, Viktor tried to warm himself beneath the thin quilt Frau Hilda Vogel had grudgingly given him. He thought of the golden-haired young woman who had led him upstairs. "I must learn German quickly," he vowed, "if I am to talk to her."

By the time he awoke the next morning, Sofia and Andrei were reunited in prison. Viktor's name was mentioned briefly in their rough interrogation, but in the rush to placate an impatient new tsar with their execution, it was soon forgotten. Sofia was the first woman hanged in Russia in living memory.

From that morning forward, young Viktor Zhelyabov was also no more. He'd written down the name of the captain of the ferry to Kiel and so became Herman Ott. At least he could pronounce it.

1

Buckingham Palace, London, Wednesday, March 10, 1897

The chamberlain was as starched as his collar. "I beg your pardon, madam, but I do not see your name on Her Majesty's calendar. Perhaps you were scheduled for a different day?" His raised eyebrow implied how unlikely he thought the possibility.

I knew that getting an interview with the queen was a long shot at best, but when your funds can only half-fill one sock, it is time to embrace long odds.

"No, sir, I do not have an appointment for today, nor any other day, but was hoping you could give me a time in the near future when Her Majesty and I might speak."

"I see." The eyebrow descended regally to its original height while the nose elevated, a minor act of facial acrobatics I could not help but admire.

"I'm sorry, Miss Harkness, but Her Majesty has no time for an interview today, or any day in the foreseeable future. Please, be on your way."

I gritted my teeth. I had known that being shown the door was the most likely outcome, but the man's air of superiority left a sour taste in my mouth. "Very well, sir," I managed to say without snarling. I presented my card in a final act of supplication. "Should Her Majesty's schedule have an unexpected opening, please reconsider my request."

I doubt the man would have accepted the card had he not been wearing gloves, and I feared it would soon find itself in the nearest dustbin, but life is marked by unexpected strokes of good fortune. The cost of a single card would be worth the wager he'd pass it on.

I heard a voice summoning the man from inside the queen's parlor as I left, and I was nearly at the bottom of the stairs outside the palace when his wheezing voice called out to me.

"Miss Harkness! Please, a moment."

If I'd told the man I saw perspiration on his brow, I believe he would have died of embarrassment. He cleared his throat as he struggled to catch his breath and fleeing dignity, then straightened to pronounce, in his most stentorian tones, "Her Majesty will see you now."

I curtsied. I couldn't help myself, and my smile must have made his collar feel even tighter.

"Thank you," I managed to say without laughing. Apparently, he'd overstepped his bounds and was being taught a lesson by his mistress—to my benefit.

"This way, miss."

I walked meekly behind, my palms suddenly clammy. *Be careful what you wish for*, I thought. It was well known that the queen did not suffer fools lightly, if at all. I was about to bandy words with the ruler of an empire spanning half the globe, and I remembered advice given to me as a student in a school production: "Remember your lines, and don't bump into the furniture." Not a deep philosophy perhaps, but it would serve for the moment.

Her Majesty was dressed all in black, the only color she'd worn since the death of her beloved Albert decades ago. I'd never been in the presence of royalty so I curtsied in front of the small woman seated before me, and hoped I'd gotten it right.

"Your Majesty. Thank you for seeing me."

The queen inclined her head and continued to pet the Pomeranian in her lap.

"Tea," she said, not glancing at the chamberlain.

"Yes, Your Majesty," he said. Now back on *terra cognita*, the chamberlain's face was the mask of a loyal servant, yet I had no doubt he'd have poisoned my drink if possible.

Her Majesty indicated a small side table nearby with a chair for me to occupy, and the chamberlain served us each a cup of steaming tea. Once the formalities of tea had been addressed, she sent the man away with instructions: "We should like a short repose before the afternoon's appointments, but see to it we are not disturbed until half-past the hour."

The man bowed, glanced sidelong at me, then turned on his heel and left, softly closing the door.

The corners of Her Majesty's mouth briefly hinted a smile before she turned to me again. "Normally we are not disposed to meet with journalists, even less so with women who enter the male workplace, but we felt the young man required a reminder as to whom he served, and his role in our household." The corners twitched again. "You have twenty minutes."

I started our brief interview with what I thought was a benign topic. "Thank you, Your Majesty. I understand you were a devoted reader of the Sherlock Holmes stories in *The Strand*."

Her regal nose sniffed as she raised her teacup to her lips. "We were quite fond of the stories. Mister Holmes is the exemplar of British chivalry, and we were most displeased at Doctor Doyle's wanton murder of him at the Reichenbach Falls. You may quote me directly and, should you chance upon the man, please implore him to resurrect dear Mister Holmes for his sovereign. As the years pass, much we once had is taken from us. The tales of Holmes's escapades were one of our few remaining pleasures. Now he has cruelly deprived us and his legions of readers of this literary treasure."

She held her cup as though to warm her hands. "As you are a writer yourself, is it possible you know the man?"

I hesitated. I recalled a warm embrace in the fog, nine years before. The memory passed as quickly as it came. "Yes, Your Majesty, though I've not seen him in some time. We do not frequent the same social circles."

She fixed me with her dark, expressive eyes. "Then tell him—tell the world, if you like—that he has greatly disappointed his monarch." Her teacup rattled slightly as she replaced it into the saucer and sighed. "It would please us greatly if this interview could affect the resurrection of the noble Sherlock Holmes, but we tire. We wish you a good afternoon."

The aged queen rang a bell and the chamberlain, who must have been listening outside, entered with a lap blanket for Her Majesty. He gently lifted the Pomeranian, who scarcely stirred, and after arranging both the blanket and the dog as she wished, he led me out as she prepared to nap.

"Good day, Miss Harkness," he said with great precision once the door was closed and we were out of earshot of his mistress. "Don't come back."

I smiled. I could ill-afford making an enemy of the man, but I replied before thinking, "That's not for you to decide, though I'm happy to profit any time you forget yourself."

I curtsied in farewell, he sniffed, and we parted ways.

I was so pleased with how the interview had gone that I indulged in a meal in a café. "Table for one," I told the waiter. He nodded and took me to a small table in the corner by the kitchen. *They always try to put me out of sight*. I sighed. *I suppose so as not to scare away the other customers.*

I gritted my teeth at the clatter of crockery and tableware being removed from the opposite side. The glare of the freshly bared tablecloth hurt my eyes. *Might as well post a sign*, I thought. *Single woman. Beware!*

The empty space across the table was, if not an old friend, at least an acquaintance of long standing.

My name is Margaret Harkness, and like most people worth knowing, I am a person of many parts. First of all, I am a woman in a man's world. Everything I have gained or have accomplished in my life has, with rare exception, been without male assistance, and often despite their resistance. I am also a suffragette. Women will only be taken as equals by the men in power when we can vote them out of office or, to their ultimate horror, replace them.

I am a writer, but a writer without a story is as useless as a singer without a song.

I am also a Christian Socialist. I see it as my calling, my song if you will, to rip away the veil of ignorance the well-to-do maintain regarding the poorest of society. My political views have estranged me from my family, and my need to pursue my own career once cost me an engagement. My books and other works must be my legacy, my "children," as romance and marriage are now dreams long buried.

My books have a limited following however, and I supplement my income with freelance journalism. The male editors of the major papers are reluctant to publish works from a woman writer, so I have often found it necessary to swallow my pride and adopt the *nom de plume* of John Law.

As I approached this my fortieth year, I noticed my strength failing. After visiting various consultants, I have been diagnosed with something resembling lupus. The exact diagnosis was a matter of academic conjecture, but as there is no effective treatment for any form of the malady, it really doesn't matter what it's called. Lupus will serve. My joints stiffen, I tire more easily, and I find it necessary to stretch every morning to remain mobile.

None of the pipe-smoking doctors I visited would promise a cure, but one suggested moving to a warmer climate might slow the progression of my condition. Therefore, I was now doing all I could to acquire funds for emigration to Australia. I'd done a brief stint there in 1891 as a foreign correspondent for the *Pall Mall Gazette*, and I knew from my contacts that newspapers were having a difficult time retaining journalists. It seemed that as soon as a reporter arrived in the goldfields, he forsook the typewriter for a pick and shovel in hopes of making his fortune.

Women have fewer restraints in the less-structured societies of mining communities, so I should have little difficulty finding employment. As I struggled to scrape together the funds for my passage, I regretted more than once that we were no longer exiling prisoners there. Sadly, a simple robbery would no longer purchase me a one-way voyage to that far-off land, though I suppose I'd soon find the darbies on my wrists a nuisance.

My interview with the queen was of no great import, but despite its brevity I was certain I could sell it to any of the major London papers. Her Majesty's opinion regarding my friend Doctor Doyle was widespread throughout the British Empire and he had already suffered much public scorn for the death of his consulting detective in a dramatic struggle at the Reichenbach Falls. He could surely withstand a little more—though it is perhaps fortunate for Mister Holmes's creator that the British monarch can no longer order a man's execution by royal decree.

I had faced grave danger together with Doyle and Professor Joseph Bell—Doyle's inspiration for Holmes—as what we laughingly called "The Three Musketeers." In 1888, some nine years ago, we hunted Jack the Ripper, only to discover he considered me his rightful prey. But that is a tale for another time. Suffice to say that, although we have gone our separate ways, we maintain a warmth and affection common among veterans of any shared danger. Only Bell and myself dare call our fellow Musketeer by the *nom de guerre* Bell bestowed upon him, "Porthos."

2

I t was a cool but sunny spring day, perfect for a picnic. Herman and Astrid, now married seven years, walked along the Spree River near the workshop, a basket of food and bottle of Riesling under Herman's arm. They found a spot beneath a tree along the river and Astrid laid a faded quilt upon the ground. Herman helped her sit, for her swollen belly showed the two would soon become three. Frau Vogel had never warmed to Herman until Astrid became pregnant. Now Herman's mother-in-law would sing in the kitchen as she prepared their dinner, careful to ensure her daughter was never hungry, and even gave Herman an extra helping of strudel with a smile.

"I love the cherry trees, Herman, don't you?" Astrid asked. "One of Father's favorite songs is about them. He used to sing it to me when I was little. He has a nice voice, if you can believe it. Odd as it seems, he was a choirboy before he became an anarchist."

Astrid began to sing a slow, sad song in French. Her voice was sweet and soft, and Herman lay down and closed his eyes to listen better. Feeling a light breeze, the sound of the river flowing, the smell of damp earth and the cherry blossoms landing softly on the two of them, he inhaled his wife's voice and at that moment was possibly the happiest man in Berlin.

Herman asked, "I've heard you sing it before. It's so lovely, yet sad. *'Le Temps des Cerises'* . . . 'the time of Cherries'?"

"Yes. It's from the Paris Commune of the Spring of 1871. For ten weeks, the city of Paris was ruled by the people. All adult men and women had the vote. Women were paid the same for their labor as men. There was no death penalty and total separation of church from state. It was a dream. The common man and woman were equal to any aristocrat before the law, except of course, all the aristocrats fled. The government of France collapsed at the end of the Franco-Prussian War, but the people of Paris refused to surrender."

"The aristocrats would never allow that to stand!"

"No, my love. The royals across Europe were so afraid these ideas would spread that the Prussian and French Armies, having just concluded a war, cooperated in the defeat of the Commune. The Prussians blockaded the eastern side while the French Army came from the West. It took one week, *la semaine sanglante*, 'the bloody week,' to take the city. That is our heritage as anarchists, Herman. And I will sing '*Le Temps des Cerises*' to our child, in hopes that the dream that all become equal before the law will someday become a reality."

She slowly sang the song again, stopping to translate from time to time. "*Les belles auront la folie en tête, et les amoureux du soleil au coeur.*"

"'The girls will have folly in their head,'" she said, "'and the lovers have sunshine in their heart.' I'll translate the rest another time. It's quite a bit sadder, and I don't want to spoil this beautiful day."

After their lunch, Herman gently laid his head on Astrid's expanding stomach and dozed while she rested against a tree and read a book by one of her favorite authors, an Englishwoman named Margaret Harkness.

Herr Vogel had insisted on Herman learning English so that he could deal with their wealthy British customers. Astrid would share her favorite passages with Herman when things were slow and he worked adjusting the firing mechanism of a rifle. She could never get Herman to read much besides the occasional dime novel, though. He was very fond of American Westerns and Mark Twain, though he had been well schooled before fleeing Russia.

Herman was an apt gunsmith and Herr Vogel was hopeful to pass the business on to him, but Herman never forgot the image of the young boy bleeding in the street, nor of the tsar's entrails splayed between his legs. He was a more than competent marksman, and sometimes his father-in-law would take him to a range outside Berlin to demonstrate a hunting rifle to a potential client. Herman enjoyed the concentration, the inner stillness required for a long-range shot, and so long as the targets were paper it was nothing more than an exercise in meditation. He would begin to breathe slowly and deeply and soon entered a state of total calm as finger and trigger became one.

But Herman saw himself as a man of the future. One of the shop's biggest customers, Herr Herbst, was an electrical engineer and he hired Herman for an apprentice program. Soon Herman was busy stringing cables and installing lights in the nearby Reichstag and other government offices. He would still work in the gun shop evenings and weekends, but as he helped to banish the darkness of night, his hours grew. Astrid grumbled over his long days, especially as the time for her confinement drew near, and Herman persuaded Herr Herbst to allow him to leave work for the child's delivery.

Herr Vogel meanwhile met regularly with "fellow travelers" among the anarchist community. Bismarck's socialist reforms during his time as *Reichskanzler* had kept their activity to a low simmer, but they kept in close contact with their busier comrades in Paris and Geneva. One evening, Herr Vogel called Herman to the shop after he came home from work.

"I have something to show you, my boy, something I'm very proud of. I'd like you to test-fire it for me this Sunday."

He produced a leather case much like that for a small trombone. Herr Vogel brought out three pieces reverently: When assembled, there was a barrel, a tubular magazine, and a hollow metal flask with a threaded brass nipple. The flask attached to the assembled magazine and barrel to form the butt. The case held two more flasks and a slender metal rod of unclear purpose, which attached to the underside of the barrel.

"What manner of rifle is this, Herr Vogel?"

"Ah, Herman, this is *Mein Meisterstück*! The finest weapon I've ever crafted. It is a long-range air rifle. I am not sure, but I believe it would be effective up to two hundred meters"—he slapped Herman on the shoulder—"in the hands of a skilled marksman. We must test it this weekend. I made this at the request of someone high up in our circles. I do not know its intended use, but if it's aimed at a crown, I wouldn't mind."

Herman marveled at the workmanship but wondered why the most beautiful devices men crafted through the ages had almost always been weapons. He admired it, as one would a cobra swaying before the charmer, but he did not love it as Herr Vogel did. It was a tool. A tool he had no use for.

"Very well, Father. We'll see what your device can do this weekend."

"Device? My son, you wound me! This is a weapon worthy of heroes. Of liberators. Yes! That's what I'll name it. *Liberator!*"

The following Sunday, April eleventh, Herman and Herr Vogel brought their wives along to *der Jägerverein*, the Hunters Club outside Berlin. It was a mild summer day and the ladies packed their picnic basket with a goodly measure of pickles, cheese, and *Wurst*. Herr Vogel lacked the wealth to be a member of the club, but he was allowed the use of the range whenever he wanted as he had several clients among its well-to-do members. *Befreier* (that is, *Liberator*) was tucked into her traveling case as the two men advanced to the firing line while the ladies sat on benches ten meters back, beneath the trees.

Herman found the pieces fit together snugly. It took about twenty seconds to thread the flask into place. A soldier in combat would find it slow to reload, but this was a weapon for hunters. Or snipers.

The small tubular magazine ran along the right side of the barrel and, reaching into a leather pouch, the gunsmith fed twenty .44 caliber lead balls down the tube until it was full. "The flask, when fully charged, is sufficient for one entire magazine. You will need a fresh one every time you reload."

"How do I recharge it?"

"*Ach*, here . . ." Vogel pointed to the metal rod attached beneath the barrel. Pulling it out, he attached the base to a spare flask and explained the rod was a pump. "Given its small size, it takes fifteen-hundred strokes to fully charge a flask."

"Fifteen-hundred? That's insane!"

"I have a larger pump in the shop. This would only be used in the field in an emergency. You shouldn't ever need to use it. Now let me shoot once to show you how to operate it."

"I know how to fire a rifle, Father."

Herr Vogel patted his son-in-law on the shoulder. "Yes, you do, which is why you're here. But the loading of this rifle is unlike anything you've ever seen before."

The gunsmith set up paper bull's-eye targets at fifty-meter intervals, up to two hundred meters, then returned to the firing line and aimed the rifle at the nearest target, his left foot forward. Lifting his left thumb, he said, "Observe."

He pressed a slim metal strut with the heel of his left hand, sliding a small block in the breech to the right while lifting the rifle barrel slightly. Herman heard the balls rattle as one fell into the cup of the block. When Herr Vogel released the strut, the block slid silently back into the breech: The rifle was loaded.

"Just remember to lift the barrel slightly when you reload. A minor incline is sufficient."

Herr Vogel fired, the discharge a hollow *thunk*. Not silent, but instead of the sharp crack of a gunpowder-fueled discharge, it was softer and of longer duration, spreading the sound out perhaps twice as long. Herr Ott lowered the weapon and smiled in satisfaction when he saw he'd hit the target dead-center.

Turning to Herman, he handed him the rifle. "Your turn." He stood behind Herman and set up his spotting glass. "Reload, and let's begin."

The rifle was well-balanced, though the round shape of the flask kept it from settling comfortably onto the shoulder. Indeed, the flask, the source of the propellant, was the weapon's Achilles' heel. If roughly treated the neck could rupture where it threaded into the firing chamber. This deadly apparatus would have to be handled as gently as a baby.

After tilting the barrel and reloading, he laid down and got into firing position, resting the barrel on sandbags. He began his breathing routine, aligning the sights. As he inhaled, the sights would rise; as he exhaled, they would lower once more. He let his breath out slowly, and as the sights approached the bull's-eye, he gently squeezed the trigger. It fired with a soft cough. Too soon. The bullet hole was ten centimeters too high.

"The trigger pull is very delicate," Herman said.

"*Ach,* I should have warned you. This has no firing pin, merely a valve that releases the compressed air into the firing chamber. Do not squeeze the trigger until you are ready to fire."

The next three shots were dead-center and within three centimeters of one another. At one hundred meters, his shot group was still a respectable five centimeters.

Herr Vogel then produced a telescopic sight and deftly screwed it into place.

After some adjustment, Herman was hitting the target dead-center once more, now with a three-centimeter variance.

"The barrel isn't even warm!" Herman marveled.

"No messy explosions," Herr Vogel said with pride. "No smoke, no flash, and very little sound. A sniper would be difficult to find. *Befreier* is truly worthy of her name."

At one hundred and fifty meters, the holes in the target were still within five centimeters of one another, but at two hundred meters the distance ballooned to twelve.

Herr Vogel clucked his tongue. "Tight enough for a shot to the chest, but as the accuracy wanes its penetrative power would also. I think we have what we came for. Hilda will be quite cross with me if we spend the entire afternoon playing with this beautiful lady while ignoring her and Astrid."

After disassembling the weapon and stowing it back in its case, Herman dusted off his hands. "Your *Liberator* has a soft voice, Father."

"Sometimes, Herman, if you want people to listen, you must whisper."

3

The labor was long and difficult, but little Immanuel (named after the German philosopher, Immanuel Kant) was, if one could judge by the volume of his screams, quite healthy.

To celebrate, Herr Vogel took Herman to a local *Kneipe* for a round of drinks and a meal. "I have someone I'd like to introduce you to," Herr Vogel said. "He has been anxious to meet you, but with you so preoccupied with Astrid I knew it wasn't the time. Now, if you'll indulge me, he has a proposition for you."

"I can think of no one anxious to meet with me unless I owe them money," Herman said. His good mood at Astrid and the child doing so well was replaced with suspicion. He knew this must have something to do with the cause his father-in-law never stopped talking about; even though Herman had made it clear his days as a revolutionary were over.

"Not to worry, Herman. If anything, you may make some money out of this. I promise you it does not involve guns or bombs, but I should let him explain. Here he comes now. Herr Grüber! Here, *bitte!*"

Herr Grüber was the best dressed socialist Herman had ever seen. His dark green wool suit and red tie were easily the most expensive clothes in the place. Despite his wealthy attire, Herr Grüber jostled among the crowd of working men comfortably, with a slight waddling gait that reminded Herman of a duck. He smiled at Herr Vogel's invitation, motioned to the red-faced waitress to bring him a beer, then settled into the chair across from the other two men.

"So, Herr Vogel, this is our young electrician. The bringer of light into darkness." Turning toward Herman, Grüber said, "I trust you are aware of the story of Prometheus? His reward for similar work was not so generous. Hopefully, I can do better for you."

Herr Karl Grüber was stout—not surprising given the easy way he drained half of his one-liter stein in a single steady go. Though still wary, Herman could not help but warm to the easy way the man had of talking to those beneath him in society. This was a man who was comfortable with anyone because he was comfortable with himself.

Herman said, "Good day, sir. May I ask why you wanted to speak to me? Do you need some electrical work done?"

Herr Grüber smiled at Herman, and when he did his entire face joined in. "Work? Definitely! Electricity is involved, but not in the way you think. I have recently been hired to emplace telephones within the Reichstag and other major government buildings in Berlin. Men with your experience are hard to come by, and I want to hire you to install and maintain my telephonic devices."

Grüber's eyebrows rose in unison with the corners of his mouth as he added, "At a substantial increase from your current salary."

"And how would you know what my current salary is, Herr Grüber?"

"I don't, and it doesn't matter. I can use you as soon as you can honorably leave your current employer. Is one week enough time?"

Herr Vogel coughed politely. "And the other matter, Herr Grüber?"

Grüber's smile did not fade, though his generous eyebrows knitted together, "We will discuss that at another place and time, if your son-in-law is as clever and loyal to the cause as you say."

Herman frowned as he cut a thin slice of dried sausage with the care of a surgeon in the operating theater. "With a growing family an increase in my pay would be welcome, sir, but I'd like to know what other uses you have in mind for me before I say yes. Herr Vogel knows my feelings on spilling blood. I am no butcher."

"Be at ease, my friend. I want grease on your hands, not blood. I will not go into details here, but to suffice for the moment I will say that a word, once spoken, may travel many places. Are we agreed?"

Herman put down the knife, stood, and extended his hand. "Then we have an agreement. I will report to you in one week. Where can I find you?"

Herr Grüber's hand grasped Herman's before presenting his business card. Herman gulped down the rest of his sausage before speeding home, anxious to tell Astrid the good news. Herr Grüber's insistence on paying for their meal only reinforcing his good mood.

4

Office of the German Reichskanzler, Berlin, Friday, May 21

Chlodwig Carl Viktor, Prince of Hohenlohe, Prime Minister of Prussia and Chancellor of Germany, was glaring. The two men sitting opposite him at the small table looked down at their hands, trying their best to avoid the heat of the chancellor's gaze.

"Explain to me, gentlemen," he said, his slow, exact speech mimicking the tone one would use with a dull child, "how our agents can plan an operation for months, only to find the nest of traitors empty? Three times now we have had good intelligence on the location of these anarchists, only to find they have slipped the net. Is there a spy in our midst?"

Oberst (Colonel) Adler, the head of the Security Service, twisted his hat in his hand. He looked out the window at a passing bird before he replied, "I've studied the logs of all who were present for meetings concerning the operations, and the only person involved in every case was"—he looked down, twisting his hat more viciously—"me."

The chancellor snorted. "Then you are either the worst double spy in history, or the cleverest, to hide yourself in plain sight. What other explanation is there?"

Adler spread his hands before him. "I have none, *mein Herr*. Coincidence is most unlikely. Somehow, they are getting intelligence from my office but are too clumsy to hide that fact effectively."

Herr Schork, the chancellor's private secretary, had kept silent until now. He cleared his throat. The two older gentlemen looked at him as though the furniture had just spoken. "Gentlemen, I have a proposal, if I may."

His superior looked down his nose but nodded. "Very well. A new idea would be welcome."

"I think we need someone from outside to look for our spy. Someone who would not be known within our usual circles and could be discrete."

"But also someone we could trust!" Adler added. "Where could you find such a person?"

The chancellor interrupted, "Herr Oberst, since you are a suspect, I request you leave the room before Schork and I continue this conversation. If you know the identity of our 'consultant,' the findings would be suspect if you are cleared."

Adler's jaw tightened as he glared at Schork, then he rose and left the room as quickly as his dignity allowed.

Once the breeze from the security chief's departure subsided, the chancellor looked at Schork with a new respect. "You know of course, once this matter is settled it is unlikely you can ever work with Adler again? Not to worry. If you can resolve this matter to my satisfaction, you will find yourself promoted. Of course, if you do not, you will have made a bitter enemy of Adler with no profit to show for it. Now, the name of this remarkable individual?"

Schork swallowed at the implication of the chancellor's words, then said, "You are aware I believe, of the fictional character, Sherlock Holmes?"

The prince of Hohenlohe slammed the table before replying, "You want to employ a make-believe detective?"

"N-No, sir!" Schork stuttered. "But the man who inspired the character is very real. He has helped the police in more than one case. I suggest we call in Professor Joseph Bell, the real Sherlock Holmes!"

5

I groaned as I arose. It takes me fifteen minutes of stretching every morning to work the stiffness out of my joints. I can still walk normally, and I've been told to stay active to maintain mobility as long as possible. The doctors said although each case of lupus was different, the one thing they had in common was progression. Despite the sale of my interview with the queen, the cheapest passage to Australia was still out of my reach. I needed one more well-paying piece before I could be on my way.

After a meager breakfast, I checked the mailbox and smiled when I saw a letter with a return address from Edinburgh. Professor Joseph Bell was a good friend but an infrequent correspondent.

Dear Margaret,

I just had an interesting conversation with the German consul here in Edinburgh. I have agreed to assist the German government on a sensitive matter, under the condition I be allowed to choose my translator and be recompensed both monetarily and to serve as a visiting professor of surgery at the medical school in Heidelberg.

I recall your familiarity with the language, and as I desire someone I know and trust at my side, I offer you the post. Given the urgency of the request, I expect our fee will be generous.

Although I do not expect this undertaking to be dangerous, having someone with me who has proven herself stalwart in a tight situation will be reassuring if I am proven wrong. Please respond by telegram within two days of receiving this letter. If you agree, I will respond in like manner to arrange our travel.

Given recent ill feelings between Germany and our native land concerning the Transvaal, I feel it prudent to inform our government of this undertaking prior to our travel to Berlin. As many in the House of Commons are advocating for war to ensure the rights of British citizens there, it is imperative we not be perceived as foreign agents. Therefore, I will make a brief stop in London en route, and we can meet at the Marlboro Club as we did in times past.

While it would be grand to have Doyle join us on this escapade, I fear he is too well known to escape notice, and too busy with his writing to allow the Three Musketeers to share another adventure.

I await your response at your earliest convenience.

JB

My mind was flooded with the memories of the other two Musketeers his letter recalled, and of Molly, my roommate and companion when I'd first met Doyle and Bell. Molly's life was saved by Bell's generosity and surgical skill from a fatal case of Phossy Jaw, and afterward I was able to place her into domestic service as a cook. She departed with our terrier, Johnny, as neither could bear to be parted from the other.

I shook my head to clear away the fog of bittersweet memories. No, it appeared our little band would never again face danger together. Still, to share even a small foray with my old friend would be a blessing. I glanced at the sailing schedules I kept beside my desk. Perhaps this would make my immigration to Australia possible.

I opened my dog-eared notebook and, after a moment's reflection, wrote my reply by telegram as requested:

AGREED STOP WHEN STOP MARGARET

No need to be long-winded, at least not until someone else was paying.

6

London, Thursday, May 27

The elderly man at the reception desk nodded his welcome to the modestly dressed, slender gentlemen before him. I hoped my clear pince-nez glasses and slight build gave me the appearance of a clerk or academic.

"Welcome to the Marlboro Club, sir," he said.

"Is Professor Joseph Bell in? He's expecting me."

"Who may I say is calling?"

"Pennyworth. Robert Pennyworth."

"I believe he's in the reading room. Shall I conduct you?"

"No, thank you. I've been here before."

Professor Bell had aged well since I had last seen him nine years ago. His forehead was a bit more pronounced, but he was trim, and his eyes had the same flash when he looked up from his reading. His smile was as warm as ever. "Ah, Mister Pennyworth. So good of you to stop by. The glasses are a new addition."

"Yes," I replied, returning his smile. "I can no longer pass as a young man, so the glasses make me look like a bookish gentleman well into his career. The glint of the lenses also makes people glance away, so that they pay less attention to my face. But to business. Who are we seeing before traveling to Germany?"

"We have an appointment at one o'clock this afternoon with Inspector James Ethington of the Special Branch of Scotland Yard. Special Branch is responsible for counterespionage within Britain, and since this affair concerns a foreign power, I felt it best to speak with someone from his agency, so that we do not become suspect of being foreign operatives ourselves. His superiors arranged for a brief conversation today, with the understanding we'll render a full report upon our—by which, I mean your—return, for I shall go on to Heidelberg once we have completed our work in Berlin. Is that agreeable?"

"Quite. Have you arranged our fee, or is that yet to be determined? I have plans for that payment, if it's as generous as you suppose."

"Twenty pounds a day for a minimum of ten days. Each. I was quite insistent on that point. If we accomplish our task sooner, we still receive payment for the entire time. All expenses paid. I have fifty pounds for you now as a retainer."

I gave a low whistle. "Then let's meet with this Inspector Ethington and be on our way!"

Bell laughed, "I've already purchased our tickets for the train to Dover and on to Berlin for Sunday the thirtieth. Why don't you join me for lunch here at the club, after we have our chat with the inspector?"

"I hope the beef Wellington isn't as rare as before," I teased, recalling when Bell, Doyle, and I had met there last after concluding our hunt for the Ripper. "Though the company more than made up for it."

Inspector Ethington arrived fifteen minutes late. He appeared to be in his mid-forties, based upon the distinguished silver edges to his light brown hair. He had a sad smile and kind brown eyes with the fine lines at the corners which reflected a familiarity with hardship. I admired his trim figure and erect posture as he strode into the room. I have always been attracted to confident men, at least when I felt their confidence was merited, and despite his tardiness I was favorably impressed until I smelled a trace of whiskey on his breath. I kept a straight face but began to wonder what made Special Branch so "Special."

"I was sent round to learn the nature of your business with the German government," Ethington said, carefully removing his hat and holding it in his lap. "Please be brief, gentlemen, I'm a busy man. Which one of you is Professor Bell?"

I colored at the question, embarrassed for the inspector that he should ask such an obvious question, but Bell merely nodded. "I am. It was I who informed your superiors of our contract. I hope to keep this all above board and not be accused of doing anything that might harm Her Majesty's government."

"Understood, Professor. We're not always on the best of terms with the Kaiser but we do cooperate with the Germans on matters of mutual interest. Nonetheless, I expect a full report when you return, but you haven't specified the nature of your assistance."

"I was told the sensitive nature of the task required I not be fully briefed until our arrival. I was given assurances this undertaking in no way compromises British interests. Should I suspect otherwise at any time, I'll terminate our arrangement and inform you."

Ethington nodded. "Quite satisfactory, Professor. I look forward to reading your report. There's not much we know about our German counterparts, not even names of their key personnel. Anything you can tell us will be useful."

Then turning his eye to me he said, "But you haven't introduced your companion. Who might you be, sir, and what's your role in all this?"

"Robert Pennyworth, Inspector," I answered. "I'll be the professor's translator. We've worked together before, and I look forward to doing so again."

Bell and I had a difficult time suppressing a laugh when Ethington narrowed his eyes. "I suspect there's more to you than meets the eye, Mister Pennyworth, but I lack the time at present to inquire further." Handing each of us his card, he finished with, "Contact me when you get back. That's all for now."

With that, the inspector carefully stood and went off on his unspecified, yet urgent business which I suspected involved a certain brown liquid.

"If that is London's finest, things have certainly gone downhill since Inspector Abberline retired," I said.

"He is in great pain, Margaret. While I do not condone his treatment, I empathize with his attempts to maintain his dignity."

"Walking in reeking of the bottle? How is that dignified?"

"I think that's a bit harsh. Describe him to me."

"Average height. Light brown eyes and hair. Slender and soft-spoken. No tremors, though he walked with the care you see in drunkards who try to pass for sober."

"Correct so far. And his clothes? What of them?"

"Light gray tweed suit. Black four-in-hand tie. Black brogans."

"And their condition?"

"His shoes were polished, the suit pressed."

"Yes, and his shirt was ironed and his black derby, though now faded from years of use, was carefully maintained. Did you notice how carefully he held it? It's of fine make, and I suspect his name is embroidered inside to denote pride of ownership."

"What of it?" I asked. "I've seen too well how drunkenness can wreak a man's life, and his family's."

"These outward signs tell me there is still a flicker of self-respect remaining. Also, consider that he must have been of extraordinary ability to have achieved his post, even if he now appears unworthy of it. The vessels of his nose are not enlarged, so he has just recently turned to drink, or only does so sporadically. I can deduce much about a man by how he walks and dresses himself, but the source of his fall from grace is beyond me at present."

"Every drunkard has a sad tale to tell," I said. "Then they create more."

Bell shrugged, realizing my opinion of the man could not be changed. "In any case, we have done our duty as loyal subjects of the Crown. Shall we to lunch? I suspect you still have a bit of packing to do. Oh, and please come 'dressed' for the journey. Your Pennyworth disguise is as effective as ever, but it is unnecessary for this adventure."

"Old habits die hard, Professor. I believe that up 'til now I have spent more time in your presence in masculine attire. Very well, but do not begrudge me a proper suit—just in case."

7

Berlin, Monday, May 31

The rooms at the Hotel Rome on Unter den Linden 10 were well-appointed, as was the establishment in general. The chambermaid told me proudly that when the hotel was built in 1876 it was the first in Berlin to have bathtubs. It was built while the new palace was being constructed, and Kaiser Wilhelm I ordered a bathtub sent to his royal apartment once a week until construction was complete. When I expressed surprise, the young woman was quick to reassure me that bathtubs were now the norm everywhere.

I was more than satisfied with the generous initial payment and relieved to find my German adequate thus far. Berlin was a bustling city with construction ongoing at a frenetic pace as it struggled to become a capital worthy of a great nation. During a recent visit, Mark Twain had dubbed it "The Chicago of Europe," and I'd heard the description was apt, save for the absence of reeking stockyards.

Professor Bell and I awaited Herr Schork in a small meeting room off the lobby, and he arrived with typical German punctuality at exactly three o'clock. He was a thin, nervous young man with an outsized mustache, trying to hide his insecurity behind a mask of facial hair. It didn't work.

"*Ach*, Herr Professor, it is good to meet you, and you as well, Fraülein Harkness," Schork said. He brushed his lips over the back of my outstretched hand, anointing it with his mustache wax. I regretted not wearing gloves. "How much have you been told, Herr Professor?"

"Very little, other than how this affair involves a delicate matter of security, and that this undertaking in no way compromises the welfare of Great Britain. Am I correct in both?"

"Indeed, Professor. I would even say this affair is of mutual benefit to both our countries, for it involves the surveillance of those who would destroy our social order entirely."

"You mean anarchists?" I asked, savoring the prim little man's flinch at the word.

Schork's eyes darted from side to side, then he nodded. "Precisely. Our efforts to arrest their leaders have consistently failed, and some informants we had within their group have disappeared. The only logical conclusion is we have a spy in the security service. We have tried everything our agents can think of to smoke out the traitor, without success. We need fresh eyes and an unbiased approach. I suggested you, Professor, as you come highly recommended both as a keen observer and a man of discretion. Will you accept the commission?"

"I've no love for bomb-throwers, young man, but I'm no spy. How can I be of service?"

"Since we have been unable to find a double agent, our chief of security, Herr Oberst Adler, has suggested we look for breaches in our handling of documents. Perhaps you can determine a manner by which our enemies could intercept instructions meant for our agents and reports from the field. It isn't much to go on, but we have become blind to the single greatest threat to our nation. I am hoping the man who inspired the figure of Sherlock Holmes can find the answer to our riddle."

Bell snorted at the mention of Doyle's fictional detective, "Holmes again! I tell you, lad, I'm fond of the character, but I'm no magician. It's your money and your purse is generous, so we'll have a look, but I promise you nothing more than that."

Very generous indeed! I thought. *I could afford a first-class cabin.*

Schork beamed. "It's settled, then. Shall I meet you here tomorrow morning at nine o'clock? The chancellery at Palais Schulenberg is nearby on Wilhelmstrasse. I can take you there by carriage."

Bell looked at me and after my nod, agreed. Hands were shaken, or lightly kissed, and Herr Schork sped away to update the chancellor.

"He's a bit tightly wound, wouldn't you say, Miss Harkness?"

"He's a young man eager to prove himself, but an honest one, I think, else he could not be so forthcoming as to their present difficulty."

"Let's hope you're right, or our time here will be more interesting than we'd like, though it's easier to be honest about the failings of others. Care to join me for dinner? Seven?"

"Seven it is," I said. "Now, if you'll excuse me, I feel an acute need to wash my hand."

8

Tuesday, June 1

The chancellery building was impressive; a virtual army of clerks and secretaries typing, filing, or transporting reports with the diligence of field hands at harvest. The din of typewriter keys and shoe leather on polished marble floors was constant, accompanied by the rumble of voices that washed over the visitor like a heavy rain, no one voice distinguishable from another.

Herr Schork conducted us through the press and led us to an Otis elevator operated by a young man in a bellboy uniform and spotless white gloves.

I felt my throat tighten as the operator opened the cage and gestured for us to enter. "Is it safe?"

Schork smiled and stepped inside without hesitation. "Entirely, Fräulein. I ride it daily to my office. It stops automatically if the cable breaks."

"The cable could break? How reassuring. And how many floors are we traveling in this two-ton steel cage operated by an adolescent?"

The operator stiffened and, with as much dignity as his youth allowed, replied, "*Zwei, Madame.*"

"Two stories." Given the height of the first floor, that meant possibly forty feet. "Lovely."

I turned to study the operator and estimated he'd only started shaving within the year. "*Wie alt bist du?*" I asked, causing the young man's cheeks to redden.

"*Neunzehn Jahre, Madame.*"

I reckoned he was probably closer to seventeen years of age than to the nineteen he'd reported. "Is this really necessary?" I asked.

Bell chuckled. "Come, Miss Harkness," he said. "Consider this part of the adventure. I've never ridden in one of these contraptions before and am looking forward to the experience." He stepped inside, turned, and extended a hand to me.

Seeing no way to delay further, I took the professor's hand, turned to face the door, and squeezed my eyes shut as the cage doors clashed together. Bell surely noted my hand was cold but was kind enough not to mention it.

I only realized I was holding my breath when the elevator lurched to a stop and the doors slid open. This birdcage suspended by a seemingly fragile cable incorporated my fear of heights in one hellish device, and the back of my neck felt cool as the fresh air of the corridor flowed over its dampness.

Herr Schork led us to a plain wooden office door labeled only *28A. I suppose it would be foolish to place a sign declaring "Secret Police" in bold letters*, I thought. Inside, a young man who resembled my Pennyworth persona sat behind a desk, guarding the entrance to a second door at the back of the room, probably that of the office of the chief of security. Four other desks were facing the left and right walls, two to a side, each occupied by an industrious male public servant.

I noticed what appeared to be recently installed electric lights hanging from the ceiling above each desk, and a shiny new telephone at the clerk's station. *Impressive*, I thought. *Spying must pay well.* The clerk sprang up immediately, but the other four paid us no heed, each occupied with ledgers and reports.

"Herr Oberst Adler is expecting you, Herr Schork. Who may I say is accompanying you?"

"You may not say, Johann. The Oberst understands why. Announce us, please."

The clerk inclined his head and led us to the door at the back of the room, marked—predictably—*28B*. He tapped on the portal and at a grunt from inside, opened the door a crack and announced, "Herr Schork, with companions."

A muttered "*Ja!*" came from inside, and the clerk fully opened the door, indicated we should enter, then closed it behind us.

Oberst Adler was a slender, soft-spoken man, mid-fifties, not given much to blinking. Adler in German means eagle, and he looked much like a seasoned bird of prey, with a dueling scar on his left cheek hinting at younger, more energetic days. He was on the telephone at his desk when we entered, and mumbled "*Auf Wieder-hören,*" before returning the receiver to its cradle. I was surprised to find when he stood that he was a half a head shorter than I am, though his short stature did not diminish the quiet menace his dark eyes contained.

I was glad German custom did not include shaking hands with women, for I knew instinctively his hands would be cold, his grip overstrong. I was struck by the bareness of his office. No family photographs adorned his desk, nor certificates or diplomas on the wall. The only pieces of ornamentation were a large light fixture over his desk and crossed dueling swords mounted on the wall behind him, perhaps as a warning to those who displeased him. He was a man who kept his secrets to himself while seeking those of others.

There was an awkward silence while the spymaster awaited introductions. Schork flushed. "Excuse me, Herr Oberst. You know why my two consultants are here."

Adler looked as though he had just bitten into something disagreeable as he nodded. "They are here to prove I am either incompetent, or a traitor. I am unsure which determination to hope for."

"*Nein,* Herr Oberst!" Schork protested. "Our enemies can be clever. Our superiors only wish for fresh, objective eyes to investigate. Your long service and loyalty are not in question."

"Aren't they? I am the only common link among all the instances we know of when the anarchists discovered our secrets. If I am not a suspect, it is only because it was I who made that conclusion."

Bell had for all this time remained silent, unable to follow the conversation. When he turned to me for clarification, I held up my hand to request a pause while I translated.

"Can't blame the man for not welcoming us," Bell said, once the gist of the conversation was relayed. "Ask him how his *rrrecords* of the conversations were handled. I assume they all occurred in this room?" Bell's brogue betrayed his unease at our cool reception.

"I can answer zhose questions directly, sir," Adler said stiffly, in heavily accented but understandable English.

"I didn't know you spoke English, Herr Oberst," Schork sputtered.

"I would be a very poor spy if you knew everything about me," he answered, the scar on his cheek blanching as he struggled to hide his smile.

"And you, sir," Adler continued, "from your brogue I assume you are a Scot, *Ja?*"

"*Ja*, I mean yes," Bell answered, nodding.

"*Ach,* I have before me a distinguished Scottish gentleman, brought in anonymously, to investigate a leak of classified information. A task requiring skill, experience, and discretion. Do I have the honor of addressing Professor Joseph Bell?"

Bell inclined his head in respect. "The same."

Herr Adler extended his hand, "I followed the events of the murder in Argyll. Your analysis of the gunshot powder I thought was conclusive, the lack of residue on the body proved the fatal wound could not have been an accidental discharge. A pity the jury was swayed by oratory."

Bell smiled at the man's honest admiration. "Yes, but the murderer's hubris brought him a reckoning of sort. But, please, let's return to the business at hand. How do you secure your notes of sensitive meetings?"

"A moment, please. As I now know your identity, could you introduce me to your female companion with the excellent German?"

Bell looked at Schork, who shrugged. The cat, as they say, was well out of the bag. Nodding toward me, Bell said, "Miss Margaret Harkness. We are old comrades, she and I, and she is someone I know I can trust."

"A quality one should never undervalue, Herr Professor. But now, as you say, to business. A pity. Perhaps, once this matter is resolved and if I stay free of prison, you can share some of your true adventures. I feel better knowing you are the one looking into this. I trust you to be objective, and if I have failed in some manner, then so be it.

"As for my notes, I encrypt them using a codebook of my own devising. I keep my codebook and notes in two different safes stored in this office." Vogel indicated two sturdy iron safes behind him, both chained to the wall.

"The safes are combination, and no one but myself knows the sequences. Since I suspected a spy, I have placed various 'tells' on the safes before I leave for the evening and look to see if anything has been disturbed the following morning. Things like a single one of my hairs lain at a specific angle along the top, which no one save myself would notice. To date, they have always been exactly as I left them the night before."

"And where do you discuss sensitive topics?"

"Only here, in my office, or in the chancellery, though only one conversation there concerned one of our raids. All the others occurred here."

"And who was present at these meetings?"

Adler turned to open one of the safes, pulling out a dark leather-bound journal before relocking the container. "There were five discussions of interest, held over a three-month period. Let me draw you a diagram."

The spymaster smoothed out a piece of foolscap and sketched our surroundings.

ENTRANCE TO 28A

Johann Müller (Clerk)

Franz Weber (Senior Agent)   Helmut Schröder (Informant)

Wilhelm Schmidt (Weber's Deputy)   Jakobs Faulkner (Informant)

ENTRANCE TO 28B

"Müller is never involved. He has an influential father-in-law who ensures his daughter is well supported. Herr Müller is not terribly ambitious, which is fortunate, as he also lacks intellect. He manages the office and keeps my appointment book, nothing more. Think no more of him.

"Next we have Herr Weber, my senior operative, and his deputy, Schmidt. Any field operation of consequence requires one of these men be present to oversee it. I have other agents in another location, but I prefer not to disclose their number or exact whereabouts at this time. Weber was present at four of the discussions, Schmidt at three. It is possible they are in collusion, but I doubt it. Although they work well together as required, neither man is over fond of the other. I will not discuss their personal lives unless you deem it necessary, Professor.

"As for my two spymasters, Schröder and Faulkner, they are a study in contrasts."

"How so?" I asked.

Adler looked up, startled that I'd spoken; then, glancing at Bell and seeing no rebuke, he answered, "Schröder is a quiet, cautious man, while Faulkner is outgoing to an extreme. Faulkner is the younger of the two, at thirty-two, while Schröder, at forty-five, is more settled. Schröder is married with two daughters, Faulkner a bachelor."

"I assume Herr Schröder is Faulkner's superior?" Bell asked.

"No, Professor, though that would be the logical conclusion. I run my informant network in parallel. Each spymaster has his own network. Only I have access to the complete list of informants, to ensure we are not double-paying our little pigeons."

"Is it difficult to get informants from the anarchists?" I asked, making sure Adler understood I was to be a full participant.

Adler snorted, whether at me or at my question, I could not tell. "Until recently, I would have said no. There is much rivalry and even animosity within their ranks. But since this leak was discovered . . ." He sighed. "Three times we have planned raids on meetings where their highest members were scheduled to appear. Each time, we found the place abandoned. Two of my most trusted informants have disappeared—one of Herr Faulkner's and one of Schröder's. This must stop if I am to prevent any major mischief."

"Who within your office is aware of this breach?" I asked.

Adler's stone face softened a little, telling me he had resigned himself to my involvement. "Weber and Schmidt, my senior agents, who planned the raids. Faulkner and Schröder are, of course, aware of the disappearance of their respective informants, though neither is aware of the other's loss."

"So it must be either Schmidt or Weber," said Schork. "They must be interrogated at once!"

Adler took a long breath before replying: "Herr Schork, until I am removed, I am chief of security. You will refrain from telling me how to do my job as long as it is mine to do!"

Schork flinched, then Adler—satisfied his rebuke had done its job—returned his attention to us. "They are both experienced agents, and each has conducted multiple interrogations. They have risked their lives more than once in service to this office, and I will not risk destroying the trust of my two senior operatives without solid proof of their duplicity. Besides, I have discussed our dilemma with them, both individually and together. Were they guilty, they would be well-prepared to cover up their betrayal.

"No," Adler said, shaking his head in frustration, "I cannot believe either man is my Judas."

Bell looked at the telephone on Adler's desk. It was the most modern of its time, a flat disc-shaped listening device above and a speaker tube below, all contained in one piece. Running from the handheld apparatus was a cloth-covered wire which led to an elaborately engraved wood and brass box supporting the cradle. It had a small hand crank on the side, used to contact the switchboard operator.

"Do you discuss classified information on the telephone? Perhaps the switchboard operator listens in." Bell narrowed his eyes in contemplation. "Also, I understand that telegraph lines can be tapped into. I suppose the same is possible with a telephone?"

"That had not occurred to me, Herr Professor. Inanimate objects do tend to be overlooked, *ja?* But I always brief the chancellor in person. There are nuances in communication that are not well expressed though an electric line. My work involves subtle shades of gray. It is as important that the chancellor understand me as I him."

"Is there an office behind your rear wall through which one could eavesdrop?" Bell asked.

"*Nein.* I chose this specific office to ensure such a thing could not happen. The other side of this wall"—he indicated behind him—"is exterior, two floors up. The wall to your right is a hallway, and to your left is another exterior. No, Professor, the walls are not a possibility. And, before you ask," he said, thumping his foot on the floor, "the space beneath my office is a toilet that sees frequent use, and my ceiling is directly beneath the roof of the building. Anyone up there would be noticed sooner or later."

Bell rubbed his hands. "A classic conundrum—a locked room."

"*Ja,* Herr Professor. A puzzle for you, a headache for me!"

I studied the room. Something wasn't right . . . I turned to Bell. "No harm in examining the exterior, all the same. Wouldn't you agree, Professor?"

"It's why we're here, after all," he agreed. "Care to accompany us, Herr Adler?"

"By all means, for both personal as well as professional reasons, though I might advise Fraülein Harkness from entering the men's toilet. I would prefer to avoid the explanations this would require."

The next two hours were spent verifying the Oberst's descriptions. No blocked-off stalls in the men's room (as Bell reported to me, after I stood watch outside), no storage closets where a listener could hide unobserved. Bell confirmed there were no recent footprints among the pigeon droppings on the roof above Herr Adler's office (as I avoided the excursion to the top of the building). Throughout our inspections, I had the feeling there was something I'd missed. Something I'd seen but only noticed subconsciously.

As we reentered the inner office I paused, looked over my shoulder to the outer room, then glanced at Bell. He looked at me with raised eyebrows until I tilted my head upward toward the ceiling, then a slow smile spread across his face.

"Please step out of your office and close the door, Herr Adler," Bell instructed.

Puzzled, Adler complied.

"Is there someplace Miss Harkness and I may talk in private, other than your office?"

"There is a small conference room I use on occasion, down the hall," Adler said, looking more puzzled than ever. "We can go there now."

"What's all the mystery? Speak up!" Schork said.

"Fraülein Harkness and the professor are here at your suggestion, Herr Schork," Adler said, glaring at the junior bureaucrat. "Let them go about this in their own way."

"Thank you, Herr Adler," Bell said, a glint in his eye hinting that he'd come to a conclusion similar to my own. "I believe Miss Harkness and I may have an answer for you shortly. If one of your staff could conduct us to the conference room and wait outside, we should have something for you in a few minutes."

I am accustomed to discomfiting men, so I took little notice of Schork's reddening face as the secretary, Müller, led us out of the office and down the hall.

Once alone, the professor turned to me, beaming. "What did you see, Miss Harkness?"

"I noticed the desk and furnishings in Herr Adler's private office were of the same make and quality of those of his subordinates. There were no diplomas or awards on his wall."

"Just so," Bell said. "Therefore, one can deduce he is a modest man, making his only two ornamentations all the more suspect."

"The dueling swords on his wall and the light fixture."

"Precisely! As I do not see how the swords could be used to convey information out of his office, it can only be the light fixture." He rubbed his chin. "How should we proceed?"

"I recommend we tell Adler privately, as he will know best what steps to take."

"Capital! I almost feel guilty taking their money." Bell winked. "Almost."

I opened the door and asked the secretary to bring Herr Adler to the conference room. Alone. Adler arrived almost immediately, his lips tightly pursed as though tensing for a blow.

Bell nodded to me. "Miss Harkness and I have arrived at the same conclusion. Neither of your senior agents are involved, sir. At least not directly."

Adler frowned. "Alright, Miss Harkness. You have me at sixes and sevens. What is your answer to our locked room problem?"

"Your light fixture, Herr Oberst," I said simply, "is substantially larger than those in the outer office."

Adler leaned in. "And?"

"And I recommend you send a man to your office tonight, long after the building is closed, with a screwdriver."

9

Tuesday, June 1, cont.

Adler agreed to let us accompany him along with Weber and Schmidt that night to his office. Schork, to his immense irritation, was not invited.

"I will update you in the morning," the spymaster said firmly, smiling at the young man's sulk. "If it is nothing, then you have been spared losing a night's sleep. If it's significant, we can brief the chancellor together. The fewer who know of this, the better. Don't worry, you'll get your share of the credit."

Schork's mustache quivered at Adler's final remark, enough that I knew there was some truth in those parting words. The young man clicked his heels, bowed, and was gone.

"I think," Adler continued, "that I should return to my office as though nothing was out of the ordinary. I can always call in my clerk to discuss something of little importance to keep up appearances." Shaking his head, he sighed, "Herr Müller excels in such conversation."

As agreed, Bell and I were waiting in the hotel lobby at eight o'clock when the rest of the party arrived together.

"I didn't want us to be seen gathering outside the building, in case it was being watched," Adler explained. "We will walk in together as though summoned to an urgent meeting and go directly to my office. Are you ready?"

"Aye," Bell answered for us both. "Let's be off."

I sat across from Adler in the carriage, Bell by my side, while the two agents followed in a cab. "What do you expect us to find, Fraülein Harkness?" Adler asked.

"I believe your overlarge light fixture and new telephone have something in common. I looked for something that didn't fit. Were the lights in your office replaced when you got the telephone?"

The spymaster's eyes widened. "Just so! My worthless clerk was told it was to allow me to take better notes of telephone conversations. I feel like an idiot!"

The carriages arrived at that moment, and Herr Adler vouched for Bell and me to the surprised soldiers on security duty. As we approached the elevator, I said, "We should take the stairs."

"Why is that, Fraülein Harkness?" Herr Weber asked. "I am quite capable of operating the apparatus."

"It makes too much noise," I said, with as much sincerity as possible.

Adler and his two agents shrugged and moved toward the stairs, while Bell did his best to hide his smile at my successful evasion of the suspended deathtrap.

When we reached the outer door of the security service office, Herr Schmidt opened it noiselessly with his key. Herr Adler's key worked just as well on his own office, and we quietly trooped inside. The office was a snug fit for five people in the dark, as Adler forbade us from turning on the light. Schmidt pulled two candles out of his pocket and after lighting them, placed one on each end of the desk, then he removed his shoes before climbing atop his superior's work space. Herr Weber handed him a screwdriver and soon the small chandelier was hanging two feet lower, suspended by its wires.

Weber handed up a candle to his subordinate, but it was difficult to make anything out of the darkness above by the dim, uneven light. Suddenly Schmidt froze, then bent down and gestured for Herr Adler to join him.

A casual observer would laugh at the sight of two distinguished

German gentlemen standing close together atop a desk in their stocking feet, but there was no merriment in the room as the rest of us watched in silence while the two conferred in whispers.

Schmidt was replaced by Weber, whose eyes widened at whatever his superior pointed out to him. Then Bell clambered up and, after a brief glance, got down and grinned at me. "A master stroke," he whispered.

Finally, I was allowed to ascend, and Adler pointed out a vague shape in the center of the hole above. Squinting into the shadows cast by the one candle, I saw a small, conical opening of dark metal. It looked familiar. Then I looked down and saw a similar device at my feet. A telephone mouthpiece.

After placing a rolled-up handkerchief into the hole, Alder descended, then motioned for us to follow him out of the office, still holding one of the two lit candles. Once in the outer room, he closed his door and led us to a far corner. Then to my amazement, he bowed and in a low voice said, "It appears you and Professor Bell are correct, Fraülein, and I can see why he brought you along. No eavesdropper adjacent to my office, but someone was listening in. The other end may be far from the chancellery building. Who knows how far the cable may run?"

He seemed surprisingly happy given the circumstances. "Imagine! Our enemies were able to listen to my conversations remotely. I admire their ingenuity. So much, in fact, that I am already imagining the possibilities!"

"What now?" I asked, in the same low voice.

"We trace the wire to see who is on the other end. Then we ask them what they heard, and who they told. We continue to follow that trail until we find the head of this particular cell. I will extract as much information from our enemies as possible, in payment for the two informants we've lost."

I shivered at the intensity in Adler's face, made more unsettling by the light of the flickering candle in his hand. "What will happen to those you catch?"

The spymaster showed his teeth. "We fight a war in shadows, but a war all the same. I will do my best to make an example of them. You have done your part, and have my thanks, but what happens next is none of your concern. I will recommend to the chancellor that you receive a bonus for your work, and then you must go. Your work here is finished."

Bell's brogue thickened in his anger, "So we're being shown the *doorrr,* is that it? Mercenaries who've served their purpose?"

"I have deep respect for you, Professor, as well as growing admiration for Miss Harkness, but in essence your summary is correct. You came here to do a job, and that job is done. That you did it so quickly is to your credit and cause for proper remuneration, but it is my task to deal with the consequences of your discovery. Herr Weber and I have some plans to make. Schmidt will see you to the entrance and sign you out with the guards."

Bell stalked out of the room, Schmidt barely keeping up, while I loitered a moment longer. Until now, the case had been an intellectual exercise. I shivered to think my solution could lead to the deaths of others. Like an archer whose bent bow has launched an arrow, the consequences were now beyond my control. I could only hope the targets deserved their fate.

10

Once the telephones were installed, Grüber arranged for Herman to remain to service the telephonic system and perform minor electrical work, and he had a small workshop in the basement of the chancellery building.

"Herman Ott?" the man standing below him asked.

Herman looked down from the top of the ladder, a fresh light bulb in his hand. "*Ja*," he answered. "Can I help you, sir?"

Herman knew the office this gentleman came from and could only think of one reason he would want to speak with him. *Stay calm*, he told himself. *Play dumb and look for your chance.* Men like these, men with soft hands and clean clothes, tended to look down on workers like Herman. It would be easy to convince this spy hunter he wasn't too bright.

The man pulled out a badge. "I am Herr Schmidt. You need to come with me. Now. My superior wishes to speak with you."

Herman was certain if he entered their office, he would lose control of his fate. "Of course, *mein Herr*. Just a moment, so that I do not leave the entire basement in darkness." Herman replaced the bulb and then clambered down the ladder. "I need to put the lights back on and store my tools unless you need me to take them along. Then I am free to accompany you."

Herman collapsed the ladder and ambled to the small workshop in the corner of the vast basement. After he hung the ladder up, he reached for the light switch with his left hand, while pulling a wrench out of his overalls with his right.

Schmidt didn't notice this sleight of hand in the dark, and when Herman threw the switch, the agent was blinded by the sudden flash of light and didn't see the wrench flying toward his head until it was too late, when he returned to darkness.

When Schmidt came to some thirty minutes later, Weber was standing over him. He reached down to help his subordinate stand. "Don't explain," Weber said. "I came to see what the delay was. Our electrician's actions tell me we are on the right trail. I'm sorry about your headache, Schmidt, but you just extracted a most convincing confession. Time to summon reinforcements, I think. Let's go to the office where you can lie down. I'll take it from here."

Soon a net of men with soft hands and clean shirts were closing in on the small gun shop on Invaliden Strasse and the small apartments above.

Herman sped home. His heart felt as heavy as Herr Vogel's anvil, making it hard for him to breathe.

Astrid was surprised to find Herman home at this hour but knew it could only mean trouble. "What's wrong, Herman? What are you doing here?"

"We must leave, Astrid. Now! The police are after me. I helped Herr Grüber with a project and have been found out. If they catch me, it will mean prison."

She paled at this. "But where will we go? Immanuel is just an infant. I can't be running down back alleys with him in my arms. Please, speak to Father before you do anything rash!"

"I should talk to him anyway. Pack your things and be prepared to leave in five minutes."

Herman found the gunsmith carefully reassembling a fowling piece when Herman rushed in. Seeing no customers in the shop, Herman bolted the door behind him and pulled down the CLOSED sign.

Herr Vogel froze when Herman locked the door. "What's this, Herman? What's happened?"

"The police are after me, Father. The work I did for Herr Grüber has been discovered. I must leave now and take Astrid with me!"

Herr Vogel grabbed a rag to wipe his hands. "I understand why you must go, Herman. But why Astrid and the child? The authorities will question her, of course. They'll also question me, for that matter, but she wasn't involved. She and the child will be safer here with us, and you'll move faster and draw less notice without them."

That brought Herman up short. Herr Vogel was right. It would be painful, but he should leave his family behind. Imprisoning them would do the authorities no good, and if Astrid fled with him and they were caught, it would make her look like an accomplice.

He took a deep breath, his chest feeling even heavier. "You're right, Father. I know you and Frau Vogel will care for them until we can be together again."

Herr Vogel placed his hand on Herman's shoulder. "You need to go, now!" Reaching beneath the counter, he brought out a cash box and thrust a thick handful of notes into his son-in-law's hands. "Don't tell me where you're going, and don't write me. The police will be sure to read my mail. Quickly tell Astrid good-bye, then go to Herr Grüber for help, and don't come back!"

"Herr Grüber?"

"He got you into this. He will help you out, if only to protect himself. He can always claim he knew nothing of your actions, as long as you are not around to contradict him. One more thing . . ."

Herr Vogel rushed to the back room and returned with the air rifle in its case. "If the police find this here, it might raise suspicion. Take it with you, I beg you!"

Herman looked at the case, and his shoulders began to ache. The rifle together with its case weighed ten kilos, but he could not deny his father-in-law. Besides, it would make him look like an innocent tradesman, so he slung the carry strap over his shoulder, embraced the older man, and went to say his farewells.

Astrid was still pale but she was ready, a single suitcase in her hand and Immanuel in her other arm, resting on her hip. Herman took the suitcase from her and embraced her, then looked deep into her eyes. "You are both staying here. The police will not harm you. There would be no benefit to them in arresting you, and keeping you and our son here will allow them to use you as bait to draw me back."

Astrid looked into his cool gray eyes and saw pure love, and his belief he was doing his best to protect her and their child. "How long will you be gone?" she asked, as tears slid down her face. "How long until we can be with you again?"

"I can never return, Astrid. But when things settle down, I'll send for you. I've made a new life for myself once before. For our family, I can do it again."

"Promise, Herman. Promise that we'll be together again."

"I promise. Not because I want you to believe it, but because I believe it. We were meant to be together. We will be."

He peered out the window. It would take bureaucrats longer than usual to assemble a police squad, but he couldn't count on their inefficiency much longer. He embraced Astrid once more and touched his young son's face. In this parting touch he tried to convey all his love for the boy, then he fled.

Herman banged loudly at the door and was glad to see Herr Grüber answer it himself. Grüber flinched when he saw Herman standing nervously on his front doorstep with a case at his feet. "Herman, what is this? What's happened?"

"The telephone was discovered, Herr Grüber, and I had to dodge a policeman to escape the chancellery building. You must help me!"

Grüber and Herman exchanged glances. *Or else* wasn't spoken, but the sentiment was understood. The wealthy man sighed, "Come in." He popped his head out the door, looked around, then once the door was closed said, "You must leave the country immediately! It's best your wife not know where you're going, just in case."

"She understands. I am ready to go wherever you advise straight from here. I told her I can never return, but will send for her once it's safe."

"That may be a year or more, but let's get you away and deal with that later. Come. The police will suspect me, and if your house is the first place they go, since I am your employer, mine will doubtless be the second."

Herr Grüber led Herman to his study, where he tore a sheet of paper from a notebook. He scribbled down an address then unlocked a drawer in his desk. After withdrawing a large purse, he thrust it and the note into Herman's hands. "Memorize this name and address, then destroy it and flee the city. Avoid trains. I recommend you make your way south to Switzerland before heading to the safe house. Tell the person named here that I sent you, and that his debt is due. Now go! The police could be here any moment."

Herman had a sense he had been here before. Once again, he was being sent far away to escape prison, or worse. He boarded a streetcar for the southern edge of the city before he glanced down at the address: An antiquities shop in London.

The police were quite thorough, and destructive. Little Immanuel cried as bookshelves were thrown over and furnishings rummaged through.

Astrid glared. "I doubt you'll find anyone hiding in our armoire, *mein Herr*. I know nothing of my husband's dealings at work. Look as you will, but please do not break things. Some of these items have been in our family for generations!"

"Your husband did not work alone, Frau Ott," Herr Weber sneered as he oversaw the destruction. "Anything you can tell us of his compatriots would lessen his punishment."

"He's a good man and wouldn't harm anyone!"

"Perhaps he hasn't spilled any blood, but my associate with a headache would disagree that the man is harmless. But it doesn't matter, as he has enabled others to do harm. For me it is the same." Looking at the bookshelf, he said, "You have several books by this woman, Harkness. Why?"

"I love her books! She writes of the common people. I dream of being a writer someday, and she is the author I'd like to emulate. I'm surprised you haven't heard of her."

Weber shrugged. "I hadn't heard of her writing, but by odd coincidence I recently met her."

"What! She is here in Berlin?"

"Not much longer, but it was she in fact who led us to your husband."

Astrid's face blanched as the spy's words soaked in.

"No. No, I can't believe she would do such a thing."

"Oh, she was paid well for her efforts, never fear. Probably better than what she gets for writing socialist fairy tales."

Immanuel must have sensed his mother's distress, for he began wailing, and comforting him allowed Astrid to turn her thoughts away from Weber's revelation. It is always painful to see one's heroes as human. It was unbearable to think that Margaret Harkness had separated her family.

"Aha!" the man cried, holding up Astrid's red leather journal. "What's this?"

"My private journal. It's where I write my reflections and exercises in descriptions. There's nothing of interest to you, please leave it alone."

He opened the journal and Astrid colored as the stranger ran his thick fingers through her most private thoughts. He smirked. "I'll find this interesting reading back at the office. Congratulations, now you're an author."

"You can't do that! It has nothing to do with you."

"You have nothing to say in this matter, and if it weren't for your brat, I'd take you in as well. The coward fled without you, let's see if he cares to come back for you."

Herr Weber and his plate-breaking colleagues left soon after, and Astrid was alone with her thoughts among the wreckage. Her parents were taken to the police station to help an artist compose a sketch of Herman for circulation. Astrid knew her mother would be as accurate as possible, for she blamed her husband and Herman equally for their current situation and wanted to protect her daughter and grandson from the authorities. As far as she was concerned, the men deserved to suffer for their stupidity. Herr Vogel was now banished to the loft above the shop, where Herman had slept when he first arrived.

Astrid was overwhelmed at how suddenly her life had changed. She was staring at her scattered collection of Harkness novels and considering whether to burn them when Herr Grüber knocked on the door. When she saw him, she nearly slammed the door in his face. "What are *you* doing here? Haven't you done enough damage already?"

Grüber shrugged. "You didn't think badly of me when I tripled his salary. May I come in, or shall the entire neighborhood witness our conversation?"

She backed away, allowing him in, and failed to notice him sliding the bolt into place behind his back. "But you said there was no risk involved. That he wouldn't harm anyone!"

"And I have kept my word, Frau Ott. His hands are clean."

Astrid paused. "But yours are not."

"True. I need to know what the police said to you just now."

"You were watching us?"

He smiled. "Of course. I cannot help you if I do not know what's going on."

Astrid collapsed onto the nearest chair as she told Grüber of her conversation with Weber, her parents' visit to the police station, the confiscation of her private journal, and her sense of betrayal by her favorite author.

"I don't think things could possibly be any worse," she said, her eyes downcast. Then she looked up at her uninvited guest. "But, you! Nothing touches you. You have ruined my life, and yet you just walk away." She stood and leveled her finger at him. "I think the police might go easier on Herman if they knew who was behind it all."

Grüber saw the rope lying atop a crate of rifles. "I think things will get better soon. Have faith."

"Why would you think that?" Astrid demanded.

Ten minutes later Grüber walked out the back door, wiping his hands with his handkerchief as he strode away.

Inside, little Immanuel was crying again as his mother swung gently above him.

11

Herman stood before the doors to another shop just after midday. He was filthy, unshaven, and weak on his feet. He must have walked twenty-five miles over the past two days and knew he looked more like an itinerant laborer than a prosperous tradesman. He glanced at the sign above the door, which read, in large gold letters, *Luigi Parmeggiani, Antiquities.*

Herman swayed with fatigue, his strength fading as he opened the door, his body aching for sleep. A slight olive-skinned man, impeccably dressed in a gray linen suit and smelling of rose water approached, his eyebrows arched in distaste. "*Scusi, Signore,* but I believe you have the wrong address. If you are looking for work, I have my own specialists already."

Herman handed the man the note from his former employer. "This is for you. Herr Grüber said your debt is due."

The man accepted the note as though it were a filthy rag. After studying it, he scowled and jerked his head over his left shoulder. "Go around back to the workshop. You can wait there."

If Herman hadn't been so tired, he would have been furious at the rudeness of his reception, but he grudgingly turned around and made his way back toward the door, where he paused. "Is there someplace I can lie down?" he asked, looking back.

The man's face softened. "There is an old sofa awaiting renovation. You can sleep there until the shop closes and we figure out what to do next."

Herman trudged around to the back and found two workmen carefully restoring a delicate French settee. Conversation with them was fruitless, as they only spoke Italian. Herman pantomimed being told by the man in front to come into this room, and they shrugged and went back to work until one noticed Herman staring at his sausage and cheese sandwich. Herman pulled out some German marks, pointed to the sandwich, and an exchange was made.

Herman ate slowly, savoring the texture of the crust and the feel of the sausage sliding around in his mouth before swallowing. It wasn't enough, it wasn't near enough, but it was a good start. After washing the sandwich down with a bottle of red wine, which the sandwich-seller offered to him without asking for more money, Herman lay down on the couch and was soon fast asleep. His running was done, at least for now.

Herman was awakened by the insistent shaking of his shoulder. He had been dreaming of the afternoon in the park with Astrid, the cherry blossoms drifting down. When he saw where he was, he groaned.

"So, *Signore*, I take it you are on the run from the authorities, yes? Herr Grüber must have been desperate to send you to me, for we did not part on friendly terms. Did you kill someone? Someone important?"

Bleary-eyed, Herman was in no mood to be interrogated. "No. No killing, *Signore*. I helped Herr Grüber spy on other spies. We got found out, and the German Secret Police are looking for me. The British shouldn't care. I'm no risk to you."

Luigi brought himself up to his full diminutive stature. "I'll be the judge of that. But for now, you need a place to stay while I find out what sort of trouble our mutual friend has gotten me into. You can't stay here. My business associates wouldn't like it, and many of my most important transactions occur after normal hours. I have a valuable piece expected within the hour. My seller wouldn't want you to be here when he arrives."

Herman understood. Luigi was a fence, his fine store a front for his other, more lucrative sideline. Herman was more likely to be arrested here as an accessory than an anarchist. Signore Parmeggiani was right; he couldn't stay.

"I need to exchange my marks for pounds," Herman said. "Can you help me?"

"*Si*. I do many transactions on the Continent. Show me what you have, and I will give you a fair rate."

Herman handed the remnants of the purse Herr Grüber had given him, plus the wad from Herr Vogel. After counting out the pounds that the Italian gave back to him, Herman had to admit the exchange was more than fair. Luigi was an honest thief, it appeared.

"*Allora*, now to your lodging, *Signore*. There is a small room above the shop, in the back. I store supplies up there, but you can take the cushions from the sofa here and make yourself a pallet for the night. Here's the key to the back door. You can enter from the fire escape without going through the shop. I open at nine in the morning but will be here by eight. Come down then and we can talk alone when I am not in a hurry and you are rested. *Va bene?*"

"*Bene*," Herman mumbled, then he gathered the cushions and staggered off. He was awkward going up the fire escape with his arms full of cushions and the rifle case hanging on one arm, but once inside the room, he laid them down and looked around. It didn't take long. The space was fourteen feet wide and twenty long, one wall occupied with a shelf of cans of paint and bottles of turpentine, and the fumes made Herman open the one small window quickly. He knew where he would place the cushions.

Otherwise, the room was bare, save for a painter's tarp on the bottom shelf with the painting supplies. The bare wooden floor was swept clean. Signore Parmeggiani was no doubt concerned about fire, as the space was free of rags or anything that could serve as tinder. Herman missed his feather bed and duvet, but lay down on the cushions, pulled the splattered painter's tarp over himself, and returned to a deep slumber.

Herman woke at sunrise and lay still, waiting for the chime of a clock to tell him the time. As he heard the sounds of a city stirring, he wondered what his future held. Alone, away from his wife and child in a foreign country, unable to return home, did he have a future? A bell chimed seven times, nearly drowned out by the rumblings of his stomach.

He stirred, and, after finding a cart selling meat pies on a nearby street corner, was at the store entrance when the bell chimed eight. When Herman arrived, Signore Parmeggiani was already inside and let him in quickly. After locking the door again, he motioned for Herman to follow him to his office. No "Good morning," or "How did you sleep?" It was clear the fence saw him as a burden. A burden to be rid of as soon as possible.

"I don't dare send a telegram to Herr Grüber," Luigi said. "That would be too easy for the authorities to trace and follow straight to . . . you. I have contacts on the Continent who can hand deliver a message to him within a couple of days. Until then, we wait. How long do you think you need to stay here?"

"Do you mean 'here' in England or 'here' in your shop?"

The little man's cold reception made Herman doubt the wisdom of coming to him, but it hadn't been his choice. He sensed the little Italian would turn him over to the police if he deemed him a significant risk, Luigi's debt to Grüber notwithstanding.

"England," Luigi answered, with a poker face.

"I don't know any more than you do. We'll have to wait to hear when Herr Grüber thinks I can send for my family. It could be a few weeks. It could be more." Looking around the shop he said, "But I believe I can be of some use to you while we wait. I see you have various artifacts that have been turned into lamps."

"Yes. Art objects and family mementos are quite popular as lamps at the moment. Why?"

"Who does the electrical work?"

The Italian grimaced as though he'd just found his wine unfit. "There is an electrician down the street who does the conversions. He is expensive and slow. I've lost customers due to his tardiness."

Herman spread his hands out in front of him. "I'm an electrician. I can wire the objects here in your shop the same day. I think you'll find my work more than acceptable."

Signore Parmeggiani looked at Herman with new interest. An honest profit was still a profit. He pointed to an old Brown Bess musket standing in a corner. "The man who sold this to me yesterday is a retired Army colonel. The walls of his study are lined with old fire-arms, and his wife insisted he get rid of this one as there was no more room. He was most reluctant to part with it, and I am certain he would pay me handsomely if I could make it into a floor lamp. Can you do it?"

Herman studied the battered weapon for a moment. He felt his fingers twitch as he considered the challenge and at the thought of having something to occupy his hands while awaiting news of his family. "Let me give you a list of what I'll need after I examine your workshop."

Herman found a workbench in the back of the shop where furniture could be repaired (or made to look older), and after taking inventory he gave the shopkeeper a list of supplies.

Luigi scowled, but then shrugged. "An investment. *Bene.* Having you work on the piece will explain your presence, if anyone should ask. I'll send one of my workers out for these items as soon as they arrive. Why don't you come back around one o'clock? I should have everything by then."

They shook on it. Herman was impressed that the Italian had seen how the electrical work could serve as a cover for him before he did, probably due to years of skirting the law.

Herman left the shop and decided to get some measure of London. This would be his home for who knew how long, and he'd best learn his way around. He heard Big Ben toll down the Thames, and the echoes made him feel hollow inside. The distance between Astrid and him could not be measured in kilometers.

After another meat pie and a walk along the north bank of the river, Herman was back promptly at one o'clock, his hands hungry to hold tools again. Luigi nodded as he entered, and Herman went straight to the bench where he found the musket waiting. First, he fashioned a wide wooden stand to which he'd attach the butt plate, staining the support to match the color of the stock. Then he bored a hole in the base of the stand, measured the length of the weapon, and fashioned a metal support from a small steel pipe which he screwed into the base, making a hole in the pipe where the breech of the musket would align once it was attached.

The breech was small, as the musket was a muzzle-loader, so Herman drilled a hole large enough to admit a thin wire and ran the cord up the barrel. He affixed the lamp head where the bulb would reside, secured the base, and stood it up. Attaching the plug would be an easy task. It wasn't a thing of beauty, and no woman would ever want it in the more public areas of her home, but it seemed quite fitting for a retired colonel who yearned for his days in front of his troops.

When Signore Parmeggiani saw the completed work, Herman could almost see the pound notes the man was envisioning. *"Bene fatto, Signore,"* he said, "Well done." He looked at his watch. "Six o'clock. I have time to send a personal note to the colonel before dark, inviting him to visit the shop tomorrow. I think he may enjoy this small victory over his wife. The price of his triumph will be of little consequence to him, I am sure."

"Does this mean I can stay?" Herman asked.

"Of course, *Signore!* Now, let's see about better accommodations for you."

Herr Grüber withstood the interrogation by Adler well. Grüber knew that he did not have to convince the spymaster that he was innocent, only that the evidence wasn't sufficient to withstand the scrutiny his arrest would trigger. His influential friends who had helped him secure the contract to install the telephones would be quick to rush to his defense, if only to protect their own reputations. He was released from custody after four hours of questioning, and Grüber began to breathe easily.

He regretted the loss of the telephone line but knew that in this game of cat and mouse with the authorities, he was more often the mouse, so was philosophical that he'd still won more than he'd lost. As Herman's former employer, he summoned Herr Vogel "to settle accounts" (should anyone ask), when he saw a new opportunity as the two men had a final drink together in Grüber's home.

"I'm terribly sorry about your daughter's death, Herr Vogel. A tragic end to our relationship."

The gunsmith appeared as though he had aged ten years overnight and looked down at his glass. "Hilda may never allow me back into the house, and I can't blame her. We have only one more matter to discuss, then I'd prefer we never meet again. You could not have foreseen the consequences, but seeing you only increases my sense of guilt." He took a drink, before continuing.

"I regret to inform you, Herr Grüber, that I've lost the rifle you requested of me."

"You destroyed it, to keep the police from finding it?" he asked, while refilling their wine glasses. "A sensible precaution."

"No, *mein Herr*. I convinced Herman to take it with him. Unless he threw it away, he still has it, wherever that is. If you still have need of it, you'll have to get it from him."

Grüber considered this new information before reaching for his drink.

"As I recall, Herman is an excellent marksman."

"One of the best I've ever seen. He has a natural ability to focus on the target so that for a moment nothing else exists. Perhaps it is just as well that he has no desire to shed blood, as he could be a very dangerous man, otherwise."

Grüber nodded, and as soon as his guest departed, he began composing the message he would send to England the next day. *No desire to shed blood . . . yet. First, I must light the flame, then I can focus its heat.*

12

London, Tuesday, June 8

Herman now had a large workbench and a drawer full of tools dedicated to his use. He was happily turning out lamps fashioned from all manner of odds and ends. The Italian delighted in something profitable being produced out of an item he'd been unable to sell, and Herman often found his ingenuity challenged, yet he was content. He was never happier than when his mind and hands were working together to resolve a problem or create something useful.

Luigi called him in after the shop closed. "Herr Grüber sent you a letter. He enclosed it in a walking stick he and I use for messages. He sells it to me with a message inside, then I sell it back with the reply."

Herman swallowed hard, wiping his hands on his apron. "What's it say?"

The Italian shrugged. "It's addressed to you, *Signore*. I may be a dishonest man, but I don't read other people's mail."

Herman took the tube of paper and carefully unrolled it.

Berlin, June 4, 1897

Herr Ott,

The hunt for you goes on, and I regret I have no good news for you. It grieves me to inform you your beloved Astrid is dead. Apparently, she hanged herself.

The last message I received before the telephone was

discovered informed me that a Professor Bell from Scotland and a Miss Margaret Harkness from England had been employed to find the source of leaks from Herr Adler's office and had sent the police to your home. Astrid was already quite despondent after they turned the house over, breaking one or two family heirlooms in the process, and one policeman confiscated her journal to see if there was incriminating evidence inside.

When I mentioned the name Harkness to her, she became quite upset. It seems this woman was Astrid's favorite author, and when she heard Miss Harkness was partly responsible for your being hunted, she was devastated. I had no idea the name had any significance to her and shall carry the guilt of her death for the rest of my life.

Your child is fine, and will be well-tended by his grandparents, but Frau Vogel holds you accountable for Astrid's death. I am certain she would turn you over to the authorities or shoot you herself to make sure you never raise your son.

Your sacrifice for our cause will be remembered.

I shall visit when I can to see how I can help you begin life anew in England.

I am so very sorry.

K Grüber

Herman stared at the paper in his hands. Ordinary paper. No fancy seals, ribbons, or illustrations, yet it was the most potent paper he had ever seen. A few marks on it, and his life was altered forever. Astrid gone. His son lost to him. A door had closed behind him he could never reopen without risking years in prison or worse. He was too shocked to cry and sat down hard on the nearest chair, incapable of thought or feeling, his mind rejecting the words on the paper for as long as it could stand to do so.

He'd never believed in magic, yet here it was. He walked into a room one man, and by the evil enchantment of this small scroll, he would leave as another. He cursed Herr Vogel, who'd led him to Grüber, whom he cursed even more. Then another name came to mind. Harkness. It was the author's name that had pushed Astrid over the edge. And she lived in England.

Herman thought of the rifle in the case put away in his new apartment. He had laden himself with Herr Ott's *Meisterstück* in deference to his father-in-law. Perhaps *Befreier* could liberate him from some of the pain in his soul. Miss Harkness had broken Astrid's heart. He would pierce hers in return.

13

I asked the desk sergeant for Inspector Ethington and was directed down a long hall lined with offices to my right. *It seems Special Branch is more interested in reports than fieldwork,* I thought. *There are more offices down this one hall than in the entire Spitalfields Police Station.* As I passed each door, I saw earnest young men with stacks of paper and photographs on their desks making notes and looking at maps. The last door on the right was closed, however, and on it was painted in black letters: *Inspector J. Ethington.*

My knock got a muffled response, then the door was opened from inside and a bleary-eyed "J. Ethington" stuck his head out. *Napping,* I thought. *We'll make this short. At least I don't smell whiskey.*

"May I help you, Madam? Have we met before?"

I'd briefly considered delivering the report dressed as Pennyworth, but as I had other errands to run that day, decided it wasn't worth the effort. An inspector in Special Branch should be accustomed to deception. I wondered what reaction I would get from him. Shock? Laughter? Outrage?

"Yes, Inspector, we have, though not in the traditional sense. My name is Margaret Harkness. I was Professor Bell's companion when you met us at the Marlboro Club." Seeing his puzzlement, I continued. "This was shortly before we went to Germany."

Inspector Ethington peered closely at me, still bewildered. "I apologize, Madam, as I am quite proficient at remembering names and faces, but I recall Bell's companion as a slender middle-aged bookish gentleman who was going as his translator, and no one else. Besides," he cleared his throat, "the Marlboro Club bans women from entering their premises unless they are in service."

"Quite so, and you flatter me that my disguise fooled a professional like yourself. I sometimes assume a waistcoat to open doors closed to petticoats."

Ethington's face pinked up in a most becoming way. *Embarrassment. How quaint.*

"I see," Ethington gulped. "Or think I do, at least. You and the professor . . ."

"Are dear friends who have faced danger together before, though there was none this time, thankfully. I was in male attire to gain entrance to the Marlboro Club. I have the professor's report here."

I handed over the three-page summary of our brief foray into espionage, then nodded toward the gap in the door he was still guarding. "I'm willing to remain while you read it over if you offer me a seat, in case you have any questions. Otherwise, I'll be on my way."

He backed into his office as he opened the door wider, nearly bowing. "Yes, of course. Terribly sorry. I was on surveillance duty last night and got very little sleep. I'm afraid you've not caught me at my best. Do sit down."

Still better than last time, I thought, but outwardly I only smiled as Ethington removed a stack of reports from the only other chair in the room. Other than this pile, his office was well-organized, the only ornamentation on his orderly desk was a silver-framed photograph of him and a young girl around twelve who shared his slender, pointed nose. His left hand rested upon her left shoulder, and she had her right hand over his: A beloved daughter, whose likeness was placed so that he could glance up and see it whenever he wanted. It was angled for his own frequent contemplation, not put there to impress others.

My father had never requested a likeness of me.

I studied the man while he read Bell's report through. My friend generously gave me full credit for discerning the source of the leak within the Secret Police, and Ethington whistled a low tone when he got to the part describing the listening apparatus within Herr Adler's office.

"That's solid work, Miss Harkness," he said. "No danger, you say, but a nice adventure all the same. Learning the name of the head of their section will impress my superiors. Do you know what happened after the device was found?"

"I heard the man they believe placed the telephone was still at large when we left Germany. I do not know his name or if others were involved. Once we did our jobs, the Germans were rather anxious that we leave. I think they were embarrassed we were able to find the leak so quickly, though grateful it was literally plugged."

I noticed the inspector leaned forward as I spoke. He didn't interrupt me. Unusual. Not unpleasant though.

There was a pause, which lengthened until he reddened again and coughed. "How did you and Bell become involved in this enterprise? Are you a detective?"

I laughed. "A female detective! Is there such a thing?"

"You seem skillful at disguise and deduction. You bested the German Secret Police and found the source of the leak before even the famous Professor Bell. If you're not a detective, what are you?"

"An author and a friend of the professor's. I've observed his methods and learned how to apply them, though not as well as he."

"Yet you deduced the solution before he did. How?"

"The light fixture was on the ceiling, of course, so out of his direct line of vision. While Professor Bell's powers of observation of people far exceeds my own, I had the advantage in this instance of being a woman. The style of the new fixture in the colonel's office was different from those elsewhere in the building and markedly larger, yet the size of the electric light bulbs was the same. The decor in the spymaster's office was spartan, yet the fixture was elaborate. Why was that so? Certainly not at the insistence of its occupant.

"I can assure you, Inspector, that no woman would have selected a fixture for the chief of Secret Police so different from its fellows, so I deduced the electrician who emplaced the fixture had his own reasons.

As it was the only possible explanation for the leak of information, it had to be the correct one."

"Brava! An accomplishment worthy of Holmes himself. And how does a lady author become a friend of a man such as Bell and go off with him on adventures?"

I found myself enjoying the man's intent gaze and admiration. He seemed genuinely interested in my intellect, and as I noted the depth of his brown eyes I felt a flush of heat that had nothing to do with the early summer weather. "We worked together once before, here in London. Though I am not a detective, I do have confidences to keep involving the matter." *And to keep me out of prison.*

"Ah, a woman of mystery. Now I recall my parting words to you at the Marlboro, 'There's more to you than meets the eye.' You and Bell must have howled once I was out of earshot."

His honest admission of his error made me more charitable then I'd felt at the time. "I took it as a compliment, sir, that I could fool an inspector from the Special Branch of Scotland Yard in good light and close quarters. Don't worry, sir, your reputation is safe with me."

Ethington flinched at the word "reputation." *There, I've said the wrong thing again*, I thought.

"Well, Miss Harkness," he said, now businesslike, "this was most enlightening. I'll be sure to pass this report on to my superiors. I believe this concludes the official matter. I do have something else I would like to discuss with you, however." Straightening himself in his chair, he said, "May I ask you to dinner, where you can tell me more about the adventures of lady authors?"

I nodded toward the photograph on his desk. "Wouldn't your wife disapprove of such a meeting, Inspector?"

He paused and looked at the photograph of his daughter. "My wife, Alice, has been dead for the past two years, Miss Harkness."

He held up his hands. I grew warmer still, but now in embarrassment. No ring.

"I assumed a woman with your apparent talent for observation would have noticed the absence of a wedding band."

I swallowed. *A nice man. He didn't deserve me accusing him of infidelity.* "I apologize, sir. Our greatest blunders usually follow hard on the heels of our triumphs."

Ethington looked down at his desk for a moment. "Yes, my life has demonstrated that pattern better than you know." Then, looking directly into my eyes, "But you didn't answer my question. Would you join me for dinner tomorrow night? Seven? Name the place, and I'll be there."

He's a good sort, at least when he's sober. Why not? Least I can do after . . . "Delighted. I know a lovely café where you can interrogate me further. A well-done lamb chop does make me more talkative, Inspector, especially if accompanied by a good Bordeaux. You've been warned."

I confess I left with a new spring in my step. I had intended to visit the ticket office to book passage after my visit to the inspector, but I changed my mind. I had a dinner engagement to prepare for. Australia wasn't going anywhere, just yet.

14

Wednesday, June 9, cont.

The day after the letter from Grüber arrived, Herman awoke slowly. He rarely drank more than two beers in an evening, but last night he'd done his best to dull the pain, only to sharpen it with every swallow. His resolve to exact vengeance on Miss Harkness went from white hot to Arctic cold overnight. He was a master craftsman. He would use his skills and patient temperament to create a precise moment of reckoning. But first, he needed to locate his target.

He explained the contents of the letter to Luigi, and the Italian's eyes moistened. Luigi told Herman to take the time he needed to mourn. He had plenty of lamps to sell at the moment and gave Herman an advance on their sale. His workbench would be ready when he returned.

It was an easy matter to locate a bookstore, and he found one of Miss Harkness's books on a back shelf, marked down. *Not so popular in your own country, I see,* he thought. Somehow, that gave him a measure of comfort. He started to buy it, then he decided he didn't want any of his money to go to her, so wrote down the name and address of her publisher, memorized her image at the back of the book, and replaced it on the reduced-price shelf, its title facing backward.

For the next part of his plan, he needed better clothes. A second-hand store provided a respectable suit and shoes that would allow him to walk unnoticed into a business establishment without a toolbox over his shoulder.

The manager at the publisher was an elderly gray man who clearly saw little sun. He was suspicious when Herman came seeking one of his authors. "What business do you have w' Miss Harkness, sir? She's under contract with us. You can give me your message and I'll send it on."

Once you read it, Herman thought. Using his strongest German accent, he said, "I vould like to ask her to write a story based on characters in Berlin. She is quite popular in Germany, und I think such a book will sell very well. It vould only help her popularity and cause her other books to become better known also. It would cost you nothing and may help you sell more of her works."

Herman noticed the man's eyes dart to a filing cabinet beside his desk. The thought of selling more books distracting him. *Thank you*, Herman thought. *I would love to play cards with you sometime.*

"Do you have a card, Herr . . ."

"Krieger, sir. And sadly, no. I did not bring a card with me. Here is my address in Berlin. I am only in London for two days. I must return to Germany tomorrow, so sadly I will be unable to meet with her while I am here. Please send her my regards and tell her I am eager to hear from her."

The manager accepted the note. He looked doubtful anything would come of this, but he promised to send the address on. Their business concluded, they wished each other a good day, and Herman left, smiling to himself. *One step closer.*

Back at the antiquities shop, he asked Luigi if he could help him meet with one of his regular "procurers" of art. Luigi thought this an odd request for a man in mourning, but shrugged and gave him a name and a pub where the man could usually be found. Ignorance of the personal details of one's associates in art "procurement" was usually wise.

"Keys" Malone was anchoring a corner table of the Dog's Head pub when Herman entered, just as Luigi had predicted. He was telling a story about his time in Newgate Prison to two mates who seemed familiar with life behind bars.

"Ah tell ye, boyos, 'twas the Black Dog himself who walked past my cell every night just after midnight."

"What d'he look like, Keys?" asked a mate well into his cups.

"He only came by at the darkest hour, so alls I can say is he weren't more'n bones. I smelled him first. Damp dirt and rotting flesh, like he'd just climbed out of his grave. Then the sound of his shuffling feet wrapped in rags. He never turned his head to look at me, thanks be to God, though he's never harmed a prisoner as I've ever heard, nor a jailer, more's the pity."

"How long's he been seen in Newgate?"

"I hear he's been there for over a hundred years. Maybe more. If he'd ever turned to look at me, there'd be another ghost soon enough!"

They laughed together, then Keys noticed the stranger overhearing his tale. "Well, lad, you gonna say something? I usually don't tell me stories to strangers, least not for free."

Herman signaled the barmaid. "Four ales, please." Then, turning to the storyteller, he asked, "Is there someplace we can discuss business?"

Malone smiled with his few remaining, blackened teeth. "This is my office, suhr. My mates were just leaving to have their ales at the bar, weren't you lads?"

His two companions went to the bar after eyeing Herman curiously. Free ale was, after all, free ale.

After the two men had the corner to themselves, Keys became all business. "What's the job, what's the risk, and what's the pay?"

"I would think the pay would be your first question, Mr. Malone."

"Pay's no good if you can't spend it. I've no desire to go walking with the Black Dog. And you haven't answered my questions."

"The job is opening a door and perhaps a file cabinet. I will write something down, then we're done. You're not to take anything. They can't know anyone's been there."

"Then the pay'd better be good, if I've naught to sell after."

"Twenty pounds for twenty-minutes' work."

"And the risk?"

"It's a publishing house. There's nothing of great value inside. The lock on the door didn't look expensive, and the filing cabinet should be child's play. No one resides nearby, so police patrols will be infrequent."

"I won't say yea or nay 'til I've seen for meself. Five pounds to have a look. Then twenty more if I say yes."

They shook hands. "How about another ale, then we go for a stroll?" Keys suggested.

Two hours later, after walking around the building from the outside, a partially sober Malone took thirty seconds before agreeing to the job. "No dogs. Good. I hate dogs. Been bit once on a job. Can never stand 'em since." He took one look at the lock on the door and smiled. "I've a ten-year-old nephew who could pick that," he said. "Sure there's naught worth taking? I'll feel naked without a sack to fill."

Herman shrugged. "You don't look like much of a reader, but if you want ten copies of some penny dreadful, I doubt they'll be missed."

Keys snorted. "Books! I'd need a wheelbarrow full just to make two pounds. Alright then, we'll do it your way. Ten pounds now, the rest when we're done. I'll be here at two. That's usually when the bobbies take a wee nap or a spot of tea. Don't keep me waiting."

Money exchanged, they went their separate ways. Herman had never been a hunter, but he suddenly understood the thrill of it. Soon he would track his quarry to her den.

Keys Malone was punctual and earned his title, opening the door almost as quickly as if he had its key in hand. The door squeaked a bit when opened, and Herman was surprised when the man oiled the hinges once inside. Malone saw Herman's look and whispered, "Most dangerous parts of a job are when you enter and when you leave. Newgate's full of men who came in careful and left careless. Lead on."

Surprisingly, the filing cabinet took the thief longer to overcome than the front door. "Smaller lock," he explained. "Gives me less room to move about." He displayed a remarkable vocabulary of swear words, teaching Herman one or two phrases Herman hoped he'd never have use for, before the lock finally yielded and the drawer slid out. "And Bob's your uncle," Keys said with satisfaction.

Herman wasn't sure he heard right but shrugged and, with the aid of a bull's-eye lantern, quickly found Miss Harkness's address among the file detailing each of the house's authors. "I've got what I need," he said, "Your Uncle, Bob."

He was sliding the file closed when a small form darted out from beneath the publisher's desk and ran across Malone's feet, causing him to scream, "Dog!" and jump onto the desk, knocking over an inkwell.

The cat squalled as it fled into the back of the office, and Herman suddenly smelled urine. The burglar had wet himself. "Get down, you fool! Now see what you've done."

Malone climbed down, clearly shaken. "Job's done! Give me my money and I'll be off."

"We need to clean up this mess or they'll know we've been here."

"They'll blame the cat. I'm leaving. Pay me!"

Herman saw there was no reasoning with the man, so he handed over the other ten pounds, completing their transaction, and the door swung open and closed without a sound.

Herman was about to go himself when a thought came to him. Perhaps Malone was right. How to convince the publisher it was the cat? He saw the black ink glistening in the dim light given off from the street, then it came to him. One more thing to do. He turned toward the far corner of the room where two eyes were studying him. "Here, kitty, kitty."

15

Thursday, June 10

After more indecision than is my custom, I chose a green satin dress with a modest neckline. A small emerald pendant and white silk shawl complemented the ensemble nicely without being pretentious. I'd paused at the door of my apartment before going out. On the spur of the moment, I dabbed a small amount of perfume behind my ears. *Enough. It's unlikely I'll ever see him again. Just relax and enjoy the evening.*

The Mistral Bistro was intimate, the tables crowded closely together, requiring the waiters to rise up on their toes like ballet dancers to deliver the orders. The table was so small I smelled his sandalwood cologne mixed with the odor of his freshly applied boot polish, a strangely masculine combination. The food was quite good and the prices reasonable for the West End, which was one reason I'd chosen it. I assumed an inspector with a daughter had to be cautious with his budget. Inspector Ethington looked at the menu as soon as we sat down, and I noticed the furrows on his forehead smooth out once he reviewed the prices.

"So, my mysterious lady, what can you tell me about your famous acquaintance, Professor Bell?"

"Do you usually begin your interrogations before the wine is served, Inspector? A poor gambit, if so."

Ethington laughed. "Very well. Bordeaux, I believe? Or will another vintage make you more talkative?"

"You'll just have to find out. The 1895 is a good year." *And not expensive.* "That is, if the condemned woman may have a last wish."

"*Ego te absolvo*, Miss Harkness, I absolve you of your sins, but confession may still aid your soul."

We laughed together in this charming dance of wit. I'd almost forgotten the steps. I felt a slight frisson of pleasure as I realized the inspector was flirting with me. How long had it been?

"I was hired for a case the professor was working on almost ten years ago. I was living in the East End and served as a guide for him and another gentleman, but our relationship matured, and I became a full-fledged member of the enterprise."

Ethington paused as the wine arrived. He and the waiter performed the necessary rituals before the inspector nodded and our glasses were filled. Once we were alone again, he said, "Almost ten years ago in the East End? The only thing that comes to mind is the Ripper affair." He leaned in, "Do you mean to say . . .?"

"Your memory serves you well, Inspector. We played a part in that sordid matter, but it is behind us now. I earned a couple of trusted friends. It was a pleasure to work with Professor Bell again, however briefly. Ah, here comes our meal. *Bon appétit,, monsieur.* Enjoy your spaghetti."

The inspector had been in enough real interrogations to know when a subject had closed the book. He accepted his defeat graciously and turned to the topic in all the papers, Queen Victoria's upcoming Diamond Jubilee. It would be in less than a fortnight: on Tuesday, the twenty-second of June.

"It will be quite the spectacle. Prime seats along the route are selling for as much as twenty-five guineas."

"Will Special Branch have any duties associated with the ceremony?"

"We're keeping our eyes on various suspicious elements, but up 'til now the queen's attackers have been madmen from our own country or Ireland. Our various continental guests may write a lot of revolutionary tripe while in England, but they tend to behave themselves to avoid being sent home, where the authorities await."

"What do you do, exactly?"

"Describe me."

"Average height. Slender, though not skinny. Light brown hair with a trace of silver, and brown eyes. Modestly dressed in tweeds. No tattoos or distinguishing marks."

"Aye, you got it right with the first word: Average. There is nothing about me that is memorable. I have stood beside a man at a pub, then four hours later sat beside him on a park bench reading a paper, and he was none the wiser. To a foreigner, I am just an average Englishman, neither wealthy nor poor, not possessing anything that might help him to recall me as soon as I pass from sight. Being boring in mannerisms doesn't hurt, either. I do not laugh loudly, have nervous tics, smile excessively, or smoke a pipe. I am a face in a crowded city. I could scarcely be more invisible."

"I disagree in one particular sense, Inspector: You are kind."

Ethington snorted. "How could you possibly deduce that?"

"The photograph of you and your daughter on your desk. It was in a place of pride, in an expensive frame, and professionally done. You are obviously very fond of her. Such affection gentles any man. She is fortunate to have a father like you. After I became an author and journalist, my father was so concerned with what people would think, he tried to marry me off without even consulting me as to the choice of groom."

Ethington laughed while signaling the waiter, "I can tell that didn't work!" Then, to the waiter he said, "Dessert menu, please."

"You are merciless, Inspector. I thought my interrogation was concluded."

"I thought something might yet slip out if I got you intoxicated on chocolate, though the crème brûlée seems popular among the regulars."

Did I just flutter my eyelashes at him? I thought. *Good grief, Margaret, don't be an ass!* I winced as I felt the tug of his brown eyes in the candlelight. *I must remember this vintage and avoid it like the plague.*

"Margaret, dessert?"

I flushed, snapping out of my thoughts. "Yes, please. The peach sorbet will do for me. Thank you. Now, tell me about your daughter."

"Her name is Elizabeth." The inspector went at some length to brag about his daughter's virtues. A good student, a more than decent cook, and a devoted daughter. Though only fifteen, she was every inch the mistress of the household. "Frankly, Margaret," he continued, "I don't know how I'd have gotten along without her since Alice died." He wiped his mouth. "I was in a very dark place, and she was my only light. That's a terrible burden to put on a girl of thirteen. For a while there, she was more a parent than I was." He looked away for a moment. "Last week, on the day we met in fact, was the second-year anniversary of Alice's death. I was so despondent she hid the whiskey after I had a glass with breakfast. That may have been the lowest point in my life. I've resolved to do better, since."

"I'm sorry, Inspector. It must have been hard on you both." I recalled my harsh words to Bell that every drunkard had a story. This man was not a habitual drinker, and his story was worthy of more sympathy than I'd been willing to grant it, unheard. It also explained why he'd smelled of whiskey when we'd first met, yet as Bell had noted, he lacked the physical features of an alcoholic.

"Was her death unexpected? Speaking as a former nurse, I know those can be the hardest."

His face clouded over as he stared into his wine. "One morning, Alice complained of stomach pains. I put it down to indigestion and left for work. Elizabeth came home from school to find her feverish and barely conscious. She summoned the neighbors, who got her to hospital, but she died of a ruptured appendix. I didn't learn of her admission until I got home and found the apartment empty and a neighbor told me what happened."

He paused for a long moment, and I was about to say something in response when he continued in a softer voice, "One of our constables was promoted to sergeant that day, and I had a drink or two with him and our fellows at a pub near the office after work. I wasn't drunk, though I'm certain Elizabeth could smell the ale when I arrived at hospital only to learn Alice was dead."

He put down his half-filled glass. "I've never had the courage to ask Elizabeth if she blames me, but I'll never forget the look on her face when I finally arrived at her mother's deathbed, smelling of drink. I failed both of them. As long as I live, I pray I never again see the look of despair she gave me at that moment."

I said nothing but laid my hand on his arm. "She must still love you very much, to care for you like she has. Never forget that."

"Aye, there's love for sure. I'm not so certain about respect. I've given her little reason for that since her mother's death."

A young man—probably a student at a nearby conservatory—entered the bistro and began playing a romantic song on the violin. The yearning in the piece, coupled with the wine and companionship, drew my attention so that for a moment there was only candlelight, the music, and us.

I sighed. "It's beautiful."

"From Schubert's *Serenade*. The young man's technique is excellent, but he's still too inexperienced to do it justice."

"How do you mean? His playing is superb."

"True," Ethington said, "but the music speaks of yearning and loss. Until he's suffered the things the music is truly about, it is just a pretty piece of music to him. If I were to recite a poem in Japanese, even if my intonation were faultless, it would not impress someone from Japan as the words would just be sounds to me. My pauses, my inflections, would not be quite the same as someone who truly felt the meaning of the poem.

"It's the same way with this music. An older man who has buried someone he loved would play it differently, because it would speak as much to him as to his audience. A younger artist may play the notes with more verve, but a mature violinist would shape the pauses better, and understand the true meaning lies in the silence between the notes."

Glancing at his pocket watch, he said, "I apologize that this hasn't been the most romantic evening you could hope for, but it's been good for me to talk with you. Thank you for hearing me out, but I fear it's time to go. Elizabeth worries if I'm away too late. Let me see you home."

"There's no need. I made it here on my own," I said.

"Aye, but it's late now, and it's dark. I wouldn't feel right saying good-bye at the nearest Underground station."

"Ah, but how could you know I traveled by Underground?"

"Your shoes are clean, so you didn't walk, and your recommended wine is reasonably priced, so you didn't take a hansom as you are sensitive to cost. What other options are there?"

I inclined my head. "Bravo, Inspector. I would love to hear how you became assigned to Special Branch. I am certain it wasn't because you were perceived as *average* by your superiors."

"I was an up-and-comer in those days." His face darkened. "Before Alice's death . . . we should be off."

As we rose to leave, I noted his glass of wine, his first and only glass of the evening, was still half-full.

The trip to my flat was a silent though companionable one, and I flattered myself that one reason he'd insisted on accompanying me was to learn where I lived. When we arrived he bowed, I laughed and curtsied, and the evening was done. *I can't remember when I have passed a more pleasant evening,* I thought as I walked up to my flat. I sighed. *And just when I finally have the funds for Australia.*

I decided to book passage the next day before my resolve weakened. I removed my dress and fingered the glowing fabric a moment before putting it away. I wondered when I would ever wear it again.

Outside, once the man was out of sight and the woman was indoors, Herman carefully surveyed the surrounding neighborhood. She seemed the right age and build for the image of Miss Harkness in the back of her books, but it was of little consequence at the moment.

He noted the light nighttime traffic and predictable thirty-minute intervals between police patrols. Satisfied, he paced to various sites from her apartment entrance where he could wait unobserved, not wanting to leave anything to chance. *Rest easy tonight, Miss. This was just a social call.*

Herman did not notice the other eyes that watched the couple at the entranceway and his surveillance after. Once he left, they did too.

16

Friday, June 11

I awoke with a cheerful heart and stiff joints. An evening with a "gentleman caller" had been a pleasant diversion, but my body urged me to seek warmer climes. Soon.

The payment from the German contract included a fifty-pound bonus as a reward for a job well and swiftly done, so I could afford small indulgences and still secure a second-class cabin to myself and be well-resourced to begin my new life in Australia. With the funds at hand, there was nothing holding me back.

After my morning rituals, I dressed to go out and headed for the docks. There was still a single cabin available for a ship leaving the following week, but after a moment's hesitation, I declined it. *I couldn't possibly be ready to depart so soon*, I told myself. Instead, I chose a ship leaving the seventh of July. I confess I was still savoring the pleasure of Inspector Ethington's attentions the night before, and decided to find a reason to visit Special Branch once more to say farewell. It was only proper.

As I made my way back to my flat, I had a familiar but uncomfortable feeling that I was being followed, and on the spur of the moment I stepped into a café. I chose a corner table and using my teacup as a screen, scanned the establishment, then the street. It was a pleasant June morning, and the passersby strode hither and yon with purpose. All of them, that is, except for a boy of around twelve who was loitering at the corner of the building across from me.

His hands fidgeted, going into his pockets, then coming out, with his arms held at odd angles or across his body. He was dressed in a flat cap, a clean shirt and vest, and baggy trousers, all made from the same light brown wool and all at least two sizes too big. I noticed his face and hands were clean. Not a beggar, nor a newsboy as he had no papers. He was no threat, but to whom did he report? Who had a reason to follow me?

Then I felt a chill flow down my back. Who had I harmed recently? The German anarchists. *Well, Margaret*, I thought, *be careful what you wish for. Now you have a valid reason to see Inspector Ethington again.*

I debated whether I should try to shake my shadow before going to Special Branch. Would it be better if he knew I had contacts there, or would keeping this knowledge from him make it easier for James—*So it's James now?*—to catch him?

I left the café striding straight for the nearest Underground, not daring to look behind to see if my ill-dressed tail was loping after. I boarded the first car I found and stood by the door. Sure enough, the lad entered the wagon just behind, so I would be ahead of him when I disembarked. The doors were closing when I leapt out, catching my skirt in the door for a moment before I pulled it free. I headed straight for the station's exit, shaking my head as though I'd forgotten something. I had just enough self-control not to look back to see whether my shadow had escaped his car.

I found James in his office studying a calendar. He looked up when I entered, startled, but smiled when he saw it was me. I rather liked that.

"Ah, Miss Harkness, a pleasure. I had a delightful evening last night and hope you did as well. To what do I owe this pleasant interruption of my day?"

"I've grown a tail," I said.

Ethington pinked up, then laughed.

"A shadow then," I said. "A follower. Someone is stalking me! You of all people should understand the reference."

He stopped laughing, though still struggled to control his smile. "Please forgive me, Miss Harkness, but the image just now . . ." Tears trickled down his face as he fought a losing battle with another out-burst, while I tapped my foot, waiting for this bout to pass. Men.

"I'm glad my situation provides you such merriment, Inspector, but someone is following me, and I'm concerned it may involve my recent adventure in Germany. I *thought* you might be interested in knowing this."

"Excuse me, Margaret," he said, startling both of us by his use of my first name. "I mean, Miss Harkness. You're quite right to be concerned. Let me think a moment."

"Yes, please do, Inspector." Then I added, relenting a bit, "Margaret is fine."

He blushed again. *He would make a terrible spy*, I thought, not unkindly. *He's so easy to read.*

"Two things come to mind," he said. "First, I must contact Herr Adler to request information on the anarchists involved in your affair in Berlin. We need to know what contacts they may have here in London. Second, I would like to set a trap for your devoted follower, to learn who this person's working for. Are we agreed?"

"Hardly a romantic stroll . . . James. But, yes, the sooner we know what we're dealing with, the better. I lost the young man on my way here. He'll probably return to my apartment. I'll go there now and depart for the market around four. You can be somewhere near to follow us. How you catch him is up to you, but the marketplace is full of stalls and vendors. You should be able to get close without him noticing. Then, when I leave to return home, you can confront him as he leaves the market."

"Excellent. I'll send a telegram to Herr Adler now. I may have a reply before we meet, and we can confront the lad with all we know."

I didn't see my shadow when I left my apartment building, market basket over my arm, but I didn't need to. I felt his eyes. Or was it James's eyes? I steeled myself against the impulse to look around for him. No. I had to play the part of an automaton, intent on buying food and nothing else. *I wonder what automatons eat?* I nearly giggled at the thought. *This man is warping your judgment, Margaret. Be careful!* I straightened and went forward bravely to buy potatoes and bread.

As I wandered amongst the vendors, I added a roasted chicken to the basket and a quarter-wheel of cheese as images of a picnic in the park flashed through my mind. Despite my foolish daydreams, I finally noticed the boy dressed as before, pretending to watch a juggler at the market entrance. He looked fit, and I wondered if James could catch him in a footrace. Perhaps a little advantage was called for.

On the way home I stopped as though to consult an address, then turned through a narrow archway into a courtyard surrounded by tenements on three sides. The courtyard was in the shade of the afternoon sun, and I slipped into the dimness to the right of the entrance and lay in wait. Sure enough, I soon heard slow, light footsteps approach and head for the same shadows I was in. I blame the darkness of the shadows for my missing crucial features as I seized a slender arm and spun my tail against the wall, blocking escape.

"Let me go!" the youth yelled. "I'll call for the police!"

"The police are already here, lad," Inspector Ethington said, puffing from his sprint. "Now, who are you and what are you about, following this nice lady?"

The boy's eyes widened when he saw the jig was up. After a deep sigh, he removed his cap. Light-brown, shoulder-length hair spilled out. "Hello, Father," Elizabeth Ethington said. "I see I still have a lot to learn."

It was no park, but the three of us were soon sitting down in my apartment enjoying the chicken and cheese while Elizabeth Ethington explained herself.

"I'm sorry, Father. I didn't mean to alarm anyone, but the way you talked about Miss Harkness, well, I was curious and wanted to know more about a lady who could make you smile again."

"Oh?" I said. "And what did the good inspector say about Miss Harkness that caught your attention?"

James sat, miserable, while we two ladies discussed him as though he wasn't there. "Perhaps he said something in confidence that had best remain unspoken? Besides you, young lady, need to explain why you aren't in school."

"He said you are a remarkable woman, and hoped to see you again." Elizabeth blurted out.

"Now that you've ruined any remaining dignity I might have, please explain your absence from school."

"Oh, that. I'm sorry, Father, but I haven't been to school since the New Year."

"What!"

"I am literate, probably more so than some of my teachers. I do well in mathematics but see no reason why I should continue to prepare myself to be a proper wife and mother, or secretary or clerk, when that is all my schooling prepares me for. I have turned to the streets to study my true calling."

"And what true calling can you learn in the streets?" Ethington asked, bracing for the worst.

Elizabeth patted his hand. "Why, being a detective, of course. Like you."

I slammed James's back as he choked on his chicken, propelling it onto his plate. After he regained his breath and speech, he croaked out, "There are no lady detectives on the force."

"I know that, Father," she said with the air of a wise adolescent who has to explain things to their beloved but simple parent. "I want to be a consulting detective, like Sherlock Holmes."

James looked to me, pleading, "Speak to her, Margaret, one woman to another, please!"

"Very well, James, but as this conversation will be from one woman to another, I'll have to ask you to go to the sitting room while we talk."

His mouth, so recently cleared of chicken, dropped open. "What! Now?"

"Be careful what you wish for, Inspector."

He stood and bowed to the two of us before walking into the sitting room like a chastened schoolboy while Elizabeth struggled to hide her smile, at least until her father was out of sight.

Once he was gone, I turned to Elizabeth. "You understand few men will hire you. That means you'll need to advertise your services in women's periodicals."

Elizabeth's mouth dropped nearly as far as her fathers as I continued, "Now, I agree that disguising yourself as a boy is a good idea when on surveillance, but you need some practice."

Elizabeth jutted out her chin. "How hard can it be to act like a man? They do it without thinking at all."

"Precisely, and you must learn to do likewise. Now walk across the room and back."

Puzzled, Elizabeth stood and did as she was bid. "Anything wrong with that?"

"Your steps are too short. You've grown up walking in skirts, so you take smaller steps so as not to trip or dirty the hem of your dress. Boys take long strides, boys your age especially, as they try to look older and larger than they are. Then there's the problem with your arms."

"What's wrong with my arms?"

"You don't know what to do with them. You're used to carrying a purse, and your arms come across your body as you step. No boy does that. Their arms are free to swing to and fro like a pendulum. Think of how soldiers march, then reduce it a bit, and you'll be about right. Remember, Elizabeth, now you have pockets, the greatest advantage men have over us. Get to know them until they are second nature, and let your arms savor their freedom."

Elizabeth drank in every word, her questions bursting out like steam too long contained.

"Men's shoes are too wide. What can I do about that?"

"A bit of lamb's wool tucked inside does wonders, my dear. I have some I can give you. Now let's see, what else? Oh, yes. Spitting."

Elizabeth wrinkled her nose. "Some boys do a lot of that, I've noticed."

"Yes, they do. If you spit, do so with authority. When men and boys spit, it is a declaration of something. Of what precisely, I've no idea, but if you spit, do so boldly."

"Disgusting."

"If you find it disgusting, which I understand, then it's best you forgo that particular male diversion. Which bring us to scratching. Boys do a lot of that, too. Please don't. It's something I've never been able to do convincingly."

"How do you know all this, Miss Harkness? I've never met a woman who knows so much about these things, let alone one willing to discuss them."

"I've had occasion to pass as a man to avoid danger, or to seek it. It is a useful skill for a woman who chooses an . . . unorthodox path in life. One final thing: Your hands and face are too clean. If you want to pass yourself off as a street urchin, you must have some dirt on your hands and under your nails. Any final questions before school is adjourned?"

"Only one, but it's for the both of you." Then, raising her voice, she called out, "Father, it's safe to come back now!" Once he'd returned, hat literally in hand, she asked, "Did you know there was a man spying on the two of you last night when you returned Miss Harkness home?"

17

"What! How could you possibly know that, Elizabeth?" James asked.

"I followed you, of course. You mentioned the bistro, so once you left our flat, I changed into my disguise and loitered outside the restaurant until you exited. I knew that a gentleman like you would see her home, so that way I could learn where she lived. I was about to leave after you parted, when I noticed a man pacing the distance from the entrance to Miss Harkness's apartment building to various corners or places where he could hide. After he measured three different sites, he left. I was afraid to follow him, so I came home. You nearly caught me, too, because before you'd have gone to a pub for a drink, but this time I barely had time to jump into bed before you came and peeked in to see if I was sleeping."

"Why didn't you say something?"

"I wanted to, but was unsure how to tell you. I was following Margaret today. Oh . . ." She turned to me. "May I call you Margaret?"

I smiled. "Yes, I'd like that very much."

"I was following Margaret today to see if he came back. I didn't see him."

"What did he look like?" James asked.

"Sorry, Father, but it was dark. He looked strong, like someone who works with his hands. But all I could really see was his outline."

James shook his head. "I want to be angry with you, Elizabeth. But I can't. I am, however, worried. I got a quick reply from our colleagues in Berlin that I am *not* going to share with you, but it makes me think Miss Harkness's recent trip to Berlin and this mysterious man are related. Now it's your turn to go sit on the sofa while Margaret and I discuss things."

"You mean while the adults talk?"

"No. I mean while confidential information is shared with the only person it pertains to."

Elizabeth strode out of the room to the exile of the sofa with her nose upturned while James turned to me.

"Herr Adler sings your praises and wishes you well. A cell of anarchists was arrested after the police followed the telephone wire to a nearby warehouse. Only one man escaped that we know of, but he could be a very dangerous one. His name is Herman Ott. His father-in-law is a gunsmith who is suspected of being an anarchist sympathizer at the very least. Ott is known as a crack shot who often demonstrated his father-in-law's wares to clients. Elizabeth's description of a man pacing off distances makes me fear he was choosing a sniper position."

"He must be very loyal to his cause to want to kill me."

"Politics isn't his motive, I'm afraid, at least not the only one."

"Then what is?"

"His wife killed herself shortly after the police came to her house looking for him, leaving a small child behind. The woman's mother blames her son-in-law for her daughter's death. In one stroke, he lost both his wife and access to his son. He probably blames you and Professor Bell. I suspect he fled to England and, after hearing of his loss, decided to seek revenge."

My heart seized at the news of the woman's suicide. I recalled the Irish prostitute, Mary Kelly. I'd unwittingly led the Ripper to her door, and the description of her mutilation would haunt me for the rest of my life. It seemed that once more I'd been manipulated by others, leading to the death of an innocent woman.

I shook my head to clear it of the memory, with little success. "I'm the closest, so it makes sense. But how could he locate me so quickly?"

"You're a well-known author. Who would have your address? Your agent?"

"I have no agent. I deal directly with . . . my publisher." Then raising my voice I called out, "Elizabeth, please tuck your hair back under your cap. Care to join us for a little jaunt?"

It was approaching closing time when we arrived at the publisher, so I wasted no time, though I took care not to antagonize the elderly man. He was, after all, the one who made sure I got my royalties fairly and promptly.

"Excuse me, Mr. Aldrich, but has anyone approached you in the past week trying to contact me?"

He looked over his pince-nez glasses. "I apologize, Miss Harkness. I meant to send his address on to you sooner, but with the disruption of my office, I've had a devil of a time setting things right."

"I'm sorry to hear that, sir. Can you describe the gentleman?"

"Certainly. A German gentleman, shy of forty. Large he was, not the typical academic one sees in our business, eh? He asked for your address and was rather put out when I refused, though I did agree to forward his request on to you."

"And when did he come by?"

"Two days ago. You'd have his note now, if not for the mess I found in my office yesterday morning."

Ethington stepped forward and showed his badge. "What happened yesterday, sir?"

Mr. Aldrich pursed his lips when he saw the badge. "Naught for the police to concern themselves, Inspector, lest you arrest cats for their willful nature. I keep one in the office to keep rats from eating the books, and this one . . ." He nodded at a tiger-striped tom licking himself in the far corner. "He took to running about and overturned my inkwell onto some correspondence I had from a promising young author whose address I cannot now recall. I was so upset and occupied trying to locate a previous letter from him, your message slipped my mind."

"How do you know it was the cat?" I asked.

"Got his paw prints in ink all over the office, that's how."

"Anything else you might be able to tell us regarding the German visitor?" Ethington asked. "It's rather important."

"He had large hands, Inspector. At one time in his life, he made his living with those hands, before he went into books. Oh, and his eyes. As cool and gray as any cat I've ever seen. I wouldn't want to see him angry."

"Thank you, sir." Then, turning to me, James asked, "Anything else before we go?"

I considered telling the man I would soon set sail for Australia, then hesitated. Given my sudden intimacy with James and Elizabeth, I preferred they not learn of my plans this way. "Not now. Thank you, Mr. Aldrich, sorry about your troubles." I took the note left for me by this mysterious stranger and once outside, James and I peered at it together.

"A name and address only. Both probably false," he mused. "I'll pass it on to Herr Adler, to see what he can make of it. I find the story of the marauding cat rather too convenient to be coincidence. I suspect its involvement was staged to hide the evidence of a break-in. Too bad the cat can't defend itself. Doubtless, this is where Herr Ott got your address. One moment."

James studied the door lock. "Some small scratches. Inconclusive, but a professional would find this lock no challenge. Yes, I think our man was here recently."

"What now?" I asked. "He knows where I live, and I have only a vague description of what he looks like. I doubt he'll introduce himself before he fires."

"I will inform my superiors, of course. Professor Bell's report was well received, by the way. When I tell them that an anarchist sniper is about, they'll increase surveillance of known anarchists in London. Ott can't have arrived without someone taking him in. He may walk in shadows, but he needs a roof and sustenance."

I sighed. "A good plan, and I wish you well, but what about me in the meantime? I can't stay where I am unless you can offer me police protection."

Elizabeth, who'd been silent all this time, piped up. "We can!"

James looked askance at her outburst. "What are you talking about? Where could I find a contingent of bobbies to watch her place?"

Elizabeth rolled her eyes. "Of course, you can't! She can stay with us. She can share my room!"

"That is very kind of you, Elizabeth, but I must warn you, I've been told my snoring is atrocious."

"I can hear Father from down the hall. Yours couldn't be worse than that."

James frowned. "What will people think?"

"And what would you think, Father, if Margaret is killed by this man, and you didn't take her in? Are you so afraid of what strangers think that you're willing to risk her life?"

James shook his head. "No, Elizabeth. That just wouldn't do. But I have an alternative solution. Margaret, there is a flat one floor below ours that has recently become vacant. I'm sure the landlord would be happy to have a tenant ready to move in immediately. It moves you from your current residence and I'm near to hand if you need assistance. Will that do?"

I stood there in a rare moment of doubt. I could probably sail sooner and assume my Pennyworth guise until safely onboard. That would be the logical thing to do. The safe thing. But if I made the move dressed as Pennyworth, the assassin couldn't track me to a new residence, and I'd have the time to properly prepare for my new life in Australia.

Also, I didn't want this Ott fellow to scare me off. I was angry at being manipulated in a way that led to a woman's death. And if I did flee, what would prevent the man from coming after me in Australia? If I didn't want to be looking over my shoulder for the rest of my life, I needed to stand my ground and assist in this man's capture. I would leave England on my terms, when I was good and ready. I looked down at Elizabeth and squeezed her hand.

"Very well. In for a penny . . ."

18

Friday, June 11, cont.

James went off to inform his superiors of a possible assassin roaming the city, while Elizabeth and I went to their apartment building to secure my temporary new home. After a brief inspection of the available flat in James's apartment building in Soho (and assuring myself it came with sufficient furnishings for a woman who travels light), the landlord allowed me to sign a renewable, weekly agreement and provided me with a key to the flat and the building's entrance. Then we two ladies went to gather some clothes and necessaries to sustain me until I could clear out the rest of my belongings. I was a bit dazed at how dramatically my life had changed since that morning but knew I could not stay in my current lodgings with a sniper stalking me.

It took about thirty minutes to fill one typewriter case and three satchels, two for clothing and one for books. I had been parsing my possessions for the past three months as I contemplated my emigration to Australia, so the sorting was mostly done. I would return to the flat one final time to claim or dispose of the rest, making sure it was in the hours of daylight and dressed as Pennyworth, so as not to draw the notice of my German shadow.

Elizabeth noted a faded pack of hand-colored Tarot cards on a shelf. "Do you give readings?" she asked, picking them up and shuffling through them.

"No," I said, carefully taking them from her hands. "They belonged to someone I met long ago. I keep the cards as a reminder of her and what she tried to teach me."

"When was that?"

I paused. It was a story I'd never shared with anyone. I looked at Elizabeth. So earnest, so full of life and questions, almost a woman. *So like me when I was that age.*

"Sit down then. This will take a few moments to do right. I was about your age . . ."

My friend Samantha (daringly called "Sam" by our classmates) and I went to the market together the day we saw the old Tarot card reader. Each of us dared the other to have our fortunes told, until finally I accepted just to shock my companion.

"How much for a fortune?" I asked.

"Depends, dearie. But I don't tell fortunes. I tell you what paths lie ahead, and what choices you'll 'ave to make. I share the wisdom of the cards. You'll make your own future."

"How does it work, then?" Sam asked. "She asks a question and you draw a card. Simple as that?"

The old woman stared at Sam until my friend began to color. "I do a pattern and, depending on the question asked, seek insight into what the cards try to tell us. The same cards won't mean the same thing to two different people, or questions." She pulled out a worn deck of cards from a waxed leather pouch on her belt. "So, ladies," she asked, while shuffling the cards on the small folding table before her. "Do either of you 'ave a question for Old Mary?"

Sam nudged me forward. "My friend has a question, don't you, Maggie?"

Mary nodded. "About love? Most young ladies your age ask about love."

"How much does a reading cost?"

"Thruppence for three cards. Sixpence for a Celtic Cross."

"Celtic Cross?"

"Aye, Miss. My hardest but deepest reading."

"I have sixpence, but two questions. Love is one, but the other is about my desire to be a writer."

"So, one Cross, or two simple passes. What'll it be?"

"A Cross, about becoming an author."

"Done. Give me a tanner and we'll begin."

"Not love?" Sam asked, giggling.

"Writing first. I *know* writing is real."

"Now quiet, young ladies, while I shuffle the cards."

I placed the sixpence coin, or "tanner," on the corner of the table as evidence of my ability to pay. We watched as the weathered old woman shuffled the cards three times, then fanned them, face down, before us: "Touch a card, pull it out slowly, then repeat until I tell you to stop."

My heart beat faster, and I feared Sam might have noticed my hand tremble just a bit as it hovered over the spread deck. I took a deep breath as I was drawn to one card in particular and pulled it out.

Mary flipped it over, revealing a woman sitting on a throne, an upraised sword in one hand, the other one empty. "Queen of Swords. This covers you."

The next card was a man with a bandaged head with a staff in his hand, eight others upright in a row behind him. "Nine of Wands. This crosses you."

The next card: "Ace of Swords. This crowns you."

This was followed by the Two of Wands, which went beneath the central cards.

I flinched when she flipped over the Hanged Man.

"Don't fret, Dear," Old Mary soothed. "I'll explain in a moment. This is behind you."

As I reached again, the cuff of my sleeve caught a card and flipped it over. "Sorry!" I said. "Do we have to start over?"

"No, Lass. This card was calling out to you." She examined the card with an odd look. It showed a woman bending over and stroking a lion. "Strength," Mary explained. "This goes before you."

The next four cards formed a column to the right of the cross, and were from bottom to top, Page of Swords, the Tower, Eight of Pentacles and the Chariot.

"What does it all mean?" Sam asked. "Which card is the most important?"

Mary snorted. "That depends on the question. Now be quiet while I walk us through."

She turned to me as she tapped the card in the middle of the Cross. "Queen of Swords is you. You'll have to make your own way in the world for most of your life. Perhaps the cards heard you say you'd ask about your dream of writing rather than love. You'll not have an easy time of it, my dear. Don't despair, there's more yet.

"Crossing is the Nine of Wands. You'll have to fight to keep whatever you earn, I reckon.

"Ace of Swords. You'll have ups and downs."

"Any good news?" I asked. "Or should I hang myself now, like the Hanged Man?"

Old Mary smiled, revealing a few black teeth and one gold crown, a reminder of better days. "Hanged Man usually means a change is coming. Notice the man ain't dead, just hanging upside down. He sees things differently, that's all. But this time he's in the past position. This means there's something in your life you need to let go of. It's finished, and you need to move on.

"Now the next card, Strength. That called out to you. You've got battles coming and must be strong to overcome them, but if you do, you'll shine. Nothing will ever come easy, but if you do your best, you'll know success."

"Finally, a good card!" Sam exclaimed. "I was about to ask for your money back."

Mary glared at her. "I've no power to summon a card, and since you're not the querent, I'll ask you to hold your tongue 'til I'm done."

She turned back to me. "Now, from bottom to top, Page of Swords means you'll need to take precautions in your affairs. Always be ready to defend yourself."

"Take precautions," I said, nodding. "Sound advice for anyone."

"Next, the Tower," Mary continued, "You'll notice the tower is struck by lightning. You'll face chaos in your life, and learn to fix what you can and accept the rest."

"Good luck with that!" Sam hooted. "Maggie has an opinion on everything!"

Old Mary glared at Sam again. Some believe that fortune tellers can cast the evil eye, and Sam fell silent.

Satisfied, Old Mary returned to the reading. "Eight of Pentacles signifies that hard work will pay off. You've the talent, and if you apply yourself, you'll do well."

"Finally, the Chariot. The time has come to seize the reins, so to speak. If you want to take this path in life, you'll need to take action soon and set upon it."

"Thank you, Mary, you've given me much to think about. Enjoy your well-earned sixpence."

Mary slid the tanner off the table and into a small bag hung around her neck, then she laid her hand on top of mine. "The Strength card called out to you. A challenge is coming soon. You mustn't waver, and if you hold fast, you can take your desired path with confidence." She looked up at the darkening clouds. "Looks like a storm's coming. I'd best be off, or the bridge'll be crowded by the time I gets there."

"You sleep under the bridge?" I asked, stunned by the image.

"Aye, lass. But thanks to your fortune, me belly'll be full tonight. Good day to you." Mary wrapped her dark shawl around her thin shoulders and was off toward the nearest pub.

That night, a fierce winter storm came growling from the north. I begged Father to open the church to the beggars under the bridge. "They're Catholics." He sniffed. "Let them take care of their own."

"They're children of God!" I shouted. "Do you think God cares if you pray in Latin or English?"

"That'll be quite enough, Margaret," he said. "I'd have to pay the sexton to stay the night to keep them from stealing. I'll not have it."

I stormed to my room on the upper floor of our home and slammed the door. My anger was made all the hotter when I heard a key in the door, locking me in. I looked out and saw the snow coming down so hard I could scarcely see across the street. I thought of Mary under the bridge with the other beggars, then grabbed the quilt on my bed, wrapped myself up in my coat and scarf, and opened the window to crouch on the ledge.

I looked down. Twelve feet, more or less. Snow was piling up already, perhaps two feet or more, but as I contemplated jumping, I froze. Too far. I tried to force myself out into the air three times but couldn't do it. The tears first burned my cheeks, then nearly froze as I grappled with—and ultimately succumbed to—my fear. I looked up at the dark skies once more, then slid back inside, defeated. I've been afraid of heights ever since.

The next morning I went to the bridge with some hot porridge in a pot, only to find four people frozen to death underneath, Mary among them. She died because of my fear, and I took her cards as a reminder of what my weakness had cost others, so that I would never hesitate to do what I knew was right, ever again.

Elizabeth had sat silent, spellbound during my recitation. She shook herself as though returning from a dream once I finished my tale.

"How could your father allow those poor people to freeze to death, just because they were Catholic?"

"Because in his eyes, they had the dual sins of being Catholic and poor. He feared the prosperous members of his congregation would be scandalized if he gave them shelter inside their very clean, shall I say, 'sterile,' church. Unlike a Catholic priest, my father could be turned out by his congregation if he offended them too severely. He enjoyed his position in the local community as well as his secure salary and took great pains to never make his parishioners the least bit uncomfortable. The storm was one of many battles he and I fought during my time under his roof. It wasn't long after that I left for London to become a nurse, which was scandalous enough for him to nearly disown me. By the time I became a journalist and author, we rarely communicated at all."

"When was the last time you spoke?"

"Nine years ago, while I was living in Whitechapel to do research for a book. My father showed up unexpectedly, telling me he'd selected a 'suitable' young man for me to marry and that I should pack my bags. He didn't like my answer and returned home without me. He died shortly after, and I'm afraid our parting words were not tender." I rubbed the back of my neck. "I was never the daughter he wanted, nor he the father I needed. I hope you appreciate the character of yours."

Elizabeth said nothing for a moment, but her eyes grew round as I stowed my derringer in my purse. "Have you ever used it?" she asked.

I laughed. "Occasionally, though the first time I didn't actually fire it. Its presence was enough. Thankfully, I've never had to shoot anyone, and I intend to keep it that way, though with this anarchist about I'd best keep it on me for the moment."

"What stories! I want to be you when I'm fully grown."

"Making your way in a man's world is difficult, Elizabeth. I've had to fight every step of the way. For every hand up there are two boots to shove you back down, some of them, sadly, other women's."

"But you're a success. A published author, a journalist, and you go on adventures with famous men. If you can do it, so can I."

The girl's admiration was touching, and I hadn't the heart to tell her what my life choices had cost me. I'd worn an engagement ring once, until the budding young politician told me that although he shared my Christian Socialist philosophy, he would not "permit" me to continue my career once we were married as I would be "too busy" supporting his. *Good thing I won't be around long enough to disappoint her.*

She next asked me about a pendant I'd made of an 1888 penny on a tri-color ribbon.

"A gift from an enemy. Odd perhaps, but your enemies can be your greatest teachers. I keep this coin to remind me of dangers I've faced, and overcome. Every woman has her secrets, Elizabeth. Let this one be mine."

I knew my answer would only provoke further questions later, but we needed to move along before it became dark.

"One more thing: I need to tell the post office where to forward my mail. Can't have a royalty check go astray, can we? Oh, and is there anything we should pick up for the larder on the way home? Although we'll be in separate flats, I'd like it if we could dine together. It would be nice to cook for more than one for a change."

Elizabeth considered the question carefully, and it was clear she'd been the lady of the house for some time. She shook her head. "No. Unless you like a lot of sugar in your tea, we should be fine for a day or so."

"Well, Elizabeth, if you don't mind carrying the two suitcases with clothes, I'll take the other with books and my typewriter, after I change my attire."

"What's wrong with what you're wearing?"

"Nothing, except that I'm dressed as a woman. If Herr Ott is watching my residence, he won't be looking for a man. Wait for me in the sitting room, please. I'll be right back."

It took but a moment for me to dress as a respectable middle-aged gentleman and return to where Elizabeth was waiting, and I admit her reaction pleased me. Her mouth dropped open before she gave a low whistle. "Margaret, I'd never have recognized you on the street!"

"Precisely the point, Elizabeth. Let me go out first and look for any suspicious men loitering about. Give me ten minutes, then if all is clear I'll be back and we can proceed as planned. If I don't return within a half hour, go to your father and tell him what happened."

"I won't leave you!"

"Thank you, but I may have left you. If I see a likely suspect I may follow him. I'm just considering the possibilities."

She nodded her understanding, her lips pale as the true nature of our situation finally sank in. I made a slow circuit outside the building, but after five minutes saw no one of interest. I returned to my flat to collect my young companion, and off we went with our assigned burdens.

The British Mail was its usual efficient self, and after filling out a forwarding address card and buying some stamps we were soon at the apartment building in Soho. Elizabeth enjoyed helping me unpack and sort my things, and we were laughing like schoolgirls when James knocked on my new door.

"It seems I've gained a second daughter," he said, smiling. "All sorted?"

"Yes, we are. Would you mind if I prepare dinner in your flat for all of us? I've always hated cooking for one. Cheese and mushroom omelets with fried potatoes alright?"

James and his daughter exchanged glances. "How long can you stay?" asked Elizabeth.

Dinner was an unqualified success, and after everything had been cleaned and put away, the three of us adjourned to the sitting room. I was careful not to sit in the chair that appeared to belong to the man of the house.

"What did your superiors have to say about Elizabeth's possible sighting of Herr Ott? Do they take our concerns seriously?"

"No. When I said my daughter was my source of the sighting, I believe they stopped listening."

"Of course they'd say that about a woman," Elizabeth snapped.

"Almost a woman," her father corrected her. "You seem to forget that at times."

"*Almost* a woman, then. And at what age can I finally be taken seriously and do as *I* want to do?"

I cleared my throat. "As for me, Elizabeth, I cannot say. Apparently, I'm not old enough yet."

We elders laughed at the echoes of conversations we'd each surely had with our own parents at some time. The question, and the answer, were still the same.

As I prepared to go to my flat, Elizabeth asked if she could accompany me. "I've not had another woman to talk to in ages. Would you mind?"

"More woman-to-woman conversation?" I said, half-teasing.

"Something like that, yes."

James waved his vague goodnight wishes as he trudged off to bed, and soon we two ladies were alone in my flat.

The girl's happiness at having another woman to talk to was touching, and we chatted away for at least a half-hour.

"It would be unfair to ask you what your father really said about me," I said, as we got comfortable in my sitting room.

"And?" Elizabeth giggled.

"Well, are you going to tell me or not?"

Elizabeth yawned elaborately, drawing the moment out. "He said that you were unlike any woman he'd ever met before, and he wanted to know you better. I could tell he was intrigued by how forthright you are."

"Some would prefer the term 'blunt,' but forthright will do. And the day after our dinner together?"

"Oh, he didn't say too much about it, but he didn't have to."

"Why is that?"

"I heard him humming as he shaved the next morning. He hasn't done that since mother died."

"He really is a good man. You're lucky to have him as your father."

She nodded. "Even at his worst he was never cruel, not to me at least, but merciless with himself. It's good to see him like he used to be."

We chatted a while longer about things best kept in confidence, until Elizabeth finally yawned in earnest and I bade her good night.

That night, I dreamt I was sixteen years old again and walking toward the bridge over the Severn the morning after the storm. I wanted to run away, but my feet moved in slow motion closer and closer to where Old Mary lay.

Her thin form lay huddled beneath an old horse blanket.

"Mary?" I called. No answer. My feet pulled me closer, my heart thrusting against my chest. My hand reached out to the still form and uncovered the head. I looked down at the unmoving visage and saw that the frozen, gray face, was mine.

19

Friday night, June 11, to Sunday, June 13

Herman stood vigil outside Margaret's old apartment building, certain she hadn't passed him since he took his post near the entrance. The rifle's case had not caused a second glance as he made his way to her residence; nor did anyone take notice of it now, as he sat on the steps of a nearby bakery. He quietly smoked a pipe while he tried not to pick at the newly formed scabs on the back of his left hand, a reminder of the publisher's cat's displeasure at being placed at the scene of the crime.

Herman rarely smoked but knew that pipe smokers were generally perceived as harmless, and the smoke helped obscure his face. He had another to kill, once the woman was dead, so no need to risk capture yet. If he succeeded in killing the two of them, a hangman's noose would mean little except an end to his pain.

Finally, as nearby church bells tolled midnight, he gave up. She wasn't here. Tomorrow was another day. He'd found her once, he could do so again.

"How may I help you?" The middle-aged woman behind the counter seemed sincere, and Herman smiled despite himself. *The British are polite, if nothing else.*

"I have a package to deliver, but the woman who lives at the address I was given appears to have moved. Could you direct me?"

"Do you wish to mail the package, sir?"

"No, thank you. I was paid to deliver it personally."

The woman clucked her tongue in sympathy. "Then I'm afraid I can't help you. I'm not allowed to give out personal addresses."

Herman knew better than to argue. He nodded and went outside to consider his next move. It appeared he needed a package. Anything large enough not to fit in a mail slot. He went into an adjacent bookstore and, on a whim, purchased a book of poetry. One poem in particular caught his eyes, John Donne's "For Whom the Bell Tolls." He was tempted to underline the final line: "Therefore, send not to know for whom the bell tolls, It tolls for thee."

No. Best she thinks the book a gift from an adoring fan so as not to scare her into moving again. With great difficulty, he wrote a brief note inside.

Dear Miss Harkness,

On behalf of a devoted reader. May these words bring you as much joy as your words have brought me.

H

His face slowly grew a tight smile. *Inspired.*

He had the bookstore clerk wrap it for him, then he returned to the post office, the book under his arm.

The same woman greeted him as before. "Changed your mind?"

"Yes, Madam, I have. If you can't trust the Royal Mail, the world is in worse condition than I care to imagine."

After Herman paid the required postage, she wrote in large block letters on the wrapper while Herman pretended to count his change while noting the new address.

He turned and as he began his journey to Soho, started humming a tune without thinking. A passing Frenchman smiled however, when he recognized an old favorite, "*Le Temps des Cerises.*"

Soho never truly sleeps, and that evening Herman could find no dark corner within sight of the entrance to the new address. This would be difficult. The rifle was accurate and quiet but clumsy to handle. He would not be able to fire off a snap shot with any degree of accuracy, and the sensitive trigger made it likely it would discharge before he was ready. He would need time to get an accurate bead on his target and sufficient cover to prevent someone from noticing. Also, his funds were running low. He needed to make more lamps to buy food.

He smelled sausages from a nearby pushcart, and as he lathered mustard on his food, an idea came to him. The fat vendor looked to be about fifty, with a prominent handlebar mustache favored by Bavarians. Herman asked in German, "Are you from Munich?"

"*Ja, ich bin.* Why?"

"Could you do a countryman from Berlin a favor? I'd make it worth your while."

After ten pounds (half of Herman's remaining funds) exchanged hands, Herman found himself the proud proprietor of the food cart for the rest of that day and the day to follow. Herman had also been required to hand over his father's pocket watch as security, and he was careful to remove the picture of Astrid holding little Immanuel before doing so, placing the photo carefully in his vest pocket.

The Bavarian walked away happy for the unexpected paid holiday. They'd agreed Herman was to surrender the cart and half the proceeds on the evening of the following day. *I should make enough money to pay for my meals for the next two days, or eat sausages,* Herman thought.

Business was brisk until eight, and it was difficult to keep watch on the entrance at times. Finally, as the late spring evening arrived, passersby thinned out and the few remaining were intent on getting home. He was packing the cart up and preparing to take it to the pub where it would be stored overnight, when he saw a slender woman leave the building. Herman took a deep breath and mentally compared her to the image in the books he'd studied at the bookstore. His shoulders tensed as he confirmed it was her.

She seemed carefree, despite Astrid's blood on her hands. Herman had to restrain himself from rushing forward and grasping her throat with his large and furious hands.

This was the first time Herman had seen Miss Harkness in daylight, and he was surprised to see a man and young woman with her. *Staying with friends?* he asked himself. That meant something had alarmed her. *I must have been observed.* He shook his head. That wouldn't stop him.

Befreier was stowed underneath the cart, just a case holding any number of possible items. It was getting dark, and the young lady with them meant they would not be out late. Herman pulled the cart into an alley across the street, and carefully cleaned and recleaned the grill, waiting for his chance. As the shadows deepened, he drew the rifle out and assembled it on the ground behind the cart. Satisfied it was as ready as he could make it, he covered it over with a tarpaulin and left it at his feet, ready to seize when the moment arrived.

His patience was soon rewarded as the trio walked back, each holding an ice cream cone and laughing at some comment the young girl had made. There was a streetlight ten feet to the right of the entrance to the apartment building, which was fortunate. It would light up the space where they would halt for keys, while casting him in shadow.

Herman lowered the top of the grill. The fire had been out some time now, so it was cool enough to serve as a rest for the rifle. As the three of them passed him on the far side of the street about forty feet away, Herman laid *Befreier* on top of the grill and assumed the proper position. The telescopic scope drew in the dim light, making it easier to see his target in the evening shadows. The three stopped when the man reached for his keys. Herman let his breath out slowly and let the crosshairs drift down until Margaret's head filled the sights. *A life, for a life*, he thought. He put the slightest pressure on the trigger, and the rifle coughed.

20

Sunday, June 13, cont.

I was teasing James for the serious expression he wore while he ate his ice cream. "Really, James, most people smile when they enjoy an ice. Why do you scowl so?"

"I'm not scowling, I'm thinking about my ice cream."

"I never considered it a meditation. You must become quite philosophical with chocolate."

James fumbled with his keys, trying to keep the melting confection from dripping onto his vest.

"Here," I said, leaning forward to take his cone. I heard a hollow *thunk* and the brick beside my head exploded into fragments, showering us with debris.

"Get down!" James shouted, drawing his revolver, while I shoved a stunned Elizabeth to the ground before pulling out my derringer, my heart racing.

I saw a man across the street resting a rifle over a cart just as James fired, lighting up the street like a bolt of lightning. My first instinct was to fire at the man with the rifle, though it would be pointless at that range. But I would not go down without a fight. "Get inside, Elizabeth!" I shouted as I rushed forward to the right to flank him.

The flame from the revolver startled Herman. He'd never been fired upon before and flinched, causing his next shot to go high, knocking off the man's derby. Herman felt the cart shudder as the heavy bullet from the Webley's second shot smashed into it. He was reloading to finish the man with the pistol when another gun fired to his left and he instinctively ducked.

Windows were thrown open and shouts rose all around, and Herman knew his chance was gone. He grabbed the case, but as he turned, he tripped on the strap and fell face-forward. He felt the flask in the butt snap, and the bark of escaping air caused James to throw himself onto the street, thinking it was a bomb.

Herman cursed while jumping up, grabbed the case, and ran into the darkness. James leapt up and charged after him, running from shadow to shadow, ignorant that his enemy was now toothless.

Herman sped down an alley and into a secluded courtyard before stopping to catch his breath. His chest heaving, he listened for the sounds of pursuit. There was much shouting, followed by police whistles, but he seemed safe for the moment. He quickly disassembled and stored the remnants of the rifle. Then he shouldered the case and did his best to look like a tradesman making his way home as he trudged toward the nearest Underground at the Marble Arch.

I had no illusions that I could hit the man with my derringer at that range and in the dark, but I was pleased to see him duck down when I fired, at least buying us some time. I was about to fire again when there was an explosion, and I crouched down beside a building. James was up and after the assassin before I had a chance to rise. He ran to the corner we'd seen the sniper dart around, then disappeared in hot pursuit.

Running was no longer in my repertoire but I hurried with a will after James, my weapon held high. After rounding the corner, I saw him about eighty yards away standing in the middle of a street showing his badge to two police constables, who had apparently accosted him for running down the street with a drawn revolver. After a brief conversation they blew their whistles and the three of them set off in blind pursuit of the rifleman.

There was a time when I'd have gone after them, but that time was past. My chest was tight and with the danger past, I felt light-headed. I sat down on the street curb and tried to slow my breathing.

It wasn't long before I saw James returning, empty-handed, with the constables.

"What's all this about, then?" one asked as James led them back toward me and the scene of the attack.

"Someone fired at us from behind a vendor's cart," James pointed up the street in my general direction. I walked back around the corner ahead of him and looked closely at the sausage wagon, when something on the ground caught my eye and I picked it up. Some sort of brass flask, the neck ruptured, its shattered top looking like the petals of an opening flower.

My back was turned and I must have been shrouded in the shadows as I heard James continue his conversation with the bobbies as he rounded the corner.

"I'll go off with you in a moment to make a report. Just let me see to my family first."

Family? I thought. *He'd said it without thinking. Still...*

"He's gone," James said as he came up to me, still wheezing from the exertion of the chase. He looked at his revolver. "I've been an inspector for almost sixteen years, and this is the first time I've ever discharged a weapon anywhere but at a firing range, and never at night. It does make a light, doesn't it?"

Then he pointed to my derringer, which I still had in my hand. "Though you certainly made a contribution to the fireworks. I didn't know you were armed, but I'm glad you were. I think your shot from the side drove him off. Well played!"

Elizabeth came out of the building James's hat in her hands as though holding a wounded pet. "Your hat, Father. Your favorite hat. I'm so sorry."

Elizabeth stuck her finger through the hole in the front of James's wounded derby. "It missed your head by only a couple of inches."

James chuckled. "And to think of all the times you blocked it for me. The hat, I mean," and our fright was released in a burst of laughter that brought tears to our eyes.

James hugged Elizabeth then, to my surprise, me. He looked at me, then nodded toward his daughter. "Thank you for seeing to her safety."

I said nothing in response. There was no need. We'd faced danger together, like a family, just as James said.

Our laughter faded as we realized how fortunate we were to be unharmed, and James became businesslike when I showed him what I'd found on the ground.

"This was behind the cart, and I'm not sure what to make of it."

James peered at it closely. "I think this made the sound we mistook for a bomb. I'll take it along to headquarters and see what they can deduce."

He gestured to the apartment building. "Let's get you ladies inside, then I'll accompany these constables to their station to make a report that my superiors can disregard with their morning tea." He rubbed his chin. "Though being fired upon may convince them there was something to my concern after all. I doubt our sniper will return, but do not use any lights, please, and for goodness' sake don't stand by the windows! I'll be back before daylight, if only to bathe and change my clothes."

I was (and still am) unused to taking orders, but these were sensible, and for the moment my major concern was making sure Elizabeth recovered from the fright. The quiet confidence in James's voice after the attempt on our lives was reassuring, and I liked the character of the man who stood before me—and between his "family" and danger.

"Right you are . . . *Inspector*. We'll be good girls until you return. Now go do what you have to do."

My stress on the title "Inspector" gave James pause, as I'd intended. It was a mild rebuke that I was not his to command. He tipped his wounded hat and followed the two constables into the night.

21

The antiquities shop, Sunday, June 13, to Monday, June 14

Herman used the key Luigi had given him to enter the shop and drag the case to his workbench. He brought out the damaged weapon and stared at it. He was furious, but admitted the weapon had not failed him nearly as much as he had himself. He had been fired at and flinched. The woman still lived and would now be more difficult to kill. Luck had not totally deserted him, however, as they didn't get a good look at his face in the shadows; but they now knew he was in London and armed—or he would be, once he repaired his weapon.

He studied the wounded rifle. Sure enough, the Achilles' heel of the weapon was the air flask. The fragile neck of the brass air reservoir had snapped where it threaded into the firing chamber. Until he could remove the remnants of the damaged one, he was carrying a twenty-pound doorstop. Fortunately, he had two flasks left.

He reached into his waistcoat to check the time and sighed. His pocket watch was now irretrievable. The license on the side of the cart would lead the police to its owner. Either the cart owner would be used as bait or would be sure to notify the police if Herman returned. *A costly mistake. I'm sorry, Andrei. Our family heirloom deserved a better fate.*

Herman worked early into Monday morning at Luigi's shop, repairing the rifle and making lamps. He allowed himself two hours' sleep but was back before opening. He could now wire a lamp in little more than an hour and had five ready by the time Luigi arrived. The Italian marveled at the quality of Herman's work and was able to sell them nearly as quickly as they were made. Herman was low on funds, so the ten-pound advance Luigi paid him was welcome.

There was a knock at the entrance thirty minutes before opening time. Luigi went to shoo the visitor away, but he let out a cry of recognition and opened the door, locking it quickly after. He and his visitor came to the back office as Herman was starting on another lamp. He was deep in concentration threading a wire through a freshly drilled hole when he heard a voice behind him.

"*Guten Tag*, Herman. I hope you're happy to see me."

Startled, Herman turned toward a familiar if unwelcome face: his former employer, Grüber.

"What are you doing here?" he said, baring his teeth. "Haven't you caused me enough pain?"

"Herman, I came here to make what amends I could. The authorities have ceased their hunt for you in Berlin, though it will never be safe for you to return. After a difficult questioning, I was released from custody as I was able to convince the police you acted without my knowledge. Fortunately, I have influential friends who spoke on my behalf. I believe the chief of the Secret Police still suspects me, but lacking clear evidence, was forced to let me go."

"You still haven't answered my question. You told me how you were able to come here. Not why."

Grüber glanced at Luigi. "This is difficult for me, Herman. Please, may we speak alone?"

Herman shrugged. "As you wish. What more can you do to me?"

Grüber flinched at this but said nothing. Turning to Parmeggiani he said, "Thank you for taking Herman in. I consider your debt paid in full."

"*Prego, Signore*. It is nothing. His skill as an electrician has already proven profitable. You may send as many such as him as you like." Bowing, Luigi finished by saying, "I have some work to do in front to prepare for opening. I will let you gentlemen talk in peace. Scusi."

Once they were alone, Grüber pulled out his wallet and counted two hundred pounds onto the workbench. "You have suffered much for our cause and at my request. I know you hadn't time to prepare, and I hadn't the time to help you as you deserved. This money will not bring your family back, but it can help you establish yourself here."

Herman stared at the money and thought of the loss it represented. No, it would not replace what he lost. That was impossible, but perhaps it could be put to good use, nonetheless. He frowned but took the money.

"What will you do now, Herman?"

"I have the air rifle. With this money, I can take my revenge on those who robbed me of my family."

Grüber paled. "Like me?"

Herman shook his head. "No. I blame myself more than you. I knew what I was getting into, or I should have. I blame Fraülein Harkness. This was none of her affair. Astrid adored her books and felt betrayed that this woman would be an instrument of the aristocracy. She will pay. Then, if I can, I will seek this Professor Bell. After that, well . . . I don't know. What else is there?"

Grüber placed his hand on Herman's shoulder. He felt like an angler about to tempt a trout with his fly. "Have you considered that you are striking out at the symptom of your pain and not the cause?"

"What do you mean?"

"Harkness and Bell were acting as mercenaries. They were mere agents. If you want to strike a blow against those who cause the death of innocents, you should attack their employers."

"You said yourself I cannot return to Germany, though killing Herr Adler would give me great pleasure."

"No, Herman, I don't mean the functionaries of those in power. I mean the aristocracy, those who employ others to do their dirty work."

"You want me to wait for the Kaiser to visit his grandmother the queen?"

"No, my friend, but the ruling class are all related. A blow against one frightens and weakens them all."

"And?"

"If you want to prevent other innocents from dying for the decadent on their golden thrones, you can do so here in London."

Herman felt a thrill move down his spine and felt more alive than he had since hearing of Astrid's death. "The queen herself?"

"Yes, Herman. Kill the queen, the mother and grandmother of half of European royalty, and you will strike at the head of the serpent."

"How will the death of this old woman make a difference? She may not even live until the ceremony."

"You miss Astrid, and killing Victoria will not fill the loss of her death. But I can help you rejoin your son if you do this."

Herman clenched his large fists, and Grüber took a step back, unsure what Herman would do next. "You are offering to trade my son for the Queen of England?"

Grüber swallowed. "I wouldn't have phrased it like that, my friend, but in essence you are correct. Kill her during the Diamond Jubilee, with the entire world watching, and not a single crowned head will feel safe again. Their sense of invulnerability will be shattered forever. Do that, and I will get your son to you."

Herman thought about Immanuel being raised by a grandmother who hated him. All his son would ever know of his father was that he had caused Astrid's death.

"How can I trust you, after all this?"

"Herman, I have always kept my promises to you. Do this for me, for the cause, and I will see to it that your son is sent to you wherever you choose to live. America, perhaps? A man and his son could easily disappear in such a large country."

"I would need enough money to buy passage and start a new life."

"Easily done. We have wealthy patrons who can give you what you need to establish yourself there. From what I have heard, a skilled craftsman like you would do quite well in America."

Grüber extended his hand. "Do we have a deal?"

"From what you say, Frau Vogel will never agree."

"Frau Vogel has no say in this matter."

Herman sighed. *What have I got to lose that I haven't lost already?* Herman looked at Grüber, then, ignoring his hand, took off his apron and hung it up. "Excuse me, I need to find a seat for the ceremony."

"Herman, wait!" Grüber pulled out his notebook and quickly scribbled an address, then tore out the page and handed it over. "We have sympathizers in Southampton who will take you in on my behalf. Wait there for me or a message after the deed is done, and I will see to it your son is delivered to you."

Herman took the note, turned to leave, then paused and looked back. "Do not forget our bargain, *mein Herr*. If I survive and you fail to deliver my son, I will hunt you next."

Grüber was struck at the hardness in the man's cool gray eyes. The thought of those eyes peering through a telescopic sight with him in its crosshairs gave him a sudden chill despite the warm June morning, but the feeling quickly passed. As he watched Herman's broad back leave the workshop, the man bent on his new task, Grüber had to restrain a smile. The trout had risen to the bait, and the hook was deeply set.

Herman bought a newspaper with a map showing the route. The procession was to begin at Buckingham Palace and proceed to St. Paul's Cathedral, the site of the actual ceremony, traveling via an egg-shaped circuit which wound from Constitution Hill, down Piccadilly, to Strand, then Fleet Street, until finally arriving at St. Paul's. On the return the royal procession would cross the Thames twice, pass the Houses of Parliament, then arrive back at Buckingham.

Herman considered the options. His target would be as dead if he shot her on the return leg of her journey as she would be on the front end, and the bridges tempted him. If he should miss on his first shot, there would be no place for the carriage to go but forward.

Obviously, he could not hold a rifle in plain sight, even one as unusual as *Befreier*. Once assembled, its purpose was plain. He would have to find a rooftop, but that would be difficult, as every flat surface along the route was being prepared as a viewing platform.

He spent the day examining possibilities within range of the two bridges and finally gave it up. Even at the sedate pace of the royal carriage a shot over one hundred yards at a moving target the size of a pie plate, among a throng of hangers-on, would be risky. No. He had to look elsewhere.

As he studied the route map again, he idly turned to the description of the ceremony. He was astonished to read it would not be held within St. Paul's, but outside. Victoria, due to her advanced age and rheumatism, would remain in the carriage, the celebrants standing on the steps above her. She would be motionless out-of-doors for about twenty minutes.

Herman stood at the foot of the cathedral stairs where the map showed her carriage would rest. He turned slowly in all directions. First, he studied the cathedral. There was one window to his right, high up, but getting the rifle inside past the throngs of clergymen and military officers would be well-nigh impossible. Next, he scanned the courtyard. Every rooftop had temporary bleachers being constructed with awnings placed above in case of rain or excessive sun. No place to hide.

He was about to give up and see what opportunities could be found close to Whitehall when he noticed a narrow street leading out of the plaza straight ahead of where the carriage would be pointing. Down at the end of the short street, on the corner, was a building with a flat roof and both first- and second-story windows. If he could see the windows from where he was standing, then he could see his current location from there. Worth a further look. He walked to the entrance just around the corner and saw a small sign: *St. Paul's Boys Choir Boarding School*, and underneath: *No Visitors*.

I need to make an official visit, I see, Herman thought. *I'll be back.*

22

Senior Inspector Murdock glared over the top of his tortoiseshell glasses. He was infamous for his glares and general ill-humor. Before his transfer to Special Branch, he had reduced more than one bobby to tears for an incomplete report.

"What's this rubbish about an assassin, Ethington? Is this your excuse for blazing about Soho with your revolver like some cowboy in a penny dreadful? Your conduct casts a garish light on Special Branch and I won't stand for it!"

James reddened at the rebuke and had to take a deep breath before responding. "I was acting in defense of myself and my companions, one of whom was my daughter. I had no intent to cast any sort of light on anyone. I was being shot at and was trying to stop the assailant using the best means available. I dare you or any other man to say they'd have done differently."

Murdock was unused to being talked back to but conceded James's point. "Well, be more careful next time. The owner of the sausage cart was most unhappy with the hole you drilled into his means of livelihood. If you patronize him in future, probably best you don't identify yourself. No telling what you might find in your sausage."

Ethington placed his derby onto the senior inspector's desk. "And I was most unhappy with the hole drilled into my hat. Two inches lower, and we'd not be having this conversation."

Murdock found himself without a ready retort. For all his long years in law enforcement, he had never been shot at. He cleared his throat. "Then I'm glad it wasn't. Two inches lower, I mean. Well, it's done." He suddenly found the reports on his desk in need of rearranging. Still looking down he said, "You know the situation best. What do you propose we do next?"

"His intended target was Miss Harkness, and she had just moved into my apartment building as a precaution before the shooting occurred. I doubt the man will try again where he has failed once, but as the lady is proficient at passing as a man, I'll advise her to assume male clothing whenever she leaves the building, at least for now."

Murdock raised his eyebrows but said nothing. He'd been on the force for many years and had seen far stranger things than a woman dressed as a man.

"The best thing of course," James continued, "would be to capture him, but right now we have a faceless man in a metropolis of six million, and he knows us better than we do him. We need a description to go with his name. Have we learned anything useful from the owner of the wounded sausage cart?"

Murdock's face twitched into something resembling a smile. "We did. He said a fellow German had rented his cart for a day. Oh, he also produced a fine gold pocket watch the man had given him in addition to ten pounds, as a security deposit. There was an inscription we think is in Russian. I've sent for an Orthodox priest to come in and translate it for us. I'll let you know what it says when I find out."

"What did you discover about the brass flask I found? Was it a bomb of some kind?"

"We sent it to the armory for study. Go down and ask Sergeant Quint what he's discovered. Be prepared for a long discussion, even if he's found nothing."

"I will, sir. But before I go, I request you contact our German counterparts for a sketch or photograph of Herman Ott, as well as anything else useful. They owe us that much. He's used deadly force here in England. When he's caught, we can choose to send him back to them, if they give us good reason, or prosecute him here. That should motivate them to be helpful."

Murdock frowned. "I don't like dealing with the Germans, but you're right. This Ott fellow is our problem for the moment. I'd not cry if we let him become theirs again. I'll send a telegram straightaway. Now be off. I'll let you know as soon as I hear back."

James sprang out of his chair, relieved at how the meeting had gone, and made straight for the indoor firing range in the basement, and the legendary Sergeant Quint.

Known as "Sergeant Q," the man knew everything there was to know about firearms, knives, saps, and archery. If it was manmade and lethal, he'd studied it. A solitary fellow, he seemed to store up any need for conversation for the moment he was asked a question. Then a flood of information, relevant or not, came tumbling out of his whiskered face, leaving it to the listener to sift for what was useful.

The smell of gunpowder and oil told James he was nearing the armory, and he found the man cleaning a large-bore rifle within the ammunition cage. This was convenient, as James needed a resupply of cartridges after the previous night's gunfire. He was only allowed the six spares besides the cartridges in his revolver. Besides, he felt the sudden need to refresh his skills at the firing line.

Taking a deep breath, he plunged ahead. "Good morning, Sergeant Q. Going elephant hunting, are you?"

The beefy man smiled as he inspected the rifle's barrel for perhaps the tenth time. "Nay, Inspector, though I reckon this piece'd do it. She's a beauty, ain't she? Martini-Henry rifle. Military issue, fires a .577/450 cartridge effective out to six hundred yards if the marksman's capable. I got Special Branch a dozen of these for, well, whenever they might prove useful. Never know. Would you be interested in some training on it?"

"No thank you, Sergeant. I used my Webley for the first time last evening. It certainly lights up the night."

"I heard about that, Inspector." Leaning in, he asked, "Hit anything?"

"A sausage cart. Dead center."

"Oh. Well, I expect you'll be needing some more cartridges then, in case you get attacked by another cart."

"Indeed I shall, thank you. Can't be too careful, what with carts loitering all over the place. Anything you can tell me about the brass flask I brought in last night?"

The man smiled like a child eyeing a full Christmas stocking. "One or two things, Inspector. But first, what did the rifle sound like?"

"A hollow sound. Like someone blowing into an empty jug, only very short."

The sergeant brought the flask up from under the counter, then a flattened large caliber bullet. "You should be flattered, Inspector. You were nearly the first person in all of England to be killed by an air rifle. A very powerful one, I might add. I've never encountered anything like this."

"You've never seen an air rifle?"

"Oh, I've seen scores of those. Most of them puny little things used for target practice or shooting rats." Hoisting the bullet in his right hand he said, "Look at the size of this. It weighs nearly as much as the one from this here Martini. If it had hit your head it would'a left a hole you could stick your thumb into. Whoever made this beauty has my admiration. Not many craftsmen in the world could have done this. Two shots in less than four seconds, if I recall your report correctly?"

"You do."

"Then it likely has an attached magazine for rapid reloading. Remarkable. If you catch the bugger who fired at you, bring me the rifle to study and I'll retire a happy man."

James cleared his throat. "And the brass flask?"

"The propellant force, Inspector. No gunpowder. That's why it was so quiet."

"So, what happened? This just broke off?"

"Seems so. The Austrians had a model like this. The flask also served as the butt, the top screwed into the firing chamber. Rapid-fire, accurate, powerful, but too fragile for a common soldier. It was only issued to elite snipers."

"I'm honored beyond words."

"Aye, you should be. Anything else I can tell you?"

"What would be its effective range?"

"Not near as far as this beauty," he said, patting the Martini. "I can't imagine how large a flask it'd take to have that much power, but I'd think a hundred yards would be possible."

"Thank you, Sergeant. You've been quite helpful. Oh, I'd like an extra twenty rounds. After last night, I'd like some practice with the Webley."

"Here to serve, sir. Blaze away. Think of me, if you get your hands on that air rifle, now. I won't forget it."

James took his pistol and the spare cartridges to the firing range, assumed a dueler's stance, right foot pointed toward the target, the left at ninety degrees, toward the left wall. He carefully aimed at the human silhouettes twenty-five feet away.

"Hold on, Inspector!" Sergeant Q yelled out. "As you might actually use your weapon, allow me to give you some advice."

James handed the pistol over as the man approached. Gesturing toward the target, he said, "Be my guest."

"After last night you should know that if it comes down to using your Webley, it won't be 'ten paces turn and fire.' You'll most likely be at short range, and if you take the time to use your sights, you'll be a dead man."

"So I should just point in my enemy's direction and pray?" James asked.

"Point, aye, but not with your hand. Point your fist at your enemy and fire immediately before your aim has a chance to waver. Like this."

The armorer faced the wall to his left, then turned sharply toward the back wall and jerked his hand up, firing twice in quick succession. Both shots hit the target in the mid chest. "Like that. It's good for one or two shots, before the barrel drifts from the recoil. Now, you try. Don't turn, just look straight at it, and fire."

James felt like a gunslinger in a "shilling shocker," but found the technique worked. If he forgot about the gun in his hand and concentrated on pointing his fist at the target, his accuracy was at least as good as when he aimed, and he got the shot off in less than half the time.

"Well done, Inspector," Sergeant Q said, smiling. "Nothing like getting shot at to motivate your student. I pity any sausage carts that get in your way."

"I've still got to figure out how to get close to a man armed with a rifle, but you've bettered my odds if I get in range, and I thank you for that."

He carefully cleaned the revolver before loading and replacing it into his shoulder holster. If he pulled it out in earnest, he needed to know it would perform.

After a brief lunch, James returned to Senior Inspector Murdock to learn if he'd gotten an answer from the Germans or a translation of the inscription of the pocket watch. Murdock looked up when Ethington knocked, and actually smiled. "Come in, Ethington. It seems the Germans are keen to get their hands on this fellow. A composite sketch will soon be winging its way to us via diplomatic pouch. I should have the man's likeness in two days."

"Anything else about him we should know?"

"He's a trained gunsmith, a crack marksman, and an electrician who has recently branched into telephony. All in all, a man of many talents."

"Do you think he's just here to escape the Germans, sir, or do you think his arrival is more than coincidence?"

"I don't believe in coincidences, Inspector. Given what we now know about the man's impressive skills and his apparent willingness to use them"—he paused to point to James's ventilated derby—"I see why you were so keen to tell us about him. I fear he may pose a risk to either Her Majesty or a visiting noble. The Diamond Jubilee procession and ceremony with its parade of royalty from around Europe is enough to make any anarchist salivate. I think we should recognize the risk he poses very seriously, both to Her Majesty and to her royal guests." Murdock clenched his jaw. "Driving him to ground now has the highest priority."

"I agree, Senior Inspector. Anything on the inscription?"

"Not much help there, I'm afraid. Just a proverb. 'A great voyage requires a great ship,' or something like that. The priest said it meant that it took a great man to accomplish great things. Let's hope our friend Ott doesn't aspire to greatness, if he even understood the inscription. I suspect he bought it at a pawnshop."

James sighed. "I agree. No help there. What do you suggest we do while we wait for a sketch of the man?"

"Don't go after him directly. Without his likeness, you could sit beside him on the Underground and never know it. Make him think he's in the clear for now. We'll get back to him soon enough."

"What should I be doing in the meantime, sir? The trail is hot, and I'm hot to follow it."

"I have a task for you until something clearer comes along. I suspect that one of our foreign anarchists has recently become active again. I want you to surveil him for the next two days or until the sketch arrives. You can make sure he is limiting his misdeeds to pamphlets and books. He's wealthy enough to hide our German sniper and supply him with explosives to create havoc during the Jubilee. Remember, Ott is an electrician. God forbid he add bomb making to his repertoire, but he's still a man. He needs a place to stay and food to eat. We find his benefactor, we find him. So, while you may think I'm wasting your time, you might be leading us straight to our assassin."

"Who is this wealthy anarchist, sir?"

"Peter Kropotkin. Here's his address in Battersea. I think you've earned a bit of rest after your recent adventure, so you can start tomorrow. Two days should be enough to see if he's behaving himself. Then you can go after Ott fullbore."

"With respect, I'd rather inquire around about any new German electricians in the city."

"Time enough for that, Inspector. Let's do this my way, shall we?"

"Very well, sir. As you like."

23

Monday, June 14, to Tuesday, June 15

James stomped into the Ethington apartment after slamming the door, then flung himself into his favorite chair. Elizabeth and I exchanged glances at his stormy entrance.

"I take it the day did not go well?" I asked, unsure how to proceed.

"Fossils! If they didn't occasionally move from behind their desks to go to their club, you could put them in a museum."

"What's wrong?"

"We are nearly slaughtered in the street, and what do we do? I'm told to wait and surveil a wealthy anarchist on the off-chance he could be sheltering the man. Piffle!"

"What would you rather do?"

"We have more information on our assassin, Herman Ott, and among his many talents he is a skilled electrician. A foreigner arriving unprepared in our country would have a difficult time finding employment as a gunsmith, but with the rapid spread of electrification in London, men with his experience have their pick of jobs. We expect a sketch of Ott in two days' time. Until then, I could inquire around about any recently hired foreign electricians, but my hands are tied. Senior Inspector Murdock has assigned me to watch a well-to-do Russian anarchist. Murdock said it could lead to Ott, but I suspect he is just having me complete his checklist of known troublemakers prior to the Jubilee. He expects a full report in two days."

"Do you have any copies of old surveillance reports here?"

"I probably have some drafts. Why?"

"Elizabeth and I could watch the man, which would free you to follow your instincts. I write the report, and you edit it to sound like you, and no one's the wiser."

His mouth gaped for a moment, then snapped shut. "You and Elizabeth?"

Elizabeth's eyes flashed. "Yes! A real surveillance. We can do it, Father. Please?"

"Certainly not! Why, the very idea of the two of you playing detective . . ."

"Is exactly what Elizabeth needs if she is to become one. Consider it a training exercise."

"I forbid it!"

"Is this assignment dangerous?"

"Well, no."

"Does it require any specific skill I do not possess?"

James glared at me. "No."

"Then is there any logical reason not to allow us to help?"

James swallowed. "I don't want Elizabeth to become a detective."

Elizabeth went to James and laid her hand on his shoulder. "I'll be an adult soon, Father, free to make decisions on my own. Wouldn't you rather I learn these skills now, while I have someone like Margaret to teach and watch over me?"

"My little girl," he whispered. "You're all I have left." He sat, unspeaking, for a moment. "Why does the world have to change so much, and so often?" Then he turned to me. "Please look after her."

"Like she was my own," I promised, my voice huskier than usual. I cleared my throat. "I need a name, a description, and an address." Then, to Elizabeth, I said, "Let's go to your room. I need to take some measurements before we go shopping. Having you try on male clothing while dressed as a woman would attract too much attention, but you may have some preferences. The shops close in two hours, so make haste!"

Elizabeth flew to her bedroom, so didn't notice James's sad smile as she left.

On the way to the Kropotkin residence the following day, I reminded Elizabeth to stop scratching three times while on the Underground. "I thought we agreed not to ape that particular male mannerism," I said.

"But my legs itch! These short wool trousers rub every time I move. How do they stand it? Don't they feel trapped in their clothes?"

"If you'd ever worn a corset, you'd feel less sympathy for men, on that account at least, but if they're so bothersome I suggest next time you wear stockings underneath. Now, be a good lad and behave." We exchanged a smile, and Elizabeth settled down.

James had advised me to favor male attire for the time being and I had just enough forbearance to pretend it was his idea. Elizabeth's disguise was agreed upon by her and me, and we were both rather pleased with the result.

She was dressed in short, charcoal-gray wool trousers with white knee-high socks, black brogans, a white shirt with suspenders, and a navy-blue blazer. I'd trimmed three inches of her hair to allow it to be neatly braided and placed beneath her flat schoolboy cap.

I was in my Pennyworth attire, a modest clerk's suit with a black derby, and wearing pince-nez glasses with clear lenses. My only extravagance was a gold watch and chain across a black silk vest. Together we looked like a father and son on an outing.

Elizabeth was still ungainly as she tried to walk like a boy, but boys that age grow so quickly they tend to be awkward, so no one noticed. As the day wore on, her confidence grew. At one point she tried to spit. I advised her to practice in private before attempting it again.

Peter Kropotkin was not a challenging subject, even for a novice like Elizabeth. He took a constitutional around the park after breakfast, a walk of about one mile. As it was a circuit, we observed his ambulation from the comfort of a park bench. I brought a book while

Elizabeth wrote in her notebook, practicing shorthand. "It'll be useful someday," she said, "for when I am questioning witnesses."

The Russian seemed to get along well with his neighbors, greeting other walkers as he passed them, tipping his hat and speaking with the musical lilt of his native tongue. After his walk he returned to his house and sat by the window of his study, writing. No visitors happened by and no men other than Kropotkin were seen passing by the windows or in the surrounding garden. For a man who wanted to change the world, his own life appeared sedate.

Elizabeth bought us meat pies from a pushcart and enjoyed gulping hers down in an unladylike way. "Being a boy is ever so much fun!"

"It has its moments," I agreed. "Do you know why we are here in male costume?"

"Sure," Elizabeth said, her mouth full. "For practice."

"Partly true. But also because men tend to pay less attention to other men, in public at least, unless they see them as a rival or a threat. But even the homeliest maiden will be scrutinized by every passing male beyond puberty. They can't help it. Thus, dressed as women, they would be more apt to remember us the next time they saw us. In our masculine façade, their eyes slide right past us. A useful fact to remember, Detective."

She laughed. "This is the most fun I've had since, well . . ." She returned to her pie.

"I'm sorry, Elizabeth, and I'm sorry we won't have more outings like this."

"I noticed how stiffly you walk in the morning. Are you sick?"

"I'm afraid so."

Elizabeth finished her meal, then wiped her face with the back of her sleeve, smiling as she did so. She turned toward me but avoided my eyes. "Is it serious?"

"It's hard to tell. I'm more apt to die with it than of it, but it will get worse over time. My doctors advise that I move to a warmer climate." I put my hand on Elizabeth's arm. "I've booked passage to Australia on the seventh of July."

She looked away. "Does Father know?"

"Not yet. I have no intention to deceive him, so I need to have that conversation soon. For both our sakes."

"Yes, I suppose so. I'm sorry, Margaret. It's been nice acting like a family for a little while. I've missed that, and it was nice to let someone else do the cooking." She sighed. "How much longer should we stay here?"

"It's only now one o'clock. We should probably move to another bench, something in the shade, so that when Mister Kropotkin looks out, he doesn't see us. Tell you what, once we move, I'll let you compose our surveillance report for your father. Do it in shorthand, that way you're practicing two skills at once."

"I'll do my best to describe the pigeons' activities with great precision."

Nothing of import happened until four o'clock, when Kropotkin and his teenage daughter went for a stroll together through the park. They made their way past us without a backward glance from the father, but the daughter paused to give Elizabeth a second look, then she smiled shyly before hurrying to catch up.

Elizabeth blushed. "That was an odd moment. I think she was flirting with me!"

"Take it as a compliment, both for your good looks and your convincing disguise. I don't get many second looks from the ladies these days, but clerks rarely do." Then in a dry voice, I continued, "Be sure to put that into your report."

"What, that his daughter is a flirt?"

"I'd put it rather more diplomatically. Say she has an eye for handsome lads her age."

We shared a brief laugh before Elizabeth said, "I wish I could go to Australia. I love their accent, and they ride horses everywhere. I have never been on one. It all sounds so romantic, to ride with some handsome young man in the moonlight as he speaks his heart in an Australian accent."

"I must be sure to write that into my next novel, Elizabeth. I believe it would double my sales."

After the Kropotkins returned home, I stood and dusted off my trousers. "I think we've served queen and country well enough today. We have a bit of shopping to do before returning home ourselves, and I need your help to do it right."

"Why? What are we shopping for?"

"An apology, of sorts. In the form of a new bowler hat."

24

Inspector Ethington was dressed roughly. Though he had the soft hands of an office worker, he hid them beneath leather work-gloves. He wore a flat cap, a rag tied around his neck, black wool trousers and vest, his ensemble completed with workman's boots and a moderately clean white cotton shirt. Usually his job required him to be unnoticeable, but today he had a speaking role.

He'd decided to start with the Municipal Utilities Department. The streets of London were for the most part electrified by this time, and a robust workforce was needed to maintain the network, making the Municipal Utilities Department the single largest employer of electricians within the city. James asked to see the department supervisor and when the secretary refused James showed his badge, explaining he was there on official business. Puzzled and awed, the young clerk knocked on a Mister Harwood's office door and said, "There's an important gentleman here who needs to speak with you."

Apparently his superior assented, as James was waved in immediately. Harold Harwood was not amused to see a common laborer ushered into his office, though his cigar nearly fell out of his mouth when he saw the badge. He turned pale and swallowed. "Inspector! To what do I owe the honor?"

James could tell the man had something to hide and made a mental note to return once his current affair was settled. "I'm looking for an electrician. German. He'd have been hired within the past month. Any of your men come to mind?"

Supervisor Harwood's shoulders relaxed as James explained his mission. *Good. Best you feel safe. For now.*

"None come to mind, Inspector, but I rarely meet the men myself. I could telephone my senior electrician. I leave such matters in his capable hands."

"Please do, sir. But I'd rather you not discuss the matter with him over the telephone. I'd prefer to speak with him in person if you don't mind. Just summon him to your office."

"Very well," he said, his hands shaking the slightest bit as he held the device.

He wants me gone. He's definitely hiding something.

Bill Monroe was in his early forties. He was red in the face and the nose, and was ill-disposed to be called into the office without an explanation. "What's this then, Mister Harwood? Not another complaint about Trafalgar Square! I can't help it if hooligans like to throw stones at the lights. Just tell me where the problem is, and I'll have me lads sort it. No need to call me on the carpet."

"I'm sorry, Billy, but this gentleman needed to speak with you. Inspector, I can take an early lunch and leave my office for your use. I'll be back at one."

And flee the scene of the crime, James thought, while outwardly smiling and reassuring the man that would be just fine. *I need to talk to my colleagues in Financial Crimes at Scotland Yard. This man reeks of guilt.*

After the supervisor made his hasty exit, the foreman and James sized each other up. "Whatever it is, Inspector, I ain't done nothing wrong."

"I have no reason to doubt you, Mister Monroe. I didn't come looking for you."

"Who then? Bishop? He's always been a troublemaker. Be glad to give 'im to you."

"I'm looking for a man, an electrician. He could be using any number of names, but he's German, and would have started work within the past month."

Monroe shook his head. "Naught like that with us. I've a Pole and a couple of Russian Jews, but no Germans at the moment. Why, what's he done?"

"I can't discuss that. Is there anywhere you could recommend I ask? Time is short."

"You could try the Electricians Guild Hall, they could tell you who's hiring."

"Excellent. Thank you for your help."

Monroe smiled through his yellowed teeth. "Seeing His Lordship scuttle out of here with his tail between his legs was all the thanks I needed. Good day."

James had been an inspector in the Criminal Investigation Division at Scotland Yard twelve years before his transfer to Special Branch, so when he walked into the Yard later that morning, several friendly faces greeted him. "Who's available from Financial Crimes?" he asked Desk Sergeant Finney, a man James had once joined in a foot chase for a burglar.

"Inspector Atkins, sir. He's new, you wouldn't know him. I get good reports, however. Next floor up, right-hand corner in the back. Any of our foreign 'guests' reaching into the till?"

"No, Sergeant, but I may have stumbled over a local gone bad. That's for Atkins to unearth."

James found his way to Inspector Atkins' corner office and found the man poring over a ledger while humming a tune from Verdi's *Rigoletto*, "*La donna è mobile*"—that is, "The woman is fickle." *A man who enjoys his work*, James thought. *I'm about to make him very happy.*

"Good morning, Inspector Atkins. Ethington, Special Branch."

Atkins looked up. Thirty years old with thinning hair and a thickening waistline, he was obviously in his element. "Good morning to you, sir. We don't get your kind up here often. I'm intrigued. Please, take a chair and tell me how I can help."

James showed his badge to establish his bona fides, then took a seat and got to the heart of the matter. "Earlier this morning, I paid a call on the supervisor of Municipal Utilities, a Mister Harwood. I was looking for an electrician, but he was twitchy the moment I showed him my badge. He's hiding something. Given his position, it's most likely financial. I think a quick look at his books would be most entertaining, judging by your obvious relish for your work."

Atkins grinned. "Indeed, Inspector. There's plenty of loose cheese in such departments to attract the odd rat. I think a couple of colleagues and myself could pay him a call this afternoon."

"He took an early lunch after I appeared. Said he'd be back at one. If you hurry, you can be there when he arrives. I think the shock of you sitting in his office when he walks in would make him confess on the spot."

"Wonderful idea, Inspector. Thank you. I'll let you know what comes of this. Nice costume, by the way. You been stringing lines yourself?"

"Not yet. Let's hope it doesn't come to that, or we'll see how well I glow. Good day."

James left feeling better about his work than he had in some time. *Feels good to help catch a thief again.* He considered requesting a transfer back to the Criminal Investigation Division after the Diamond Jubilee. He'd gone into Special Branch as the hours were more regular and it left him with more time for his family, but Elizabeth needed him less now and would soon go her own way, and Alice . . . was gone. Perhaps he should consider how he wanted to end his career—not as someone's shadow—but as a policeman.

25

T he custodian at the boarding school was hauling out the dustbin when a man carrying a toolbox on a strap stopped him at the front door. "Excuse me," Herman said, "I'm the electrician. I was asked to perform a safety examination of your wiring."

John "Jack" Connery was a man who didn't like surprises, so he didn't like this stranger with the German accent popping up on his front doorstep and interrupting his day. "I weren't told naught about it. Be off!"

Herman shrugged. "Sorry, sir, but if I don't do my job, I don't get paid. Surely you can understand that."

Jack had enough experience with bosses to believe the man. "Awright, awright. Just give me a moment to dump the leavings from these spoiled brats. Trust me, lad, just because they can sing like angels, don't make 'em heavenly."

Herman nodded in sympathy, "Yes, I agree. Looks can be deceiving, can't they? I'll wait right here."

After the most recent pile of dirt which the boys regularly tracked in had been tossed away, Jack wiped his hands on his trousers and led the waiting electrician into the foyer on the ground floor. "You want to check the whole building, or just the basement where the lines come in?"

"The entire building, please. There was a fire last week in Brighton, and as this building is occupied at night, someone thought a safety check was in order." There had in fact been such a fire, though not in a boarding school, but it sounded truthful enough. Close enough to truth that the custodian swallowed it without a qualm, and they began their tour.

"Where'd you like to start, then? Top or bottom?"

"Basement first I think, though you've no need to follow me about. I'm sure you're a busy man."

Jack shrugged. "Fair enough. There's always something. I'll have to be with you when you're in the dormitory. Can't have strange men poking around there, you understand. I'll be cleaning on the ground floor. Follow the stairs here down to the basement. After you've done the basement and the ground floor, we can go up to the dormitory together."

"It's very quiet for a school."

"Aye, for now. Lads are all off to practice for the big ceremony. Keeps the young hellions off my back and out of mischief. Now off with you. We've both got work to do."

Herman found the wiring recently installed and in good order. He estimated the building had been electrified within the past two years. He could look at the swirling mass of lines and see an order that was close to religious. Everything connected to something else, each an indispensable part of a larger whole, and it hurt his craftsman's heart to create a flaw in the system. He added a small loop and a switch that opened it, connecting it to the main cable. Then, with the switch closed, he stripped the insulation from one side, and fastened the bare copper to a water pipe. When the switch was opened, the entire building would lose power.

After reconnecting the building's wiring to the outside cable, he performed a safety check of the entire system in the basement. He wished the boys no harm, and it ensured he got his hands dirty and didn't finish his work too quickly. Once done, he kept the power on and returned to the ground floor to perform various voltage checks to the satisfaction of the custodian. "I sleeps here meself with my missus, so good to know we're being looked after."

After the ground floor was complete, the two men climbed to the first of the two floors containing the dormitory and classrooms.

"I'm also here to check your protection against lightning strikes, so I'll have to look at the outside of the building to check the cables and connections between your lightning rods and the ground."

"Makes sense," the custodian said, "It's all electricity, ain't it?"

Herman relaxed at the man's ready acceptance of his explanation for his need to inspect the exterior. *The hardest part's done,* he thought. The window in the corner room on the first floor was possible. Just. The second floor was perfect. The direction was dead on, and the angle would allow him to fire over the crowd and mounted escort. The boys had bunk beds, and as the window was six feet above the floor, he would need to fire from the top bunk adjacent to the window. He would check the roof, but he reasoned he would likely be spotted from an adjacent building if he took any time at all to fire. Here he could lie back from the window and wait for the perfect moment. *I won't miss this time.*

As Herman had suspected, the roof was a poor choice for a position, as the flat portion was skewed too far to the left with a large tree partially obscuring the view. The rest of the "inspection" went quickly, and the custodian was relieved the building got a good report. Herman handed the custodian two copies of a form to document the work that had been done. He used a blank invoice from Luigi's previous electrician to give his visit the air of authenticity and to provide the custodian with an address near the antiquities shop.

"Keep a copy of the form," Herman said, "should you require further work, though everything seems to be in perfect order."

Jack "made his mark," and they shook hands, one working man to another.

The long-suffering custodian went back to his endless task of undoing the damage the troop of bored young boys regularly inflicted on their home. If he had taken a moment to look out a window, he would have noted the electrician pacing back and forth between the steps of St. Paul's and the corner of his building.

Eighty-eight paces, Herman wrote in his notebook after three trials. Then he reaffirmed his earlier thought, *I won't miss, not this time.*

That afternoon, when the custodian submitted a copy of the form veri-fying the work on the boarding school had been completed, a clerk in the dean's office found no record such work had been requested. He sent a strongly worded note to the address listed on the form denying payment, mentioned it in passing to the dean, then promptly forgot about it.

26

nce we'd reached the entrance to the apartment building, I was surprised when I found a package in my mail drop. "Looks like a book," Elizabeth said.

I examined the address written on the package. It had been forwarded from the postal office closest to my previous apartment. I accompanied Elizabeth to the Ethington flat to store away my peace offering to James before opening the package. Inside, as Elizabeth had predicted, was a book, this one containing poetry. I noted a bookmark leading my eyes to John Donne's *For Whom the Bell Tolls*. The inscription gave me pause, "May these words bring you as much pleasure as they do me." The sender had signed the inscription only as *H*.

So that's how he found me. I thought. *God bless the Royal Mail. They brought him right to the front door.* I looked at Elizabeth. *And her.*

"What is it, Margaret? What's wrong?"

"I know how our assassin found me."

"All this from a book? Explain, please."

"Let's go inside, in case the killer is loitering about. Then, Detective, you can study the evidence and tell me what you make of it." *God, I miss Bell right now.*

Once inside my flat, Elizabeth carefully studied the book and the wrapping, her brows knitted in concentration.

"Don't tell me what you deduce," I said. "Not yet. Just describe what you see. If you jump to a conclusion too soon, your mind will filter out anything that contradicts your hypothesis. Look. Analyze.

Then deduce. Professor Bell taught me well. You could find no one better to emulate than him."

"The package was forwarded from your apartment's address."

"Too soon. You're making deductions. First, describe the handwriting on the cover."

Elizabeth took a breath, then studied the addresses again. "Two different hands. One bold with heavy strokes. The other lighter, precise."

"Which address for the bold hand?"

"Your previous apartment. The lighter hand for the one here."

"What does that tell you?"

"Heavy Hand didn't know your forwarding address. The lighter one is probably the Post Mistress."

"Good so far."

Elizabeth sat back, her eyes looking far away. "He watched her write the address down. That's how he found us."

"Precisely. By leaving a forwarding address, I left a trail straight here. Straight to you and your father. I am so very sorry." Suddenly I felt exhausted. "My first instincts after the attack were right. Ott is clever and relentless. I should probably leave for Australia on the next available ship. That would be the smart thing to do, but I'm not going to be scared off by this man, only to have him hunt me wherever I go. I do think however, that I should change my lodgings again until he's caught, to throw him off my trail."

"You can't go! Not yet. He revealed himself when he fired at us. This is probably the safest place for you now. He knows Father and you are armed and will go after him. Please don't go, at least not until you speak with Father."

I was torn. Elizabeth reminded me of myself at her age. Her companionship would be missed . . . and James's.

"Very well," I said. "Besides, we have a fine derby hat to present him. It's the least I can do after his former treasure fell honorably in combat on my behalf." We laughed together, the cloud of parting's sorrow gone for now. "What should we have for dinner?"

James came in just then, smiling.

"Did I hear someone mention dinner?" he asked.

"Yes, Inspector, you did, though the jury is still out as to what that might be."

"Might I make a plea before the court?"

"Plea away. If we don't have the ingredients, however, you'll be overruled."

"Then if it please the court, I plead for suckling pig with truffles."

Elizabeth and I laughed. "Out of order!" I said. "The court has no such provisions. Care to plead insanity in your defense?"

"Your Honor, I plead hunger. Perhaps you could reduce the sentence to roast chicken and potatoes?"

"I'll grant you clemency this one time, if you agree to thirty-minutes' servitude washing up afterward."

"Hard labor! Very well, Madam Judge, I accept, though next time I'm getting a better barrister."

I glanced over at Elizabeth as she stared at the two of us teasing each other like children.

"Excuse me," she said, and rushed out.

James looked after her, then he turned to me, his hands splayed out. "What did I say?"

"Nothing, James. Sit down. You'll find Elizabeth's notes in shorthand of our day's activities. Mister Kropotkin was a fairly tame assignment. Whatever you did today was surely more profitable than our labors, if sitting on a park bench can be described as labor."

James rubbed his chin as he perused the hieroglyphics. "Kropotkin's daughter flirted with Elizabeth?"

"Well, no, not exactly, but she did give her a second look and a smile. Elizabeth's disguise was quite convincing. Her report is thorough, wouldn't you agree? You might want to mention that when she comes to supper. Give me an hour to prepare dinner. That will give you time to transcribe the report into your hand and style to turn in."

"Capital. I did, in fact, have a very productive day, though not on our current case."

I smiled when James said "our" case. I hadn't been involved in such adventures since the Ripper affair, nor had such close companionship. I shook my head and returned to the chicken. "How so?" was all I could say.

"I believe I identified an embezzler in the Municipal Utilities Department. Turned it over to Financial Crimes at Scotland Yard. I reckon I'll hear back in a couple of days. The man nearly jumped out of his skin when I showed him my badge. Felt like a policeman again. Useful."

Dinner was a success, and Elizabeth glowed with her father's praise. "Well, my girl, if you are dead set on being a detective, then be the best one you can. It seems you are well on your way." Turning to me, he complimented, "Thanks to your excellent instructor."

There was an awkward silence as Elizabeth and I exchanged glances, then I stood up and said in a too-loud voice, "And now for dessert!"

James patted his stomach. "I couldn't possibly, but . . . well, I wouldn't want to hurt your feelings. What are we having?"

Elizabeth perked up. "I'll go fetch it, Father. It's in my room."

James looked at me. "Well, I hope it isn't ice cream."

A minute later Elizabeth returned, carrying a box tied in a red satin bow.

James reached out and carefully opened the box, then pulled out a handsome new black derby.

"Your name's inside, Father, just like your old one!"

James said nothing for a moment more. Then he looked up at the two of us waiting for his reaction. He stood, placed the derby on his head, and bowed deeply. "Thank you, ladies. Assuming I avoid snipers from now on, it should serve me well for many years."

James placed the derby on the hat peg by the door, where the previous one had rested, before sitting back down. "All in all, this has been one of the best days I've had in a long time. Thank you. Let me finish my tea, and I'll serve my sentence in the kitchen."

Elizabeth cleared the table. This done, she turned to her father.

"You're granted a stay of execution, sir. I'll do the dishes while you and Margaret retire to the sitting room." She looked at me, "I'm sure you have much to talk about."

Curious, James ambled to his favorite chair and waited for me to join him. "Yes, Margaret, what is it?"

I looked into his face. It was open. Trusting. I took a deep breath before the plunge. "I have lupus."

"Lupus?" James asked. "What's that?"

"Doctors can't really say, but it is an inflammatory condition which gradually involves the entire body. As it is, I have to stretch every morning before I can walk normally."

James swallowed. "Is it fatal?"

"Not necessarily. Some do die of complications after many years, but for most, it affects one's ability to walk and care for oneself. I should have some years yet of fairly normal activity before becoming bedridden. It is crucial I remain as active as I can for as long as I can, to maintain the function I currently have."

"I understand. It changes nothing as far as I'm concerned."

"My doctors have recommended I move to a warm climate to prolong my mobility." At this, I placed my hand on his shoulder and said, "I've booked passage to Australia on a ship sailing the seventh of July."

"Oh . . . I see." James stood up and went to the kitchen. I followed, puzzled. He pulled out a bottle of whiskey from the cupboard. Opened it. Smelled it. Elizabeth was busy with the dishes when he entered and she froze as she watched him, her face pale.

Then he handed the bottle to her. "Pour it down the sink. Please."

She did as he asked. He watched intently as it splashed away, out of reach. "Funny," he said, as though to himself. "I never really liked the taste." He turned back to me. "You've helped me remember what my life was like, before . . ." He pointed to the now-empty bottle in Elizabeth's hand.

"I've returned to being a father, and a policeman. I found myself in time and I'm not going back. I will be the man I was for Elizabeth, if not for you, but I am still in your debt."

Elizabeth's eyes filled with tears as I took his hand. "I'm sorry, James. Truly. You are a good man, and Elizabeth and I have become fast friends. I never meant to deceive you."

James released my hand. "No blame of yours. I'm glad you moved into the same building so that we could spend some time together. Ott would have surely killed you on your own, and I got to know you better, while I could."

"I've liked that as well. But Ott might come back here. I received a threat today which could only have come from him." I showed James the book I'd received and its sinister inscription. "I think I should move again. I can't bear the thought of placing you and Elizabeth in further danger."

James thought for a moment. "I think you should stay. My own selfish motives aside, I think he'll lay low. He had a chance to stand his ground and risk dying or killing you. He fled. I am certain he'll try again when the chance presents itself, but he knows we're looking for him and that we're capable of armed resistance. I believe you're in the safest place you could possibly be, at least for now.

"We understand one another. I cannot leave my position and lose my pension. You can't stay in this climate. I would like for us to part as friends. Besides, I might need your help with this Ott fellow. I am uncomfortable with him wandering the streets of London armed with a high-powered air rifle so close to the Diamond Jubilee. Please remain near us until it's time to sail."

I considered his offer. "All right, I'll stay, but I need to help pay for our food."

James chuckled. "Your cooking more than pays for your meals. It's a week until the ceremony. I see no further need for you to watch Mister Kropotkin parade around a park. Tomorrow you can join me as Pennyworth and Elizabeth can watch our Russian one day on her own. We need to run our sniper to ground."

"Where do we start?"

"The Electricians Guild Hall. They should know of any new craftsmen in the area and who's hiring them. I may be recognized from my old days on the regular force. I'll need you, the manager of a wealthy estate, to seek out workers to upgrade his residence. Are we agreed?"

"Agreed, James. Thank you for letting me assist. It's my fault the man's here."

"It's nothing you could have foreseen. We'll get him . . . together."

After James and I returned to the sitting room, I glanced back and saw Elizabeth smiling in the kitchen. A storm had passed, and the way ahead—though difficult—was now clear.

27

"I'm looking for an electrician," the slender, well-dressed Mister Pennyworth said to the clerk at the Guild Hall. "I'm upgrading my employer's lodge and need to install electricity throughout the main and outer buildings. An acquaintance of mine mentioned a fellow, a German, recently arrived. Sadly, my friend couldn't recall the chap's name. Can you help me?"

The clerk's right hand was gone, a cheap hook in its place. *The price of progress, I suppose.* I had no personal experience dealing with electrical burns, but my acquaintances still in the nursing profession told me the smallest of external injuries often hid extensive damage of the underlying tissue, and amputation was frequently required if the victim survived the initial jolt.

The clerk scowled when he heard me inquire for a foreign worker, but opened his roster of active electricians all the same. If the man were a guild member, his dues paid the clerk's salary. "I have three German sounding names here, sir," he said. "Wasserman, Schmidt, and Heller. Any of those sound familiar?"

"Afraid not. Any of them recent members of the guild? My acquaintance said the man had only arrived in England within the past month and had been an electrician in Germany."

"Then I can't help you, sir. It takes at least a year as an apprentice and a reference from a guild member before one can apply for membership. Even if he was a master electrician in his own country, we require them to undergo the same program as anyone else."

"Do you register apprentices?"

"No, sir. Many don't complete their training. It's not easy, and . . ." He held up his hooked hand, "not entirely safe. We don't track 'em 'til we ask for dues. We have several skilled workers I can refer you to, if you'd like."

I sighed. *Another dead end.* "No, thank you. Not yet, at least."

I had just turned to go when a red-faced man burst into the office and rushed toward the one-handed clerk, nearly shoving me aside.

"Simmons! I've a complaint to lodge!"

The clerk eyed me with an unspoken apology before turning to his new customer.

"Aye, Jimmy. What's got your tail up?"

"Someone's been using my name and billing people for work they didn't ask for. They're hurting my good name."

I touched the brim of my hat in farewell. As I headed out the door, I caught just the last bit of the conversation.

"What's this about?"

"I just got a letter from the secretary to the dean at St. Paul's . . ."

The rest faded away as the door closed behind me and I walked across the street to rejoin James on a park bench.

"Anything?" he asked.

"No one may join the guild until after one year of supervised employment and a recommendation by a member in good standing, not even a skilled worker from another country. So, Herr Ott could not have joined the guild for now."

"An apprentice, perhaps?"

"Perhaps, but there is no roster kept of apprentices. He may be working for a master electrician, but we have no way of knowing. What now?"

James closed his eyes in concentration. "The sketches of Ott are due tomorrow. The man's also a skilled gunsmith. I suppose I could ask around some of the high-end gun shops, but I'd just as likely scare the man off."

I enjoyed seeing him at work, his well-trained mind sorting

through various courses of action toward tracking his quarry down, and I gazed with a growing respect for this very decent and courageous man.

He reopened his eyes just in time to catch me looking at him.

"Best we admit defeat for today," James said after a pause, "and await the drawings from Germany. Let's pay Elizabeth a call to see how she's faring."

Elizabeth had brought a sketchbook and was doing her best to play the part of a struggling artist on the same park bench she and Margaret had used the day before. She became so engrossed in getting the texture of the brick walkway right that she was startled when she felt the breath of someone looking over her shoulder.

"Back again? I didn't notice you drawing yesterday. Was that your father with you?" The English was perfect, but with the lilting musical intonation of a native Russian speaker.

Elizabeth turned and looked into the Kropotkin daughter's deep blue eyes inches from her own. When the other girl saw how she had taken this handsome young man unawares, her eyes, full before, fell half-closed and a light pink flush crept up her throat.

Elizabeth stammered in surprise, which only extended the coral hue past Miss Kropotkin's neck and onto her cheeks. "I, um, I wasn't drawing yesterday, no. My father was reading a book to me, and we were discussing it as he went along."

"Really? My father reads to me all the time, and it's all politics and economics. I hope your session was more interesting." She looked down at her shoes for a moment, as though surprised by her boldness.

"Poetry. He was reading a recent translation of *The Odyssey*. We were at the part where Odysseus put on the lambskin to escape the blinded cyclops."

Katarina looked up again, her eyes batting twice. "I don't know that part. Could you recite it to me?"

Elizabeth felt the girl was standing closer now, though she hadn't moved a step. "Sorry, I can't recall it word for word."

The girl's lower lip protruded a fraction. "Not even a little bit? For me? I *adore* poetry."

"Trust me, it's not the romantic kind." Elizabeth coughed. "But where's your father? You walked together yesterday."

"Oh, so you *did* notice." She nodded toward the far side of the small pond. "He said he was meeting someone, and for me to promenade on my own until he signaled for me to join him." She looked down at Elizabeth. "I'd rather wait here." Then, extending her hand like royalty, palm down, she said, "My name is Katarina."

Elizabeth stood and took the hand awkwardly, in *terra incognita*. "James, like my father," she said while she nodded a welcome, trying to look neither too eager nor reluctant. She looked across the pond and saw Kropotkin sitting on a bench reading a paper. She would be able to see a secret meeting, but at the same be forced to engage this forward young woman while hiding her gender. She smiled, forcing her jaw to relax. "Please join me. I'd be delighted to draw your likeness."

As Elizabeth had expected, Katarina found the opportunity to serve as a muse for an artist irresistible. "What pose would you prefer, *monsieur?*" she asked, while posturing with one hand behind her head, the other on her hip. "But no nudes. I don't know you that well."

Katarina giggled at the open-mouthed reaction to her last remark. Elizabeth swallowed hard as she gestured for her unexpected model to sit on the end of the bench, so that she could sketch Katarina while keeping an eye on the girl's father.

"Are there any poems you can recite while I sit here, James? This is boring."

"Art requires patience, Katarina, and sometimes silence. I want to catch how your hair falls upon your shoulders, please."

Katarina began to object, then looked down at her left shoulder, smiled, and kept quiet. That bought Elizabeth a good ten minutes of peace.

Elizabeth's eyes caught the movement before the clear sight of a man walking toward the senior Kropotkin. It was difficult to look across the pond with Katarina focused on her. "Turn your head to the right, please," Elizabeth said. "I want to catch the curve of your chin."

Katarina obeyed in silence, straightening as she turned, her eyes now looking back toward her house. "James?" she asked, holding her pose, "how much longer do you think it will take?"

"About five more minutes," Elizabeth answered, as she made notes on the page underneath Katarina's sketch, which had been finished five minutes ago. It wouldn't win any prizes, but at least it resembled her. Given her apparent ego, Elizabeth knew it would be close enough.

Elizabeth's attention was focused on the stocky man in the black suit and derby who had sat down next to Kropotkin and produced his own newspaper. She was certain the two were talking, shielded by the papers, but was unable to say who was talking at any given moment. The meeting lasted no more than three minutes, by which time her model was blowing her hair out of her face and tapping her hand on her thigh.

"Here you are, Katarina. A poor rendering of your good looks, I am sorry."

Katarina was all smiles again when released from her pose, and after scrutinizing the drawing for twenty seconds, said, "Well, not a masterpiece, but a good likeness all the same." Then shifting her gaze back to Elizabeth, she said, "I am sure you would do even better with practice. Same time, tomorrow?"

Elizabeth half-bowed. "If I'm lucky."

"Then let us both pray for good fortune. May I have this?"

"Certainly. Something to remember me by."

"At the very least."

Elizabeth half bowed once more. "But now I must go. Until we meet again?"

Katarina inclined her head. "Until."

The stocky man in the dark suit was walking at a brisk pace back in the direction he had come. Despite his rather ducklike gait, he waddled at a good clip. Elizabeth was hard-pressed to keep up without being too obvious. As the man left the park and returned to the busy city streets, she lost him.

Suddenly, a thin hand seized her arm from behind. Before she could resist, she was spun around and brought face-to-face with a stern Peter Kropotkin.

"Who are you, young man, and what were you doing with my daughter?" The paternal Kropotkin was keeping a firm grip on Elizabeth's arm, and although she had violated the first rule of covert surveillance, that is, to go unnoticed, she had to choke down a laugh of relief that his concern was his daughter and not her proximity to him or his meeting.

"Beg pardon, sir!" she said in an uneven voice. She had intended it as a tenor, but in her surprise tightened her vocal cords: Her pitch quavered, much like that of an adolescent whose voice was changing, a serendipitous piece of authenticity. "I was practicing my drawing, and she agreed to pose for me. We were out in public, and there was nothing improper, I swear! Ask her yourself."

The man released Elizabeth's arm but continued to glare at her. "She said you gave her the drawing and schemed to meet again tomorrow. Is this true?"

"She asked if I would be here tomorrow. I said I might. Is that a problem?"

"Meeting with young boys without my knowledge, from families I do not know? How could that be a problem?" He pointed his finger inches from Elizabeth's nose. "Especially if he does not return. Do you understand me?"

Elizabeth swallowed. "Perfectly, sir."

He nodded. "Good. Now go. I will be looking for you, and next time I will have a cane. You are fortunate. In Russia, I would have a whip!"

28

James and I halted in midstride as we saw Elizabeth in the grasp of Peter Kropotkin, in the midst of an animated discussion. James tensed, about to rush forward, and I grabbed his arm. "Wait a moment. Have some faith, and let's see how she handles this. He won't harm her in public."

Kropotkin released her, and as he spun in our direction, we both turned our attention to the various instruments of feminine torture in the window of the nearest millinery shop.

In the window's reflection I saw Elizabeth tug at her cap and as she turned to go, she spied us across the street. She made it a point to walk behind us. As she passed us by, she whispered, "Meet me at the Hound and Hare around the corner."

Five minutes later, Elizabeth and James were each enjoying a ginger beer while I awaited an ale. "Well, Lizzie, that could have gone better," James said. "I think that's the last time I'll ask you to follow Mr. Kropotkin."

Elizabeth started to protest, but before she could do so in full, James began laughing out loud. "While your ability to blend needs some work, your disguise held up perfectly! I thought he was about to strike you right there. Did I understand he thought you were paying too much attention to his daughter?"

Elizabeth ground her teeth. "If this is what it's like for the male species, it's a wonder humanity hasn't died out. *She* was flirting shamelessly with *me*, yet her father accuses me of inappropriate behavior. I have a newfound sympathy for men, Father. She was as predatory as any shark."

148

"Cheer up, lad," I said, savoring the moment with my almost-family. "You are officially relieved of any further duties involving the Kropotkins. The sketches of Herr Ott are expected tomorrow, isn't that right, James? Once we have them, we can resume our hunt more efficiently."

Elizabeth stared into her ginger beer for a moment, then she looked up. "In all the excitement of my romantic escapades, I forgot to tell you: Kropotkin had a brief meeting with a strange man who walks like a duck."

James's drink was halfway to his mouth when Elizabeth spoke, and he set it back down. "What's this, then? What happened?"

"He was dressed all in black and made me think of an undertaker."

"Describe him," I said.

"Stout, less than average height, with a prominent handlebar mustache. He sat down beside Kropotkin and raised a newspaper, as the Russian was already doing. There they sat for around three minutes. Then the stranger lowered his paper and walked off to my left the way he'd come. I was trying to follow him when a protective father accosted me, and the man slipped away."

"Kropotkin is a skilled player of the game, Elizabeth," James said. "While you used your interaction with his daughter as a screen for your surveillance, he may well have played the protective father to hide his discovery of you, and to allow his accomplice to escape." James paused, then he chuckled. "As I consider the matter, it's likely that despite your obvious charms, Lizzie, his daughter was detailed to keep you occupied."

Elizabeth finished her ginger beer in a manly gulp and replied. "I'm not sure which is worse; to think I am irresistible to women, or that I am so easily duped."

Her father patted her back. "Either way, you can no longer shadow him. He would detect you immediately. Besides," James grinned, "we must protect you from his predatory daughter. I can see you have a lot to learn about women."

Ale squirted out my nose, and I was grateful I was dressed as Pennyworth at the moment. "And you think yourself a competent teacher on the subject?" I shook my head. "Based upon recent experience, Inspector, I'd have to disagree."

His jaw dropped, then he joined me in laughter. "Well, based upon recent experience, your doubts are probably justified. But back to more pressing matters . . ." He turned back to Elizabeth. "Would you recognize this stranger again if you saw him?"

"I'm not sure. He wasn't there long, and his clothes seemed too large for him. If he were dressed differently, I doubt it."

James nodded. "Good. Not good that you're not sure, but good that you recognize your limitations. The worst disasters I've seen are usually caused by someone who is sure of their abilities or information without good reason. If you are to be a detective, you will be a shadow, fumbling in the dark. Always keep clear what you know, what you don't know, and what you think you know, and you'll never go wrong."

"So, Detectives Ethington," I said, "what next?"

"If I may speak for the Ethington Collective," James began.

"Or the collective Ethingtons," Elizabeth interjected.

"Indeed," James acknowledged, "I think we should *all* retire from the field of battle for the day. I will compose the surveillance report on Kropotkin to give to my superiors tomorrow, and I'll receive Ott's likeness in return. I fear the visit by the mysterious undertaker may lead to my being required to remain Kropotkin's shadow, but I can argue he needs a fresh man to prevent him from becoming suspicious. Ott is my focus, and while Kropotkin speaks of revolution, his own hands are clean. He deals in words, not deeds."

That agreed, the trio set off for home. They were in such a good mood they failed to notice a man in black with a prominent handlebar mustache waddling a discrete distance behind them. Once the three reached Chez Ethington, he carefully scribbled the address in a small notebook and turned on his heel.

29

Kropotkin answered the door on the second knock. "Come in quickly!" he hissed. "What if they see you?"

Herr Grüber smiled. "They may be policemen, but they are also public servants. Your shadows are home for the evening. There are three of them, two men and the lad. Interestingly, they all live in the same apartment building. I suspect one of the older men is the father of the young man who caught Katarina's eye. That was cleverer than I would give them credit for, though Katarina played her part well."

The Russian conducted his guest into his study and closed the door before answering. Shaking his head, he said, "She enjoyed her part rather more than I'd like. I daren't tell her to throw away the crude sketch the young man made of her. I suspect she has already perfumed it and placed it within her jewelry box." He shrugged. "Are all girls her age such hopeless romantics?"

Grüber chuckled. "Being a confirmed bachelor, I have no expertise in the matter. But she deserves her trophies, and now that we can speak unobserved, we can conclude our business."

"Yes, by all means. Why were you so desperate to see me? A dead drop usually suffices."

"I didn't have time. Or rather, *we* don't have time. I have set something in motion that requires you to leave England for a short while, quite possibly much longer. You need to have an absolute alibi for the next week."

"The next week? What happens . . . Oh." Understanding came over Kropotkin's face.

"Yes. I have a plan in motion. The man is very skilled and highly motivated. I am confident enough in him that I am moving some pieces off the board and out of danger."

Kropotkin looked over his glasses. "So, this is just a game to you?"

"Yes, but with the highest of stakes. Freedom." Grüber pointed to an ivory and teak chess set on a sideboard. "I see you play chess."

The Russian snorted, "Who from my country does not?"

"Then you are aware of the Queen's Gambit?"

"Of course. The queen's pawn is advanced two spaces to begin the game."

"And what is the purpose of the move?"

"To gain control of the center."

"Exactly. But, to succeed, what must happen next?"

"The pawn is sacrificed."

"And with this queen's death, we will control the center. I have already chosen my pawn. I need you safe, to press our advantage afterward. How soon can you leave?"

Kropotkin stood, walked to the window in his study and looked out into the darkness. "That depends on where I'm going."

"Geneva. I have requested a conference to be held there on the twenty-third of June. Nothing of consequence will be discussed, but it will draw our leaders into one place to protect them from charges of involvement in this matter."

"What exactly do you hope to accomplish by the murder of an old woman? I'm not squeamish regarding her death, mind you, but the condemnation our cause will suffer should have some redeeming feature."

"My goal is a war that topples the old order forever."

"And how will the queen's assassination accomplish that?"

"Once the British learn it was a German who pulled the trigger, nothing less than war will satisfy the mobs."

"And how will the mobs learn his nationality? What if he escapes?"

"If he is not immediately apprehended or killed on the spot, he'll seek our comrades in Southampton. They'll see to it he is found."

"But won't he implicate you and our network?"

Grüber spoke as though they were discussing the weather. "Not as long as his son is within my reach."

Grüber went to stand beside his host as they both contemplated the formless dark outside. "Only you will know the real reason you've been summoned. Please keep that to yourself, though it would be wise to plan for what comes after the queen's death. Do not take a large amount of baggage with you, but be aware it may be a year or more before you can return."

Kropotkin increased the distance between them slightly. "I pray you never find me as useful as this pawn you've chosen."

"Never fear, *mein Kamerad*. He is useful. You are indispensable."

The Russian looked back at his chess set. "Killing her will be extremely difficult. If he is unable to act and escapes, you'll have lost your chance. Have you considered that your objective may be achieved just as effectively if he is caught with proof of his intent?"

"I see that I am in the presence of a chess master. What do you suggest?"

"Surely you have more than one pawn in your box? The right words whispered into the ear of a known British informant should guarantee your man's apprehension. The news could not be suppressed, and the papers would be demanding war against your country for the affront."

Grüber rubbed his chin as he considered the Russian's words. "An excellent idea. I have just the man in mind, but please go to Geneva anyway. If the reaction is as strong as you predict, we will have much to discuss."

The two men stood silent as they peered into the blackness of night, each deep in their own thoughts.

"It is easy to destroy, Herr Grüber. But once the old order is shattered, what will we build in its place?"

Grüber rested his hand on the Russian's shoulder. "A world where the people finally control their own destiny, my friend, though I expect that men of vision such as you and I will have a role in guiding it. Whatever form that new order takes, it can only be better."

Once Grüber returned to his hotel room, he considered his options. Luigi had been helpful in the past, but given his sentimentality could not be trusted to inform on Herman, and might well warn him of Grüber's planned betrayal if he learned of it. He pulled some foolscap out of the writing desk and began his letter. He'd post it first thing in the morning, and it should arrive at its destination by the afternoon of the same day.

To Special Branch, Scotland Yard
From a concerned citizen . . .

30

Special Branch headquarters, Thursday, June 17

enior Inspector Murdock was in rare form when James presented his surveillance report that morning. "I must compliment you, Inspector," he said as he gazed over his spectacles. "You seem to have accomplished the miraculous."

"Beg pardon, Senior Inspector?"

"I mean to say that you are apparently capable of being in two places at the same time." Murdock produced a memo and laid it down beside James's report. "This morning I received this memo from Senior Inspector Danforth, chief of Financial Crime, praising your good work and interdepartmental cooperation. Your suspicions of the head of Municipal Utilities were confirmed. It seems the man has been dipping into the trough for the past three years. Inspector Atkins said there are at least £5,000 unaccounted for, and the man is in custody as we speak. Well done, that. It never hurts to foster goodwill among our colleagues."

Then he held up the report on Kropotkin's movements. "But here I have a report from you describing the Kropotkin subject's activities at the same time you were either at the Utilities office or sharing your suspicions with Financial Crimes. How can this be?"

James swallowed. "I sent an associate to surveil Kropotkin the first day so that I could follow a possible lead on Ott. They gave me their report, though I did arrive at the park where my associate was just after the departure of the Russian's mysterious visitor."

"So, you cannot personally verify the appearance of the second conspirator?"

"No, Senior Inspector, I cannot."

"Which begs the next question: Who can? Who is this unknown associate?"

James felt like a condemned prisoner on the gallows. Seeing no escape, he braced for the drop. "My daughter, sir, Elizabeth."

Murdock's face went from pale to purple in the space of two heartbeats. "What! You entrusted surveillance of a suspected enemy of Her Majesty's government . . . to a child?"

"She's fifteen, sir."

"An adolescent, then. I'm not sure which is worse, that you entrusted this affair to your daughter, or that you submitted an official report fraudulently under your own name. I'm at a loss as to how to respond to this breach of faith."

"As you said, sir, I couldn't be in two places at the same time. We've less than a week until the Diamond Jubilee. We both believe Ott is a serious threat, and I felt that directly pursuing him should have the highest priority. My daughter, Elizabeth, wants to become a detective and the first day of surveillance she was with Miss Harkness, who has aided the Metropolitan Police before."

The senior inspector rose from his seat like a whale breaching the surface. "Miss Harkness, too? Why not the custodian of your building? Your daughter's math tutor? Is there anyone else you invited to do your job while you disobeyed my orders?"

"No, sir. No one."

Murdock stuck his finger inches from James's nose. "You are suspended pending a hearing of this matter." He turned his palm up. "Give me your badge. Now. Then go to the armory and turn in your Webley. Report back to my office tomorrow at nine and you will be given the date and time of your hearing. I would not be optimistic, if I were you."

Dazed, James stood and placed his badge into the man's waiting hand.

"May I ask one favor before I go, sir?"

"You dare, after all this? It must be deucedly important. Very well. Ask."

"May I have a copy of the sketch? I could look around for Ott on my own, while I await my hearing."

Murdock let out a soft snort. "You're tenacious, I'll give you that." He reached into his inbox, plucked out a manila envelope and extracted from it a copy of a sketch. "Here. One more set of eyes can't do any harm—besides, the likeness has already been shared with the press, asking for information on the man suspected of attacking you. Just be certain you don't introduce yourself as 'Inspector' Ethington until we get this sorted out. Understand?"

"Perfectly, Senior Inspector. Thank you."

Murdock sat down, his chair groaning at the sudden burden. "I take no pleasure in this, Ethington. Your recent work has been exemplary, and God knows we need every man we can muster as the Jubilee approaches. We'll talk more tomorrow, after I've calmed down. Now go."

James trudged out, head down, the sketch clutched in his hand.

He told Sergeant Q the cylinders of his Webley were loose, and it needed to be looked at. The armorer shook his head. The Webley was well known for its reliability. He'd recited more than once the old saying, "A poor workman blames his tools," but he accepted the revolver and promised to inspect it. "I can have it ready tomorrow morning, Inspector. Will that be soon enough?"

"I hope so," he said, and left.

Once outside the armory, James sat and inspected the sketch. Other than a prominent handlebar mustache and a square, solid chin any boxer would envy, Herr Ott was rather unremarkable. Five-foot-eight, about one hundred eighty pounds. Muscular. His hair was parted in the middle, ears small, nose unbroken, eyes . . . silver-gray. Hair could be cut, dyed, or shaved, but eye color was fixed. People would notice, as the elderly publisher had. *Finally*, he thought.

Margaret and Elizabeth were waiting for him across the street in a pub, both "undressed." He'd resisted Elizabeth's joining them until she made it clear she would just follow. It suddenly occurred to him that Margaret now had the only firearm.

He pondered his next move. *Time is short. Best to accept reinforcements.*

The pub had only two other customers at the far corner of the bar and a bartender reading *The Illustrated Police News*. The customers had a racing form spread out on the bar and were deep in discussing their investment portfolio for the afternoon. Neither one raised his head when James walked in to join Elizabeth and me at a table.

"Did you get the sketch?" I asked. "Your troops are ready to sally forth, General. Just say where!" My smile faded however when I noted his long face. "What happened?"

James seemed to have shrunken into himself, and the transformation unnerved me. He collapsed into a chair before speaking. "I'm suspended. I had to surrender my badge and revolver. I'm to return tomorrow to learn when my hearing will be, to see if I lose my post permanently."

He held up his hand to hold off our outcry. "My suspicions about the head of the Utilities Department proved true. Apparently, he had been dipping into the till for some time. The chief of Financial Crimes was so grateful he sent an internal memorandum praising me for my assistance."

I felt a chill. "And the time of the report on Kropotkin coincided with the time you were speaking with your colleagues at the Yard. How did you explain the discrepancy?"

"I'm not a clever man, Margaret. I confessed that you and Elizabeth performed the surveillance and composed the report. Senior Inspector Murdock's reaction was so extreme I may have shortened his life. My revolver rests in the armory 'undergoing maintenance' until tomorrow. Murdock allowed me a copy of Ott's description and sketch, but I had to surrender my badge, and cannot use the title of 'Inspector' until further notice. For the moment I am a civilian, with no more authority than you." He spread his hands. "I may have lost everything by catching a thief."

Elizabeth sat silent, one tear sliding down her cheek.

I was stunned by the news, made all the worse by my sense of guilt. James was a good man, trying with all his might to do the right thing, and in my desire to play detective and enjoy some time with Elizabeth, I'd cost him his reputation with his superior and quite possibly his livelihood. He deserved better.

Then I had a revelation that froze my heart and tongue. Since his career with Scotland Yard was probably finished, he would soon be free in a way he might never be again. I thought of my old acquaintance, the empty space across the table, and how much I'd enjoyed filling that space with my almost-family.

I was attracted to the man, and knew he was to me. I imagined what it might be like, to marry at my age when many women were already widows. I shook my head. It was too late for me. Given my condition I did not wish to become a burden on another, and it would be selfish to ask him to accompany me to Australia. We might have been very happy together, had we met in another time or circumstance, but we had not.

Still, if the hearing went badly for him . . .

"So, what shall we do in the meantime, James?" I asked. "Are we still on the hunt for Ott, or have you given up?"

James straightened. "I may not have a badge, but I'm still a policeman, through and through. I'm on the case, at least until I'm thrown off the force for good. Let's wait and see how long it is before my hearing. Given how close it is to the Jubilee, I might get a stay until afterward. If we catch Ott in the meantime, it could well save my position."

He sipped his ginger beer for a moment before continuing. "I've some contacts in Whitechapel who might prove useful. They won't know of my suspension, and I may be able to get them to sniff around there for our quarry. At this point, I've nothing to lose."

Meanwhile, the two gamblers at the end of the bar completed their strategy session, paid their tab, and walked out of the bar, while the bartender returned to his paper. It seemed odd how we three could be plotting to save a monarch, while the rest of the world took no notice. We paid our tab and James headed off for Whitechapel while Elizabeth and I headed home. I recalled Old Mary and her tarot cards, and how I was once again waiting to see what hand fate would deal me.

31

When James stepped outside into the warm spring sunshine after leaving the bar, he had a clear mission. Stop the assassin, with or without a badge. He thought back to his days as an inspector under Abberline in Division H in the East End. He'd learned the truth of the old saying, "It takes a thief to catch a thief." Ott wasn't a thief, but perhaps he was hiding with one.

I wonder if he's still alive? James thought. Last he'd seen Billy "Peg Leg" Fisher, his liver was giving him fits, and he'd had to cut back on the gin. That'd been, what, three years ago? Well, nothing ventured . . .

Peg Leg had once been a sailor, but a leg crushed by a falling mainsail years ago before steam engines took over had left him with a wooden leg and a powerful thirst, though perhaps the thirst had always been there. Now Billy was a fence, and a good one, for three young burglars who were loyal to him due to their blood relation. They were his sons.

Little happened in the East End that Peg Leg wasn't aware of, or had a hand in. Though he would steal the crown jewels given the chance, he was careful to never spill blood, and he and James had an armistice of sorts. There were criminals far worse than he and his progeny, so in return for the odd bit of gossip, he'd been left alone. Time to renew old acquaintances.

When James had first been assigned to the East End, he'd been surprised how much business took place inside pubs. On reflection, however, it made sense. Rooms were usually crowded, and two men surrounded by loud, drunk customers could carry on a conversation in greater privacy than was possible back at their digs. Besides, it allowed both sides to keep their residence concealed from the other party.

James was relieved to see the old salt in his favorite corner of the Ten Bells, his wooden leg propped up on a chair while he smoked his pipe and chatted with his three sons, who were between seventeen and twenty-one. The difference in their hair color told James no two had shared the same mother.

Billy looked up sharply as James approached. The inspector wasn't surprised by the fatherly advice the fence was giving his boys. "Aye, lads, while the bands a'playing and the crowds 're cheering, 'twill be a fine time to . . ."

"Hello, Billy. Glad to see you're such a patriot."

"Inspector! Good to see you!" he said, raising his pipe in mock salute. "I'd heard you'd moved on to higher things than us poor lot 'ere in Whitechapel. You here to sweep the streets before Her Majesty rides around the town? If so, you're off your map, shipmate. Her course is charted far from 'ere."

The three sons smirked but remained silent. They knew of the truce their father had with the inspector and, having no stolen property on them, they sipped their ales and listened.

"Do you see a broom in my hand, Billy? No, I haven't been transferred to the sanitation department, but this visit does concern the queen. Did you see the paper today?"

Billy nodded, stroking the stubble on his chin. He could smell a deal a mile away, and knew one was coming. "I might 'ave at that. And?"

"Did you see the sketch of a man?" He pulled out the police drawing of Ott. "This man?"

"Aye, I did. Took a shot at one of yours, I believe." He winked. "Missed."

"Not by much. I was the target."

Billy clucked his tongue. "Ah, as popular as ever, Inspector. Well, you can't expect a man to change his ways just 'cause he got a bigger badge. But you still haven't told me why you're here."

"I think he's hereabouts, and I want you to help me find him."

Billy spread his hands out in front of him. "And why should I help you? What's in it for me?"

"Because I believe he's here to kill the queen. If he does that, and if he were hiding here . . ."

Billy sighed. "Every constable in London will sweep in here and tear the East End apart. Aye." He rubbed his forehead. "I still recall how I had to scramble when you lot were looking for the Ripper. Bad for business, that. Not to say it was good for the ladies either, mind you." He gazed fondly at the three wooden figures sitting around him. "But I had hungry mouths to feed, so had little time to mourn their troubles, you understand."

"Then, if you don't want bad times again, you'd be wise to look about, Billy. We don't have much time, the ceremony's next Tuesday."

"You're no more fun than before, Master Ethington. All right. I'll sic my boys on his trail. What can you tell me to help us find this poor marksman? I'm sure you know more than's in the paper."

"He's German. He's an electrician, and he uses an air rifle that makes very little noise. He's dangerous, Billy. If your boys find him, leave him to me."

"My boys can take care of themselves, sir. But thank you for the concern. Where should I send word if I learn something?"

"Here." James wrote down his address, hoping he wasn't extending an invitation to be burgled at a later time. "Any time at night. During the day, send word to the station at Spitalfields and they'll telegraph my office."

Billy extended his hand. "I'll see what I can find out, Inspector. Oh, and the conversation me and my boys were 'aving when you came in . . ."

"I didn't hear a thing, Billy, as long as no one's harmed."

"A pleasure as always, Inspector, and proud to do me civic duty. Good day."

James appreciated the relatively cleaner air of the London streets after the close confines of the pub. He reflected that he now had the best sleuths in London on his side. Billy had a nose for profit and whom to profit from. If someone in the East End was being paid off to shelter the killer, Billy and his lads would hear it on the wind. If Herr Ott's benefactor was a believer in his cause and not sheltering the German for pay, then it was hopeless, and James would just have to do his best on the day of the ceremony.

Let's hope greed wins out over politics.

32

Herman was awakened by a knock at the door. The sun was barely up, so it couldn't be past six.

"Who's there?" he asked, out of sorts by his abrupt return to the waking world.

"Parmeggiani," whispered a voice. "Get up!"

Herman staggered to the door and let the small Italian in. He seemed more animated than usual, which took some doing. "What is it? What's wrong?"

"This is what's wrong!" he said, thrusting a copy of *The Star* into Herman's face. "You're a wanted man, for attempted murder of a woman and a police inspector! You said your hands were clean."

"My hands *are* clean. I missed. But hers aren't!"

"I don't care. Your likeness is all over the city. In the *Times* as well. You can't come to the shop. You must go. Now!"

Herman rubbed his eyes, still unsure he was awake. "Go? Go where?"

"I don't care, and I don't want to know. If someone sees you at my shop and summons a constable, my entire operation would be placed in danger. Here." He shoved fifty pounds into Herman's hands. "For the lamps. If you left anything at the store, tell me and I will bring it to you, but you must be away from here as soon as you can."

Herman took the money without reaction, trying to grasp his situation. "No."

"No? What do you mean, no?"

"If I leave now, I wouldn't remain at large for one day. I agree I can't stay here for long, but give me until tonight. I have nothing in the store which concerns me. Bring me some food for the day, and when you return tomorrow, I'll be gone."

Luigi clasped his hands together. "Madonna!" he cried. "You're killing me, but alright. Stay inside today, and I'll bring you food. But you must be gone tomorrow."

"Agreed. Now go while I prepare. I've been hunted before. I doubt the British can be any more capable than the *Okhrana*. At least the English don't torture their prisoners anymore."

He laid his hand on the Italian's narrow shoulder. "Don't worry, *Signore*. If I am caught, I will not turn you in. You were kind to me, in your fashion. Besides, turning you in would not help my situation. Now go!"

Luigi sighed and shook Herman's hand. "*Mille grazie, Signore.* It is good when kindness is remembered. I regret my words just now. Fear is stronger than charity, at least in me. I make a good living but never forget I am always one step away from the dock and a magistrate peering down at me. *Arrivederci!*"

Herman went to the basin to wash his face. He stared at his exuberant handlebar mustache and sighed. No hot water. This would not be pleasant. He lathered up the soap in a cup and began laying it onto his mustache like a plasterer finishing a wall. He studied his face as he gave the soap a chance to soften the bristly hair. The hair on his head was thinning in front, a feature not shown in the sketch in the paper. He stroked his razor as he considered how much to take off the top. *I'm no barber. Best take it all.*

When Luigi returned with a couple of sausages, a bottle of wine, and a loaf of bread his knock brought only a curt, "Leave it outside and go. Best you not see me. Thank you, and good-bye."

After the footsteps faded away, a clean shaven, bald gentleman snatched the food inside.

Senior Inspector Murdock was preparing to depart for the day when a junior clerk came into his office, a letter in his hand.

"What's this, then?" Murdock asked, his hat already in his hand.

"This letter arrived around noon today. It contains a threat against the queen, and we get so many letters like this without return addresses I was just going to toss it, but it has some specific information most threats don't contain. It's probably nothing, but I thought I'd leave that for you to decide."

Murdock sighed. He'd better things to do then to read an anonymous letter from some crackpot, but he'd not be able to rest that night, knowing it was waiting on his desk.

"Very well," he growled. "Your timing needs improvement. I'll have a look before I go, now get out!"

The clerk made his escape, doubting his wisdom at bothering the man this late in the day, while Murdock put on his reading glasses and slumped back down into his chair. As he read the message, he began to sit straighter, and by the time he'd finished his back was ramrod.

To Special Branch, Scotland Yard
From a concerned citizen

Sir,

> *I'm not the most patriotic Englishman in the empire, and I admit that I've fallen in with a bad lot and attended some socialist meetings, but there are some things I cannot abide. I feel it my duty to tell you that there is a German anarchist named Herman Ott who is here in London to kill Her Majesty during the Diamond Jubilee. He has a rifle and knows how to use it.*

> *I beg you take this letter seriously. You can easily see if my words are true, for he is working for an antiquities dealer named Luigi Parmeggiani at the below address. If you perform a search of his lodgings you should find a high-powered air rifle in his possession.*

> *I've done a lot in my life that I have reason to be ashamed*

of. I hope somehow that this letter may put my misdeeds into balance.

God save the Queen!

An address followed near Charing Cross station. Murdock hadn't been on the streets in over ten years. He unlocked a drawer in his desk and brought out his Webley and shoulder holster. Time to see if he was still a policeman.

Herman left the flat as the sun set. He had to steel himself to go out into a world where everyone was a potential risk. He was more alone than ever before. In Russia or Germany, he could at least hope for a sympathizer. Here, he was not a revolutionary—just a criminal. He must look as uninteresting as possible until his mission was done.

He stepped out into the darkness without hesitation. He knew any jerky motion would draw people's attention. He needed to walk as though he owned the ground beneath his feet. He entered the Dog's Head and found Keys in his usual corner, dispensing wisdom as he sipped an ale. Not wanting to draw attention from the three men sitting with him, Herman sat at the bar and told the barman to send a whiskey to Malone, figuring the others wouldn't get a good look at him from across the smoke-filled room.

When the drink arrived and the barman nodded at its donor, Herman raised his glass in salute and turned his back. Now all he could do was wait. He had nearly finished his first ale of the evening when a hand came down soft on his shoulder. "Evening, boyo, and to what do I owe the pleasure?"

Herman turned and was relieved to see no flash of recognition in the Irishman's eyes. "We've done business before. I need your services again."

Keys started at the sound of Herman's voice and studied his face.

Then he nodded. "Aye, we have. You're a sight different, though handsome as ever. My office, alone?"

"Yes, to both. Do I need to buy your friends another round of ale?"

"Nay. Don't want to spoil 'em, anyways. They're used to being shooed off when I have business associates here." They walked back to Keys' corner table. "Bugger off now, lads. I need to seek me fortune." The three hangers-on shrugged and took their custom to the bar without a backward glance.

"Your friends are agreeable," Herman said.

"Long practice, nothing more. Any one of 'em would sell his mother for a drink. It's a rare treat to do business with a gentleman what keeps his word. Now, what's it this time, another lock to be greased?"

Herman leaned in to reduce the chance of being overheard. "Quite the opposite this time."

"How's that again? You want me to secure something?"

"Not something. Someone. Me. I assume you've read the papers?"

"Nay. There is naught in the papers of interest to me. Besides, I can't read. What's in the papers got you so worried?"

Herman considered how to answer. He knew the higher the risk, the higher the price, but best the man hear his reasons now, rather than go asking about them later. He sighed. "I took a shot at a police inspector. My picture's in the paper, or my likeness before this . . ." Herman waved a hand over his face and bald head.

Keys laughed. "Is that all? So, you missed then? More's the pity. Well, I can find you a bolt-hole well enough; it ain't cheap nor fancy, but I reckon you've got no cause to be picky. How long you reckon you've got to hide?"

"Five days."

"Ah, figure on slipping out during the big to-do for the queen? That's clever." Malone nodded, satisfied. "Five pounds a day for five days is twenty-five pounds." He snorted. "Maybe I can't read, but I can do me figures well enough." Then he laid a finger aside of his nose. "We might be busy later on. Best pay me now. Do we have a deal?"

"Ten now. The rest when I see the place and am satisfied."

"It's not like I've a string of houses to choose from, but all right. I'll take the ten now. I owe the barman near as much, and then I'll conduct you to the royal suite." Winking, he continued, "Sorry, lad, but you'll have to carry your own bags."

Soon Herman and the Irishman were walking through a dark courtyard in the East End, and Herman wished he had something besides a disassembled rifle to hand. Keys noticed Herman's nervous glances as they passed alleyways. "Not to worry, lad. There's honor among thieves here. 'Sides, I usually don't have the scratch worth fighting over. Not far now."

My safety depends upon the goodwill of criminals. Have I really fallen so far? Herman mused. *But then, to their eyes, I am one of them. So yes, I suppose I have plummeted into the abyss.*

They passed through a narrow entrance into another courtyard, this one larger, and Malone led Herman to a dim doorway on the far side. He pulled out a large key, and the well-oiled lock opened without a sound. The doorframe bordered a pitch-black rectangle, and Herman heard something scurry in the room. *Rats. I'll be lodging with rats.*

Malone pulled a candle stub and matches out of a pocket, lit the candle, and handed it to Herman. "I trust you'll find your lodgings to your taste, sir," he said, bowing.

The room had one single bed with an iron frame, a washbasin, a table, one chair, and a bedpan. The entire room was hardly larger than a cell, but at least his only roommates would be rats. He saw a particularly large one sprint under the bed.

"It has rats," Herman said. "Big ones."

Malone shrugged, "'Tis the East End, boyo. There's more of them 'ere than people. Get used to it. Now, about those other fifteen pounds . . ."

Herman gritted his teeth. He could lodge at one of the better hotels in London for five pounds a night and he might get away with it. He might. Malone stood there waiting, his hand out. Herman paid, accepted the key, and made sure he could lock himself in.

The Irishman turned to leave, but before he could, Herman caught his arm and asked, "Now what?"

Malone smirked. "You leave by the twenty-third, lad. Keep quiet and no one here'll bother you. Half the families here have someone on the lam. Now, unless there's something else, I've a terrible thirst and the bar closes in an hour. Good night, and don't mind your room-mates. They won't eat much!"

"Speaking of eating," Herman said, "bring me some food every day, and I'll pay another three pounds. Nothing fancy, but a day's worth. Agreed?"

"Hope you're not expecting steak and kidney pie, but if honest food's good enough, then I'll do it. That'll be another five pounds now, Governor." Keys smiled. "Just so we understand one another."

Herman grumbled a bit, enough to keep the man from realizing he could charge twice as much, then he paid. "Once a day, in the morning by eight."

"Right you are, then. Eight, sharpish." Malone tipped his cap, then strode off into the darkness. Herman closed the door, locked it, and eyed the darkness beneath his bed, wondering how long the candle stub would last. He saw no others in the room. *It's going to be a long night. I should have asked for more candles.*

Luigi was closing the shop for the day when a burly older gentleman accompanied by two police constables confronted him at the entrance. The badge the older man flashed in his eyes was impressive, but the large-caliber handgun he carried was even more so.

33

Friday, June 18

James sat outside Murdock's office promptly at nine, his new hat in his hands.

Senior Inspector Murdock was in a dark mood when he opened the door. His eyebrows knit together when he saw James sitting outside his door like an errant schoolboy summoned to see the headmaster. "Come in," he said, his head jerking toward the chair in front of his desk. "We have much to discuss."

James entered, thinking of Daniel in the lions' den, yet doubting he had divine protection. "Aye, Senior Inspector. About the hearing . . ."

Murdock grimaced. "There'll be no hearing."

James's mouth gaped and he bolted upright from his chair. "I'm to be discharged just like that, after all my years on the force?"

Murdock looked over his glasses. "Sit down, *Inspector.* You're not to be discharged . . ." He took off his glasses and rubbed the bridge of his nose, "but promoted."

James melted into his chair. "Promoted? How? Why?"

Murdock replaced his glasses and glared across his desk. "Why, indeed. You might even be knighted at this rate.

"First, the chief of Financial Crimes, Senior Inspector Danforth, spoke with the police commissioner before I did. It appears the chap you sniffed out wasn't alone in his chicanery, thus the extent of corruption is broader than it first appeared. You're a hero, apparently. Danforth wants you in his department and promoted to senior inspector and his assistant, as soon after the Jubilee as possible."

"But I'm no clerk! Why would he think I'd be of any use in that department?"

"He says he has plenty of clerks. He needs a proper policeman in charge."

Murdock coughed. "Secondly, your suspicion regarding Ott's risk to Her Majesty was verified last night in a most unexpected manner. Due to an anonymous letter received yesterday we have the man who was sheltering our assassin in custody at this very moment. He was most talkative, but Ott was already gone."

Murdock opened his desk and slid James's badge over to him. "Take it. Your Webley is waiting for you down in the armory." The senior inspector straightened in his chair, a sour look on his face. "Given these new developments, I've decided to keep your indiscretion *entre nous*. Based upon your body of work over the years, and your instincts regarding our anarchist, I think you merit the promotion.

"Our informants tell us that several senior anarchists in London are heading to Geneva for a hastily called conference. While none of our sources know the precise reason for the meeting, the timing coincides with the Jubilee, and I see this as further confirmation that your concern about this assassin was correct. I suspect Kropotkin and his kind are seeking high ground to avoid the fury a royal assassination would provoke. I've informed the police commissioner that it was you who unearthed this threat against the queen, so if catching errant bookkeepers becomes wearisome, I could find you a post here, as my deputy."

"While I'm gobsmacked at my good fortune, Senior Inspector. Don't you find this anonymous letter a bit too convenient?"

"Aye. It smells to high heaven. I suspect this betrayal is an act of revenge by one faction against another, but at the moment I'm not inclined to be too choosey as to who helps me protect our sovereign. The enemy of my enemy, as it were."

"If you don't mind, Senior Inspector, I'd like to question the man you brought in last night to see what he can tell me about our assassin."

"As you like, Ethington, though I doubt you'll learn much. He has much to hide, doubtless, but it seems he was kept in the dark concerning Ott's true purpose here in England."

James looked at the badge on the desk in front of him. He recalled the day he'd made inspector and how proud Alice had been when he'd taken his police constable uniform off for the final time, what they'd done after, and the baby who followed. His badge lay there, gleaming, waiting for him to pick it up, even as another waited to replace it. Senior Inspector. He'd be in charge of a section and lead his men into battle.

Murdock continued. "The promotion becomes effective at the start of a new pay period, July the fifth. Until then you are still a member of Special Branch, and your only concern until further notice is Ott. If you can't catch him, at least keep him on the run so he doesn't interrupt the Jubilee next Tuesday. Once the Jubilee is over, you can take the rest of the time off with pay until your promotion becomes effective.

"We may sing God Save the Queen, but for the next four days, Special Branch will do their part. That may not make us angels, but at least we'll be on the same side."

James thought of the stern old woman who represented a nation's will and nobility. His hand seemed to move on its own as he watched it place his badge back onto his vest.

"Thank you, Senior Inspector. God save the Queen."

"God save the Queen!"

Luigi Parmeggiani was haggard and twitchy when James sat down with him in an interrogation room. His linen suit was badly wrinkled, and he smelled more of prison soap than rose water.

"Please, *Signore,* why am I still here? I've told you everything I know."

"How did Ott come to work for you?"

Luigi knew that only Grüber could have betrayed him, but the fence would not turn him in to the authorities. In Italy, revenge was almost an art. Justice would be served in due time, but at a time and date of his choosing. He'd worked out his cover story before he'd reached the police station.

"I needed an electrician. This man showed up, was quick and proficient, so I hired him. I see no crime in that."

"Yet you turned him out once his likeness appeared in the papers, so you knew you were harboring a wanted criminal."

"I was unaware of the picture, and once it was shown me, it's not a very good one. Ott, you say his name is? He told me it was Schmidt. Anyway, he'd just learned of his wife's death a couple of days before. I gave him an advance on some lamps he'd made for me. I assumed he'd gone off to drink away his sorrow. He may be back at the shop even now."

Just then there was a knock at the door, and a sergeant stuck his head in.

"Beg pardon, Inspector. Mister Parmeggiani's barrister is here to see him."

A well-dressed gentleman came through the door with a briefcase and an umbrella, ready to do battle. He flourished a card identifying himself as Richard Baxter, Esq.

"Good day, Inspector. May I ask why my client is still in custody?" he asked in a mild voice, his public-school accent declaring his class as surely as an Oxford tie.

"He was harboring a man suspected of attempted murder, sir. Surely that warrants further investigation."

"You have proof my client was aware he was a wanted criminal?"

"Well, no."

"Has he answered all your questions to the best of his ability?"

"He has answered all our questions," James said, "though his ability is still in question."

The barrister showed his teeth in what may have been a smile, or a polite snarl. "Nice turn of phrase, Inspector. I'm requesting his release in court this afternoon. Unless you have something more than an anonymous letter that could have been written by a competitor of my client's, I expect his release today. If you have any further questions for him, I must insist on being present. Do you?"

James knew he'd get nothing more from the little Italian.

"No, I'm done." He turned to Luigi and handed him his card. "If you think of anything further which may help us locate the man, please look me up."

James walked down to the armory where Sergeant Q and James's Webley awaited. "I'm here for my revolver," he said. "What did you find?"

The armorer shrugged. "Needed a bit of oil, which is your responsibility, and the spring on the extractor needed replacement. The cylinders were tight as a drum." He handed over the cleaned and well-oiled weapon, whereupon James reloaded it and replaced it in its holster.

It felt right there somehow. He hadn't realized how he'd missed its reassuring weight until it was back in place.

Rearmed and bearing his badge, Inspector Ethington set forth to save a queen.

When James returned, Elizabeth was practicing walking like a boy in her urchin costume.

"How did your meeting with the senior inspector go, James?" I asked, "Will your hearing occur before the Jubilee?"

"No need," he smiled. "They're promoting me!"

"What!" Elizabeth said, round-eyed, and they embraced.

As I watched Elizabeth congratulate her father, I recalled my foolish thoughts from the day before, of asking James if he'd join me in a new life in Australia. I was glad that for once my head had won out over my heart.

"How is that possible?" Elizabeth asked.

"Where to begin? The embezzler had collaborators, and I was credited for their arrest. The chief of Financial Crimes wants me as soon after the Jubilee as possible, as his deputy."

"That's wonderful!" said Elizabeth.

"Oh, there's more than that. An anonymous letter received at Special Branch yesterday led to the arrest of the man who was sheltering Ott."

"But not Ott himself?" I asked.

"No, he escaped. The man we arrested readily admits to hiring our anarchist as an electrician, but we can't find any reason to hold him. He's probably free already. I suspect his hands aren't totally clean, but I don't have time to pursue that, at present."

"So close," I said. "His luck can't hold out forever. Anything else?"

"Our informants report that several prominent anarchists are suddenly leaving London, and Murdock believes that it's to get them safely away before the assassination. He now agrees with me that the man is a definite threat to Her Majesty, and Ott is my only responsibility until after the ceremony. After the Jubilee, assuming all goes well, I get nearly a fortnight's paid holiday before my promotion takes effect." He hugged Elizabeth again. "Things couldn't be better."

A fortnight before my ship sailed? Time enough to consider canceling my booking, enlarging it for three, or sailing alone as planned. Apparently, my head and heart were still not in full agreement. I bit my tongue and remained silent, forcing a smile.

Josh, Ben, and Harry—Billy Fisher's three sons—had fanned out into the markets and pubs of Whitechapel. It wasn't long before Josh heard that Keys Malone was paying off his debts and buying drinks. Not like him at all. Before the night was over, Keys had a shadow.

Herman cleaned and oiled his rifle. Once it was ready, he began pressurizing his spare flask. Fifteen-hundred strokes of the small pump would take at least a couple of hours.

The rifleman was far enough away from the route that the late-night hammering of bleachers being erected by electric light didn't bother him. Banners were being hung from buildings, and hawkers were busy selling the few remaining seats. Nearly everyone in the city was in their own way preparing for the big day to come, now just four days away.

34

Friday, June 18, cont.

Herman was pleased to see his landlord come to call that morning with a couple of hot sausages covered in mustard, a small loaf of bread, and a quarter wheel of cheese. "You are a man of your word as well, Herr Keys," Herman said.

"Nah. I just like getting paid. It's easy enough to snag you something to eat. Anything else?"

"A half-dozen candles would be nice. The rats avoid the light."

"Still going on about them rats? I thought you'd all be getting on well by now. Fair enough. Six candles tomorrow, with food. How's that?"

"Would later today be possible? The short candle you left me is used up." Herman gritted his teeth, not wanting to beg. "I wouldn't want to face the whole night in the dark. Please. And a box of matches."

Malone wasn't overfond of rats himself and relented. "Right you are, then. Candles and matches. Give me an hour or two, but I'll be back today before noon." He cleared his throat and added, "Five more pounds."

"Done," Herman said, and he paid, handing the money over without thinking about it. "Thank you," he put in, but Keys was already gone.

Josh Fisher, the youngest of Peg Leg's acknowledged progeny, noted the door Malone had knocked on. The door was solid, and the window beside it was covered by a filthy muslin curtain. Did he take this to his da, or should he try to get a look at whoever was inside? He'd get the back of Billy's hand for wasting his time if it wasn't the man they were looking for. Best try to sneak a peek.

Josh waited for the Irishman to leave and followed him for a half-mile, just to make sure he wasn't coming right back, then he made his way to the corner he'd hid behind previously. No change. He summoned up his courage and knocked at the door. No answer. He knocked again, and called out, "It's all right. Keys sent me."

"Open Sesame" could not have been more effective. The door opened, and a powerful arm seized his and snatched him inside. The man staring at him was different than the one in the papers. No mustache, bald . . . Then he saw the square chin and looked up into gray eyes. Josh swallowed hard. He'd planned on some made-up conversation outside, then he would go, but he had no idea what to do now that he was inside the room, alone with the man.

"Yes? Do you have them?" Herman asked.

"Uh, no. Not yet. What kind did you want again?"

Herman smelled a rat, and not the ones frolicking under his bed. "What kinds are there?" he asked, noting his visitor's eyes darting about. *A liar,* he thought.

"Is white all right?" Josh said, licking his lips. The man had a broad chest and the thick arms of a laborer. Picking pockets and sliding through open windows hadn't given the thief a comparable physique. He was overmatched and knew it.

Both started when there was another knock at the door.

Herman sidled past his nervous guest to stand between him and the door. "Who's there?" he asked, his fists clenched.

"Who would it be? Are you daft? Let me in," Keys whispered.

Josh waited until Herman turned his back to open the door, then sprang forward, an open straight razor in his right hand. Herman sensed the attack and ducked. Keys walked into the blade, and his nose spouted blood.

"What the hell!" he screamed, as Herman, underneath his attacker's arms, sent Josh flying with an elbow. Keys kicked the door shut and pulled out his own razor.

The cramped room gave no space for fancy maneuvers. Josh, with the bed frame pressing against the back of his knees, was unsteady. He waved the razor in the air between them. "Back away! My da knows I'm here. We're with Inspector Ethington. If I go missing, they'll know who to look for. One more step, and I'll shout out for all I'm worth, I swear I will."

Malone laughed. "And who'll care? Someone screams in this courtyard at least once a week. You know no one will come. So talk. What's this about an inspector?"

Josh saw no way out. He pointed at Herman with his razor. "The inspector says he wants to kill the queen. If he does, the bobbies will tear Whitechapel apart. We'll all lose business."

The Irishman whistled low and looked to Herman. "That so? You here to kill Her Majesty?"

Herman kept his fists up but nodded. "*Ja*. That's so."

"Well, boyo, why didn't you say so? After what the Brits 'ave done to my people, a little payback would be a welcome sight." He looked at the young man waving his razor at him and pressed a rag against his bleeding nose. "Just one problem. What to do about little Josh here?" He winked at the young Fisher. "You think your da will miss having another mouth to feed, especially one as worthless as yours?"

Keys removed the rag and scowled at the blood that soaked it, then spat at the young man's feet. "You'd best tell us what you knows, if you wants to live. What else did the inspector say? What does he know about my new friend here?"

Josh's razor hand began to shake and his mouth was so dry he could barely speak. Keys was known as a man not to cross, and Josh could see in his eyes he'd killed before. Josh swallowed to get enough spit in his mouth to talk.

"Said this man Ott was a German, an electrician, and he was here to kill the queen with some sort of strange rifle. I didn't understand that part. Da said for us to hunt for him, to keep the peace down here. I'd heard you'd come into some money, so I followed you here to see if you was being paid to hide him."

Malone leered at him. "Clever of this inspector to get your da to do his dirty work. Anything else?"

"No, I swear! Let me go and I'll tell no one. Not even me da."

Malone shook his head. "He'd smell you were hiding something. Pity you're not as clever as your father. If we let you go, the police'd be here in less'n an hour looking for Mister Ott here. And me." He turned to Herman. "What do ye say? Shall we let the rabbit go, or kill it?"

Seeing his moment, Josh barreled into Malone and knocked him back. He was leaping for the door when Herman's solid right fist slammed into the boy's face, and he collapsed.

Keys straightened up and looked down at Josh, who lay face down on the floor. "Nicely done." He smiled. "Well, that certainly makes things easier." Before Herman could react, Malone slit the young man's throat like a farmer slaughters a hog. "Might want to stand back a bit," he advised, "to keep it off your clothes. It'll stop directly."

Before Malone could say anything else, however, the sudden return of Herman's breakfast sausage joined the spreading pool of blood on the floor.

Keys snorted. "Some killer you are! Will I have to hold your hand when you've got Her Majesty in your sights? Come on, man! This's what you came to do. If you can't stand the smell of blood, you'd best go back home and leave me your fancy toy. I'll find a use for it."

"I'll be far enough away I won't see the blood," Herman managed to say between gasps, "and I'll be running away before she even falls. You don't know what I'm fighting for, or you wouldn't doubt me." He took a deep breath and looked down at the dead young man. "What do we do with him?"

The Irishman rubbed his chin. "Can't leave him 'ere, that's for certain. Wait 'til night, then you won't 'ave to carry him far. Nothing to tie him to us. Dump him a few alleys away and be done with it."

"Me? You killed him."

"Aye, and with no help from you. Well," Keys allowed, "you did lay him out. That was handy."

"But why me?"

"'Cause I ain't sticking around. If Peg Leg Fisher's looking for you, he'll find you, 'specially now his son's missing. You could hide from the bobbies down 'ere forever, but Master Fisher has friends everywhere. I'm feeling a sudden fondness for the Old Country. Stay 'ere as long as you want. I'll not be coming back for some time."

He turned to go, but before he could exit, he stopped, reached into his pocket, and handed Herman a small parcel. "Your candles and matches. Light one for little Josh 'ere . . . to keep away the rats. Good hunting, boyo. Don't miss!" With that, he was gone.

Herman dropped onto the one chair in the room, as far from the dead man and the pool of blood as space allowed. He considered his situation. He looked over at the mess and consoled himself with one piece of Malone's wisdom. *He's right about one thing. It does stop, eventually.*

Herman grabbed the moth-eaten blanket and mopped up the blood as best he could, then he wrapped the dead boy in it. He sighed and lit two candles, placing one on each side of the corpse. He cursed Grüber and the day he'd met him. He thought of little Immanuel. Would he still be fit to hold him when all this was done? He looked out the window, but the shadows had barely moved. He dared not leave the room in daylight.

He took out the pieces of the rifle, carefully cleaning and oiling every part that moved and tightening every part that shouldn't. Not that the weapon needed maintenance, but it was something to do. Giving his hands a purpose calmed him and took him back to the mechanical world, where everything made sense. He hated this device, this *Liberator*. He snorted. Until now, it had only enslaved him to the will and purpose of others.

Sometime later, Herman looked out and saw it was finally getting darker. The two candles had concealed the approach of night. He counted the toll of a nearby church bell. Eight. Still too early. To his surprise, his belly grumbled. *Maybe I needed this*, he thought. *Maybe Malone was right about that, too. I need to get comfortable with death if I am to bring it to another.*

He ripped off a stretch of blanket and tied it like a scarf around the dead boy's neck to hide the wound. Soon it was nine and fully dark. Herman raised the corpse to its feet and was grateful the boy was so slender. He draped the right arm over his neck, opened the door, and together they staggered down the street like two friendly drunks.

Herman was surprised how easy it was to walk with a dead man beside him without attracting attention. Drunks were commonplace in Whitechapel, and most people didn't give them a glance. After fifteen minutes of shambling away from the room, he found a narrow passageway and collapsed against a wall with his pale, silent companion. He propped the dead boy up, patted his cheek, and mumbled—loud enough to be overheard, "I'll go get us another drink, my friend. You wait here." Herman had to remember to stagger now that he'd been relieved of the corpse, while the body faithfully did as it was told, and waited right there.

35

Friday, June 18, cont.

I did my stretching slowly as the sun came up, reaching for my toes. *Good thing I'm not taller, or I'd never get there.*

After I convinced my body to move, I went upstairs to the Ethington residence to prepare breakfast, as had become my habit since moving in below them. I looked in on Elizabeth, who was yet to stir. I gazed down at her tousled hair. It was a light brown that shone when brushed, but the wild tangling of it just now was endearing all the same, like the mane of some wild horse.

I tweaked her nose before heading for the kitchen. "Latecomers to breakfast get cold eggs."

"Does that apply to the Lord of the Manor as well?"

"For Lords, I might make an exception." *The simple rituals of the day,* I pondered as I cracked eggs. *I never knew they could be so fulfilling.*

James came trudging down the hall. Apparently, the Ethington tribe was not at its best at sunrise, but both could be moved to action by the smell of eggs and bacon.

As I dished out portions for each, they gathered at their places, but each waited until I sat down. "What are your plans for today, James?"

He paused, fork hovering over his plate. "Today I want to walk the route of the procession and look for possible sites for a sniper to hide."

"That's six miles, Father," Elizabeth said. "It'll take half the day to do it right, with the traffic and all. May I go with you?"

"Yes, James," I said. "Let's make it an outing."

James did his best to look severe. "What kind of family considers looking for a sniper a normal pastime?"

"You might as well give up, Father," Elizabeth teased. "We've got you outnumbered."

"And surrounded," I said, as I took his empty plate. "The exercise would do us good."

"Well, broad daylight this close before the event should be safe enough, I suppose," he said, admitting defeat as graciously as possible. "But bring your derringer along, just in case."

"My dear sir, you know what a careful person I am. I always take precautions." Then I turned to a grinning Elizabeth. "So, Elizabeth, what's it to be today? Dressed, or undressed?"

When the girl's mouth gaped open, I laughed. "Meaning do we wear male attire of course, hence no dresses, or 'undressed.' What else could I mean?"

James rubbed his forehead. "You're quite right, Margaret. I am outnumbered and surrounded. But please, ladies *do* wear *something!*"

"Pants it is, then!" Elizabeth giggled. "I'm getting rather used to having pockets."

James shook his head as his daughter rushed to her room. Looking at me, he said. "I blame you, of course."

I laughed. "I have rather upset your world, haven't I?"

"Aye, and thank God for that." While his daughter was probably flinging clothes about in her bedroom, we exchanged a look that reminded me of what could have been.

We two gentlemen—along with the young lad who accompanied us—seemed a companionable trio walking along together beside the procession route. Banners made the path easy to follow, and starting from Buckingham Palace it took two hours to walk the three miles to St. Paul's Cathedral, as James stopped every hundred yards to survey the rooftops.

During one of these pauses, I noted a poster announcing a three-night engagement by Samuel Clemens, otherwise known as Mark Twain, at the Royal Victoria Hall. I recalled my interview with him during my involvement with the hunt for the Ripper, along with his sparkling performance of his works the night that adventure came to a head. Nine years ago seemed a lifetime away.

When we finally arrived at the cathedral, we stopped to survey the buildings which lined the large plaza facing the entrance.

"Look at the bleachers going up atop the buildings," I said. "No place for a sniper to hide up there."

"Aye, but the queen will be stationary here for twenty minutes." James pointed out. "This is the place of greatest danger. If I were a sniper, here's where I'd have the best chance of success."

"Perhaps he'll try to hide in the cathedral, Father," Elizabeth suggested. She pointed to a large window to the right as we faced the front of the building. "He could shoot right down at her from there."

"Now you're thinking like our adversary. That's good. But the stairs that pass in front of the window will be full of people looking down at Her Majesty. The roof would be slightly better, but clergy and city officials who aren't part of the ceremony will be granted access to that space. He couldn't possibly go unnoticed long enough to fire, and escape afterward would be impossible."

James looked around the courtyard again. A moving procession with guardsmen on horseback screening the target would be a challenging shot, all the more so as the queen was not a large woman. Never over five feet, age had shrunken her height as it had expanded her waist. She was quite likely the smallest person engaged in the entire affair, other than the members of the boys' choir who would be standing on the steps above her.

"Do you see anything, Margaret? I feel as though there's something right in front of me, but I'm missing it."

I shook my head. "Then I'm as blind as you are, James. I agree this is the perfect killing ground for our hunter. The only possibility I can consider is that he would be in one of the windows in the square, but I can't imagine any being unoccupied. He'd have to have a delegation of conspirators filling the room to be allowed to fire. And some windows will have an impaired view due to the statue of Queen Anne in the plaza, so we can rule those windows out entirely. Plus, a man with a rifle at a window would be seen by the onlookers on the roof of the cathedral." I sighed. "All in all, your security precautions seem airtight. I see no flaw."

James shook his head. "But if that were so, why would Ott still be here? Either he's intent on killing you, or he's seen something here that we haven't."

My head hurt. I half-remembered something, something about a false claim . . . then it left. I shook my head.

We finished the route, taking four hours to travel the remaining three miles. James stopped about twenty minutes at each of the bridges the procession would cross, seeking any place a sniper could fire while the procession's mobility was reduced. Nothing.

As we approached the royal residence once more, Elizabeth asked, "How do you know he hasn't fled, Father? Perhaps he's made the same conclusion you have. I bet he's across the channel and in Paris. You may have defeated him already, without even knowing it."

"I can't afford to think like that, dear," he said. "'Pride goeth before a fall,' and that would be a disastrous fall indeed."

We completed our walk shortly after two o'clock and after a light lunch at a bistro, James declared a parting of the ways. "I should go into the office to see if there're any messages for me or any new information from Germany on Ott. I doubt it, but I'll take whatever comes our way that might help us find the man. What about you and Elizabeth?"

"As for myself, I have a couple of letters I want to send to Australia. I made contacts among the journalist community while I was there in '91 and I should let them know I'll be returning soon and needing employment. As for Elizabeth," I winked, "I think she needs to practice her spitting."

Elizabeth and I laughed, bowed to James, and left a perplexed Inspector Ethington in our wake.

36

Friday, June 18, cont.

Back at home, we found a letter from Germany forwarded to me from my prior address. I recognized the Professor's precise handwriting and noting the letter was sent a week prior, I tore it open on the spot.

Heidelberg, June 11, 1897

Dear Miss Harkness,

I've had a stimulating week as a visiting professor at this historic university. A Professor Holman was assigned to me as translator and guide. Or, using his proper German title, "Herr Professor Doktor Holman." More than one of the students was confused by our British tradition of referring to surgeons as "Mister," a relic of the days of Barber Surgeons. One student, doing his best to address me properly in English, referred to me as "Mister Professor" Bell, and the title stuck. I've been called worse, and I accepted my new title with a smile.

As I shall have to travel through London on my way back to Edinburgh, I thought you, Doyle, and I could dine together and stage a brief reunion of the Three Musketeers. Doyle, as you may know, now resides in South Norwood, a short distance from London, so he could easily join us.

I joined the Marlboro Club during our prior adventure, so

I plan on staying the night there on Saturday, the nineteenth. Fortunately, I made the reservation prior to our departure for Germany, for it was the last room they had available until after the Diamond Jubilee, and I can only stay the one night.

I shall be traveling at leisure for the next week, so please leave a message for me at the club's reception. I estimate my arrival around noon.

If you are unable to meet with me, I understand, but request that you RSVP so that I may plan accordingly when I arrive.

Respectfully Yours,
JB

I read the letter over twice, the first time quickly, savoring the memory of his voice as I imagined him reading it to me. The second time I read it over more slowly, in order to fully grasp the content. Bell was arriving tomorrow! It would be good to sit around the table with my comrades once more. Then I frowned. James and Elizabeth should not be excluded.

Elizabeth could tell by my smile the letter was significant. "What is it, Margaret? Who do you know in Germany?"

"A dear friend," I said. "Though he resides in Edinburgh. He was with me in Germany recently, and stayed behind a few days once our business there was settled. He'll be in London tomorrow and wants to dine with me and our mutual friend, Conan Doyle, tomorrow night."

Elizabeth's eyes bulged when I mentioned my other old comrade.

"Oh, Margaret, you must go! Could I go? Could I meet him? Could Father come too?"

I laughed at her enthusiasm. Elizabeth did nothing by halves. "In order of your statement and questions, I agree I should go, and yes, yes, and yes! The diversion would do us all good."

Elizabeth danced up the steps to the building entrance while I mentally composed my response. I would have much to relate to my two old friends on how I had spent the last fortnight. I'd have to move quickly to get a message to the club and be back in time for dinner. I stopped Elizabeth as she started to change back into a dress. "If you want to accompany me," I advised, "don't change. I'm leaving as soon as I dash off a note."

I wanted to re-create the episode of the Three Musketeers as closely as possible, and as I was soon leaving for a new life in Australia, I felt a little indulgence was called for. With that in mind, I sat down and composed the following note:

Dear Mister Professor Bell,

I am delighted to have the chance to break bread with you and Doyle one last time before my emigration to Australia on July seventh. As it's possible this will be our final farewell, I will take the liberty of requesting that you task your doorman to purchase five tickets for the eight o'clock performance of our mutual acquaintance, Mark Twain. I shall reimburse you for all when we arrive.

I can see your abundant eyebrows ascend after reading the number of tickets I require. While you have been teaching in Heidelberg I have been rather busier, to wit—I have survived an assassination attempt by an anarchist and acquired a dear friend in Inspector Ethington, who has a remarkable fifteen-year-old daughter. I trust you have no objection to them joining us for the evening. I recall our conversation regarding the inspector after our initial meeting with him, and once again your perception, and generosity of spirit exceeded mine.

His daughter, Elizabeth, desires to become a detective like her father. As such, she is already adept at passing herself off as a young man, and I would ask you make a reservation at the club for the five of us, to allow me to coach her on how to behave as a male in more formal situations. I would be grateful if you didn't share Elizabeth's gender with Doyle, to see if she can fool him for the evening.

As you can tell, I aspire to be as entertaining as always.

My current address in Soho is attached. Please send one of
the club's couriers with your response to inform me if my plan
meets with your approval and, if so, what time we should arrive.

Affectionately Yours,
Margaret

I folded my note and placed it into an envelope, wrote the flat's address on the outside with my name, and looked up to see Elizabeth ready to go. "Come, Elizabeth. We need to buy you some theater attire while we're out."

Elizabeth hesitated at the entrance to the Marlboro Club, holding back and asking me, "Are you sure?"

"Don't be afraid, Elizabeth," I soothed. "The residents scarcely look at one another. A young man your age will be completely beneath their notice. Besides, I want you to get a good look at where we're having dinner tomorrow night."

"What!" Elizabeth's pale face turned paler. "Impossible! I wouldn't be able to swallow."

"How else are you to meet Doctor Doyle?" I teased.

She sighed and followed me into reception where I exchanged pleasantries with the clerk, then explained I had a note for a guest arriving tomorrow. We left, Elizabeth mute the entire time.

"Now, that wasn't so bad, was it?"

"No, but I didn't have to say anything. Are Professor Bell and Doctor Doyle agreeable to two females joining them for dinner in a men's club?"

I patted her shoulder. "As for me, I've dined there with them before in male clothing. Knowing Professor Bell as I do, I think he'll find it excellent sport."

"And Doctor Doyle?"

"Oh, he won't know. I want to see if you can fool him the entire evening."

Elizabeth gave me a look somewhere between amazement and terror as she froze on the sidewalk in midstride. "Margaret! How could you? What if he finds out!"

I pulled gently on her arm to restart her motion before we were overrun by other pedestrians. "I sincerely doubt that will happen. First, Doctor Doyle has a robust appetite and will be much occupied with the meal. Second, he will be more interested in the recent adventures of Bell and myself in Germany than mine here in London. He's apt to give you a friendly nod, then focus on other matters. As long as you don't scream, you should be fine."

"But my hair! I can't wear a cap to dinner."

"Quite right. I have a wig I can lend you. Now, let's go, we have much to do!"

I swore Elizabeth to secrecy regarding the next evening's plans until after dinner. When James arrived home I asked, in my most innocent voice. "So, any news to report?"

"No news from Peg Leg or his brood, nor anything new from Germany. I spent more time studying the route of the procession, and I am convinced more than ever that if Ott strikes, it will be during the ceremony. Besides, that would make the greatest impression. Unless he's a distraction for some bomb-throwers along the route?"

"We can't afford to discount the threat," I said. "Anything else?"

"Various administrative tasks that I fear shall only multiply once I am promoted. Heavy rests the head that wears the crown, I suppose." He shrugged.

"So," he asked, "how was the rest of your day?"

37

Friday, June 18, cont.

Elizabeth was all aquiver, and I feared if I didn't tell James about our invitation for tomorrow night right away, she would burst. "I received a letter from Germany today," I began, wanting to draw the moment out.

"From the Secret Police?" James asked. "Another bonus, perhaps?"

"Nothing so mercenary. The letter was from my dear friend, Professor Bell."

"Oh, is he still in Germany? What on earth for?"

"He was awarded a week as a visiting professor in Heidelberg. Now he's on a brief holiday. He'll be back in London tomorrow, and has invited us to dinner."

"Us? Why would he invite us?"

"Well, he's invited *me*, but I wouldn't go without you and Elizabeth."

"And you accepted without consulting me?"

His reply brought me short. "James, there wasn't time. I got the letter late, due to transferring my mail here. I needed to get the letter to the club where he'll be staying before his arrival . . ." I glanced at Elizabeth. "And I needed to make certain preparations."

"Tell him the rest," Elizabeth said, her eyes trained on me, offering encouragement.

"Doctor Doyle will also likely be there, in remembrance of times past, when the three of us worked together."

James's smile was replaced by a clenched jaw and crossed arms.

"The Doyle who makes Scotland Yard look like a haven for the feeble-minded? That Doyle?"

"Yes, James," I said in a mild voice. "My dear friend and comrade, Conan Doyle. I'm sorry I didn't consult you. I thought you'd be excited. I was planning on the five of us going on to a reading by Mark Twain afterward. My two companions and I have a bit of a history with him also."

"Margaret, I'm in the middle of a manhunt. A man who, by the way, tried to kill us in the street. I'm unavailable tomorrow night. I hope you and Elizabeth have a wonderful time."

"Elizabeth is very keen to meet Dr. Doyle, and I think you should come, if only for her sake."

"Yes, please Father. Tell him the rest, Margaret!"

"Is there something else I should know?"

I cleared my throat. "Elizabeth and I are going in male attire, as we'll be having dinner at a men's club."

Silence. James sat frozen in his chair for at least three ticks of the clock, then a low rumble from deep within his chest exploded like a volcanic eruption as he laughed long and deeply. Tears ran down his cheeks as he hugged himself in the release of pure joy. He clung to the moment as long as he could, and I sensed that he was letting go of far more than the troubles of the day. After he had finally regained his composure and his breath he asked quietly, "Is that all? Very well, then. I look forward to it!"

Elizabeth told me later it was then that she knew he was truly her father once more.

Peter Kropotkin and his daughter caught the evening train to South-ampton. They would catch the morning ferry to Calais, and then travel on to Geneva to join fellow anarchists from throughout Europe. Although the various leaders moved with discretion, their journeys, and gathering, were noted.

The bleachers around the steps to St. Paul's were nearly complete; the odor of freshly sawn pine made the square smell like an Alpine forest.

The choirmaster had the boys of the choir march to their places for the ceremony several times. No singing on the steps . . . yet. It was vexing enough just getting the little hellions to walk in a line without tugging on each other's robes or causing mischief. They would be in place before the queen arrived, but thousands would already be there, and the choirmaster didn't want the papers to remark upon their deportment.

Herr Grüber was disappointed to learn that Parmeggiani had cast Herman aside when the man's likeness appeared in the paper, allowing him to avoid arrest. As Grüber expected, the fence's familiarity with skirting the law had allowed him to emerge a free man after a brief incarceration. His message of condolence to Luigi went unanswered, which Grüber put down to the Italian's caution after his recent brush with the authorities. Grüber would alert his contacts in Southampton to keep an eye out for Herman, though he had faith the man's love for his son would keep him on task. His pawn was in play, and it was a move he could no longer recall.

Troop ships were arriving and tying up along the Thames. Soldiers from the far reaches of the British Commonwealth would ride along the route before the queen to demonstrate the extent of her empire to a watching world.

That night, soldiers from around the globe met in London's pubs, ready to defend the honor of their various regiments against one another, sometimes with fists when words proved insufficient. Still, at the end of the evening, before staggering back to their respective ships, they linked arms and sang:

> *God save our gracious Queen!*
> *Long live our noble Queen!*
> *God save the Queen!*
> *Send her victorious,*
> *Happy and glorious,*
> *Long to reign over us,*
> *God save the Queen.*

38

Saturday, June 19

James answered a knock at the door and found Harry Fisher, Billy's oldest son, waiting for him.

"You found him? You can take me to him?"

Harry spat at the inspector's feet. "Me da's waiting. You can talk to him." He eyed Margaret and Elizabeth in male attire, turned back to the inspector. "Only you. These blokes can bugger off."

Elizabeth blushed, and James had to bite his tongue not to play the outraged father. *Time she became accustomed to such language, if she's to work the street,* he thought.

"Right you are." Turning to the "blokes," the inspector said, "Won't take long."

"Maybe it won't, and maybe it will," Harry said. "Let's be off. Da's waiting."

The elder Fisher was in the Dog's Head at his favorite table, his other son, Ben, and a bottle of whiskey beside him. Billy's eyes were red and his cheeks wet, but the paleness of his face flashed to red when he saw James enter. His wooden leg slammed to the floor as he stood and shook his fist in the inspector's face. "You killed my boy, you bastard!"

James was knocked back, partly by the strong stench from the man's mouth and partly by the spittle. He resisted the urge to wipe it off. "What's this then, Billy? Your boy? Which boy?"

The man poured himself another drink from a half-empty bottle and downed it before answering. "Which one ain't here, you idiot? Josh, my youngest. Found this morning in an alley with his throat slit.

Police Constable Williams was good enough to come to me right away after he recognized him, just lying there like an old sack." He started sobbing. "I know it was that German you're looking for! No one in the East End would have the bollocks to kill a son of mine. It's my fault. I shoulda never listened to you. I tries to do right by queen and country, just once, and what happens? My son pays for it!"

Billy grabbed James's lapels and shook him. "And for what? Josh weren't the brightest, but he was a kind lad. Never gave no one cause to do this to him." He stopped to wipe his nose. This done, he stood as straight as his peg leg allowed. "I want to slit that bastard's throat meself, right after I whisper my boy's name into his ear, so it's the last thing he ever hears."

He collapsed back into his chair and mumbled, the whiskey finally overpowering his rage and grief: "Me and me boys'll find him. We'll find him."

Harry caught his father before he hit the floor and picked him up by his arms, while the other son picked up his legs, wooden and flesh. "We've no more business with you, Inspector," Harry said through clenched teeth. "If we find this German first, we'll deal with him on our own. Best you not cross our paths again."

"Before you go, can you tell me where he was found?"

"You can ask Constable Williams to show you. We're off. Got to see to Josh's wake and funeral. Now go away, Inspector!"

With that, the two sons carried their unconscious father off. Peg Leg was a criminal of the lowest class, yet James was touched by the tenderness his sons showed as they bore him away. *Well, there's some good in all of us, I suspect. I hope.*

James was used to violent death, though usually it was the result of drunken brawls or two criminals falling out. Although he had no blood on his hands, he knew that Josh would still be alive if he hadn't asked Peg Leg for help. A father's tears at his son's death were no less sincere in Whitechapel than in Whitehall.

It was now approaching ten in the morning. The tragedy of the young burglar's murder made it clear why Ott had to be caught as soon as possible and James felt the need to rush somewhere, to do something heroic and save the day, but where, what? His quarry was no more tangible than smoke but every bit as real. James had been a policeman long enough to know that doing nothing was sometimes the best thing to do, though it can also be the hardest. *I can at least talk to PC Williams and have him show me where the body was found. That counts as doing something.*

When he arrived at the Spitalfields Station, he saw Sergeant Bean at the desk. He recalled when he worked there, how the bobbies called him "beans for brains," and James had to stifle a smile when the sight of the man brought the memory back. "Good day, Sergeant," he said. "Constable Williams report in yet?"

"Nay," Bean said. "I reckon you'll be wanting to speak with him about the late Master Fisher he found with his throat slit. Body's probably still at the morgue, if you want to see it. Williams said it was done with one slice. Whoever did it was as cool as an adder and just as deadly. Don't know what an idiot like Josh did to have an experienced killer use his blade on him, but there's no mistaking the work of a man who's killed before."

James shuddered when he thought how closely he and Margaret had come to being added to the assassin's list. "I reckon you're right, Sergeant. Thank God we don't get many like him. I'll pay my respects in back. Please call me when Williams gets in."

"Aye," the sergeant said, calm and inscrutable as always. He'd seen the world's misfortunes on the beat, and now they were paraded before him while he sat on his lofty perch in the station. Inspectors, bobbies, and criminals all came and went, and as time passed they looked more and more alike.

James found his old comrade, Inspector Harry Caldwell, having a spot of tea, his feet up on his desk. "Good thing Abberline's retired, or he'd pound you into the ground . . ."

"Unsharpened!" Harry replied, laughing as they recalled the old chief inspector's favorite threat. "You're a long way from the Yard, my friend. What's this about?"

"Fisher."

"What? The death of one of the busiest burglars in London merits your shoe leather?" Harry put his feet down. "Have some tea and tell me why."

"I'm partly to blame for his death."

Inspector Caldwell whistled at this. "Now that's a tale I'd like to hear."

"I asked Peg Leg to find a man. I think Josh found him."

"You hired Fisher to find someone?"

"'Hired' isn't the word I'd use. I explained how it would be good for him. He saw the light and agreed."

Harry gave a sitting bow. "They must teach mind control over at the Yard. I don't recall you having a silver tongue."

James sat down with his tea. "So, what have you found out?"

Caldwell shrugged. "Not much. No one saw him arrive there. An old woman, probably meaning to pick his pockets, discovered the man she thought was a passed-out drunk was actually dead. Williams found the throat wound. Oh, and his pockets were cleaned out, so she probably picked his pockets anyway. Her reward for being a good Samaritan, I suppose."

"Good citizens are hard to find. Anything else?"

"Not so far. To be honest, I reckoned it must be someone with a grudge against his father, and I figured before I could sort it out Peg Leg would deal with it himself. Justice isn't very patient in the East End, if you'll recall." Harry leaned forward. "Now, Special Branch Inspector Ethington, why did you ask our mutual acquaintance, Master Fisher, to help you hunt down someone? I'm deeply hurt you'd turn to him before you would me. I carry a set of darbies, if you recall. Fisher's only experience with manacles is wearing them, though not as recently as I'd like."

"I reckoned it takes a thief to catch one. He's the best, and he has—or had—three sons to be his hounds. You already have the flyer for the man I'm looking for."

"Ott? You think he's down here?"

"He's hiding somewhere. He knows we're after him. We almost caught him yesterday, so I reckon he's either fled to the continent or he's in the East End, where people don't ask too many questions."

"Took a shot at you, eh? Taking this rather personal, I see."

"You ever been shot at, Harry?"

Caldwell rubbed his chin. "Well, no. Not as I recall."

"You'd recall if you had. And yes, I am taking it personal, but that's not the only reason."

Harry sipped his tea, waited a moment, then set his cup down. "All right, James. Out with it. What else?"

"I have intelligence that he's here to kill the queen during the Diamond Jubilee, either during the procession or at the ceremony itself."

"That would make him, what, the eighth man to try to kill her? If I were him, I wouldn't like my odds. Her Majesty eats assassins for breakfast." Harry raised his cup of tea. "A woman to respect, with or without a crown. God bless her."

"God save the Queen, Harry, but help Him the best you can."

Inspector Ethington was into his second cup when PC Williams stuck his head through the door. "Sergeant Bean said you wanted to see me, Inspector?"

"Yes, Williams. I need you to show me where you found the body before I view it in the morgue. Won't take a moment."

Williams shuffled his feet and looked down. "Well, Inspector, could it wait until tomorrow morning? My wife's pregnant, due any day now. The closer she gets to delivery, the more she worries about me. I've only got two more hours on my shift today."

James coughed. "Sorry, Williams. I must insist. You can go straight home from the scene if your time's up. I can go to the morgue on my own. Is that fair?"

Williams nodded, the creases on his forehead smooth again. "Aye, sir. It's on the way. I was afraid you'd drag me off to the morgue after. It's in the opposite direction."

"Then it's settled. You don't want to be late for lunch with your wife. Unless her mother's near to hand, it may be the last hot one you have for a couple of weeks."

Williams smiled at that. "Her sister lives close by, so I doubt I'll go hungry. Let's go!"

James turned to Inspector Caldwell. "Well, Harry, are you coming, or do you need a formal invitation?"

Harry sighed. "Things were so quiet here once you went away." He stood, picked up his bowler, and nodded. "Since you asked so nicely."

Ten minutes later, they were standing in the alleyway, looking at the spot Josh had been laid to rest.

"Was he just dumped here, Williams? You'd think he'd have been noticed before sunrise."

"Nay. He was propped up, sir. Posed, you might say. The cut on his neck was covered up by a strip of wool wrapped to look like a scarf. Folks figured him as just another passed-out drunk."

"Hum. Couldn't have gone far encumbered by a dead man without drawing people's attention. Anyone notice when he was put here?"

"I've asked about. Sure, drunks ain't a rarity here. A hundred people coulda seen him and not recall. Sorry."

"I had some of our other men ask about as well, James," said Inspector Caldwell. "I honestly didn't expect to find his killer, but we did the usual, at least."

Which is why you're still at Spitalfields, James thought.

James noticed the constable shifting his weight from side to side like a little boy needing the toilet. "All right, Williams. You're free to go."

"Thank you, sir. I'm off to log out then." Williams touched his helmet and was gone in an instant, leaving James alone with Inspector Caldwell in the dim alley. *How far could I walk with a dead man beside me?* James wondered. *How big a circle do I need to draw?*

"Harry, I need you to roust out enough men to search every room within a four-street radius. Make sure each man has a sketch of Ott. We need to complete this before dark. I reckon he stays inside during the day, so the next five hours may be our best chance to catch him."

"And where are you off to?"

"The morgue. Time to pay my last respects to young Josh Fisher."

39

Saturday, June 19, cont.

Herman had fallen into a troubled sleep once he'd returned. Now his stomach was grumbling and he fretted, waiting until full dark to go out and buy food. Keys would not be making any more deliveries.

Then he heard voices, shouts, knocks on doors, and he peered out the dirty window. Three constables with nightsticks, a flyer in their leader's hand, were entering homes and asking questions. Herman knew whose likeness they carried. He saw them come to a door and knock. After no one answered the third knock, a pale man with rings of keys and a set of picks set to work. The door opened after about five seconds. A senior constable went in with the locksmith and the constable carrying the flyer, while the other constable stayed outside to watch the courtyard. After a minute or so, the other three came back out again, the locksmith secured the door, and they proceeded to the next residence. In the West End, the police would not enter a locked residence without a warrant. In Whitechapel, such formalities were the exception.

Herman knew if he tried to leave while the others were inside the constable watching the courtyard would call out. His room was in a corner of the yard and the only way out was forward, past the search party. He was trapped, and the constables were making their deliberate way toward him. Unless . . . It was time to see if he could do what needed to be done.

He assembled the rifle. When the next door opened and three

other men went in to perform their duties, he cracked open his door and sighted on the head of the constable outside. He swallowed hard. Then, with the slightest pressure, the rifle coughed and the man fell onto the street without crying out.

Herman quickly disassembled the rifle and threw it into its case. He was out the door and almost to the entrance to the court when the senior constable found his colleague dead on the doorstep. The East End was a violent place, and Constable Harris had seen his share of dead men, but never one taken silently and behind his back. He pulled out his whistle, but his hands shook so that it took him a couple of breaths before he could blow into it. By that time Herman was around the corner and into the street, just a tradesman with an odd tool case and a satchel with spare clothes.

Well, he thought. *Now I know I can kill. Satisfied, Keys?*

It was clear where he had to run from, but where to? Somewhere a good distance from here, anyway. He caught a horse-drawn omnibus, not caring where it went, and rode for fifteen minutes before hopping off. He'd bought a sausage and was sitting on a park bench when the shakes hit him and he had to lay the sausage down beside him before he dropped it. *I've killed a man. There's no going back, now. If men have a soul, mine's damned.*

He lay back on the bench, shivering from the cold sweat. He covered the sausage with a rag in his pocket before the sight of it made him gag. *Even damned men have to eat,* he thought, and he spied a pub across the park. Suddenly, he wanted a beer more than anything else in the world, and made for it. He may have been born in Russia, but when it came to beer, he was a converted German.

His stomach settled down after the beer, so he had a second and felt even better. Seated on a bar stool, he considered his options. Returning to the East End was out. Keys had apparently known the young man he'd killed, which meant the family knew the Irishman. Herman had no doubt the burglar would turn him in to save his own hide if either the police or the dead man's family caught up with him, and Keys knew what Herman looked like now.

Then it occurred to him. Where is the best place to hide? The place least expected. Herman drained his beer and left to find a secondhand clothing store. He hoped he still had time.

40

Saturday, June 19, cont.

James showed his badge to the clerk and asked to see the surgeon who'd examined the body brought in that morning with the slit throat. The man at the counter was as gray as the majority of the morgue residents, and only slightly more animated. He waved his right hand toward the back. "Hopkins," he said, and returned to his study of a copy of a penny dreadful with the picture of an American cowboy on the front cover.

Police Surgeon Hopkins was dressed in a smock that had once been white. Now, after multiple washings with blood on it, his "uniform" was a mottled burgundy. He was of average height but had an impressive set of flaming red side-whiskers that would have disqualified him from passing unnoticed in a crowd.

James showed Hopkins his badge of office, and when he inquired about the young man's death, the surgeon nodded.

"Lad hadn't a chance. The incision was so clean, I reckon he was unconscious when the deed was done. If he'd moved his head or struggled, the line wouldn't have been so straight and even."

"So, not a knife fight, then?" James asked.

"Nay, Inspector. He was bled like a lamb, and whoever did it had done it before. Brought to mind the bad old days of the Ripper in his surety of hand."

"Anything else you can tell me?"

Hopkins was about to answer when he was called to the back: "Mister Hopkins," a constable said. "Sorry to bother you and the inspector, sir, but I'm here on a sad duty."

Hopkins's brow furrowed. "Constable Harris, after all you've seen, it must be a terrible thing indeed. What've you brought me?"

Harris looked down and shook his head. "One of our own, sir. Constable Williams."

"What!" James said. "What happened?"

"We were too short-handed to do the search with the men we had, so I ordered Williams to stay after his shift. He was with me as we did a search around the site where the Fisher lad was found this morning." Harris cleared his throat. "As you suggested, Inspector."

James felt his gorge rise. *Another death at my feet*, he thought.

The surgeon removed the oiled canvas tarpaulin covering the body and whistled. The single bullet hole above the right temple was obvious. He rotated the head from side to side.

"Note the absence of an exit wound on the opposite side. The small amount of blood around the hole tells me the man died instantly." The surgeon took a ruler and laid it beside the hole.

James stared at the hole and reflected that Sergeant Q had the right of it, the hole would easily accommodate a man's thumb. Then he recalled Constable Williams's words to him earlier that day, about fearing the inspector would "drag him to the morgue," and let out a long, shuddering breath as he fought to keep his composure.

"Large caliber weapon," the police surgeon continued, "probably around a .44. No gunpowder around the wound, so the shot was fired from some distance. Have you apprehended the shooter, Constable?"

Harris shook his head. "No, sir. Thing is, I couldn't have been more than twenty feet away when Williams was shot, and I never heard a discharge. I went inside to look for anything suspicious, and while I think the occupants of the room are probably thieves, I didn't find anything that led me to think they was involved with our assassin. They were as surprised as I was when I walked back out to find Williams dead."

"Were there any witnesses?" James asked. "As crowded as the East End is, surely someone saw something."

"One old woman whose eyesight ain't the best says she saw a man lean out a door three doors down for a second, then she saw the constable fall and the man hightailed it out of there. We found traces of smeared blood on the floor of the room she says he left, but the description she gave didn't fit the man we're looking for—though, as I said, her eyes ain't the best. She did insist he hadn't a mustache."

"He could easily shave that off. Who lives in that residence?"

"An old acquaintance of ours, Inspector. None other than Mister Keys Malone."

"Now that's a name I'd not expected. Keys is a businessman, first and last. There's no profit in dead bobbies."

"I agree, sir. And he don't look nothing like this Ott fellow we're searching for."

James sighed. "He's proving to be as dangerous as I feared. With the Fishers and the police both looking for him to avenge one of their own, he'll flee if he has any sense."

Constable Harris nodded agreement. "I'll do my best to capture the man, but . . . God forgive me for saying this . . . I hope Peg Leg and his lads catch up to him first. They won't play by Marquis of Queensbury rules."

"I understand how you feel, Constable, but I need him alive. I need to know if he's working alone. The safety of Her Majesty may be at stake."

Both the surgeon's and Harris's eyes widened at this announcement. The bobby sighed. "Aye, sir. I'll tell the lads. We'll do our best. Just let us know when you're done with him."

"I'll do no such thing. But please, let me know when the funeral is. Williams was, as you say, one of ours. When you take up a collection for the widow, I'll be sure to do my part."

Harris touched the bill of his helmet in farewell and left, his silence expressing how he felt about inspectors who sent young constables to their deaths.

41

Saturday, June 19, cont.

Herman was able to outfit himself in a fine suit of moderately worn clothes, including a matching cravat and bowler. He purchased a carpet bag that made him appear more profitable, then headed to the Underground. The car was jammed with people of all classes heading home from work. Most were looking forward to a brief stint of freedom, what with the next day being Sunday. There would be one day of work on Monday, followed by the Jubilee on Tuesday. With all of this, the car was in a festive mood.

Herman bypassed the first two hotels he saw once he left Kensington Station. He reckoned they'd already be full, due to the upcoming festivities, but when he saw the Kingsmill Hotel along North End Road, it looked just shabby enough to offer some hope of a vacancy. Herman had a good store of money in hand but felt it best to keep much of it in reserve for his flight after the deed.

There was one room left on the top floor next to the loo, assuring frequent disturbances as his neighbors used the facility, but the space would serve. When the clerk remarked on his case and asked his line of work, Herman replied, "Insurance."

The queen's police protective detail had walked the route that afternoon, along with police commissioner, Sir Edward Bradford, the assistant commissioner, Alexander Bruce, and the commanding officer of the Household Guards. Intervals of soldiers and policemen were double-checked. An officer on horseback could usually contain as much of a crowd as ten constables on foot, but for the ceremony the ratio was halved.

Bradford was a slight man. The left sleeve of his coat was pinned to his chest, the empty sleeve a reminder of an encounter with a tigress while in India. Despite the loss of his arm, he was able to continue his military career, even hunt boars afterward with a lance while on horseback, placing the reins in his teeth when the lance was called for.

"Why are we inspecting the route tonight, Commissioner?" the guards' commander asked. "Wouldn't tomorrow be more informative?"

Sir Edward had served in the cavalry, and he was favorably disposed toward those who served astride a horse, yet he frowned at the man's question. "By detecting a flaw now," he said, with some forbearance, "we give our subordinates sufficient time to address any problem, and for us to reassess the situation tomorrow."

"You mean to say . . ."

"Yes, Colonel. Even if we find no flaws, I shall repeat my assessment tomorrow, this time by horse to give us a different perspective. I want to see the route through Her Majesty's eyes." Seeing the man's disappointment, he said, "You may send your executive officer tomorrow if you wish, Colonel. I'm sure you have a lot to inspect within your own ranks."

The guards' commander nodded, unaware of the rebuke inherent in the commissioner's remarks. "Thank you, sir. He will be at your disposal."

Bradford personally approved the measures in place. Special Branch had shared their concern about a possible assassin, and his experience as the chief of the Viceroy's secret police in India taught him to respect the danger one motivated man represented. He saw in their precautions no flaw a would-be assassin might exploit, but he would return tomorrow, nonetheless. Queen Victoria was his sovereign, and his four years as her aide-de-camp had only strengthened his devotion to her. He would rather lose his other arm than fail her.

42

Saturday, June 19, cont.

Acourier from the Marlboro Club arrived shortly before two o'clock with a brief message from Bell:

Dear Miss Harkness,

I vow not to frighten the gentleman with lurid tales of your derring-do, though I can make no such assurances regarding Doyle, who has confirmed his attendance. He is a storyteller, after all.

I look forward to seeing if the young lady can pass muster for the evening as a young lad. If so, the torch will be well and truly passed to the next generation of audacious females.

It will be pleasant to enjoy Twain's performance tonight and not have the shadow of the Ripper hanging over us as it was before. You deserve a fond, carefree farewell from the male Musketeers. Though we have parted ways, knowing you were never far away was comforting. I'll miss having you in the same hemisphere.

As for the tickets, consider them my farewell gift.

Until this evening.

Affectionately,
JB

"Bell said yes!" I exclaimed to Elizabeth. "I must teach you how to tie a proper four in hand cravat."

Elizabeth and I exchanged glances when James stumbled through the door around four, our excitement for the coming evening withered as we noted his slumped shoulders. "What is it, James? You look like Death himself."

He collapsed into his favorite chair. "With good reason. A constable was shot and killed today, while following my orders. No one heard the discharge, so it must have been Ott. I was right about where to look for him, but that gives me no comfort." He rubbed the bridge of his nose, "The man's wife is due to deliver their first child any day now, and I sent him to his death."

I put my hand to his shoulder. "I'm so sorry, James. Our enemy is clever and cruel, but you couldn't have known this would happen. It's to your credit you care for this man as you do. How can we make his killer pay?"

Elizabeth came up beside me. "By stopping him and catching him, of course!"

"Bell sent me a message agreeing to dinner tonight and the Twain reading after," I said, "but I would understand if you'd rather I canceled."

James shook himself out of his stupor. "I'd forgotten. I'm not in a jolly mood, but I know how important it is to you to see your friends one last time. Perhaps I could corner the professor long enough to ask his advice on our search. Give me a few moments to rest, and I'll wash up and change."

Elizabeth squirmed in her seat as we rode in a Clarence cab to the Marlboro. "What have you talked me into?" she groaned. "I'll be humiliated if someone finds me out!"

I squeezed her arm. "Don't worry, dear. Inspector Ethington and Mister Pennyworth are here to help. And as for your nervousness, Doctor Doyle is well accustomed to having that effect on his public. It will only add to your authenticity."

Elizabeth and I wore short wigs beneath our flat caps. We were modestly dressed in tweeds for the theater, but, as Twain's readings were considered somewhere beneath opera but above a Christmas pantomime, it was enough. James surprised me by wearing a proper smoking jacket and a top hat, and I had to remind myself I was temporarily male, so as not to admire him too openly. He certainly didn't look "average" this evening, and even Elizabeth seemed impressed.

James managed a small smile as he sat across from the two of us ladies "undressed" for the theater. "I think I needed this diversion," he said. "Perhaps when I have the professor to myself, he and I can make a small wager. I'll offer him two-to-one odds Lizzie can fool the creator of Sherlock Holmes for the evening."

I knew how hard it had been for him to submerge his grief, and he was putting on a brave front. Courage takes many forms.

We arrived at the Marlboro promptly at six, and when I informed the receptionist that "Mister Pennyworth and friends" were expected as dinner guests of Professor Bell, he gave Elizabeth a close look. I was proud of how she stared back at him with wide, innocent eyes. She did not flinch.

"How old is he?" the receptionist asked, squinting.

"Sixteen," I answered. "Doctor Doyle is joining us, and I promised my nephew he could dine with us to meet him. This young lad," I said, patting "his" shoulder, "wants to be a detective like Sherlock Holmes, and I couldn't refuse him the honor."

The receptionist eked out a weak grimace. "I can well understand that. I miss his stories in *The Strand*. We normally don't admit patrons under the age of majority, but if the lad limits himself to the dining room and the loo, I'm willing to bend the rules." The man winked at Elizabeth. "Tell Doctor Doyle we need Holmes back, will you, lad?"

"Aye, sir!" Elizabeth managed to say, though I thought I saw her flinch when the loo was mentioned. A detail I'd failed to consider. Elizabeth and I would have to sip our drinks modestly.

Bell was already inside when we entered. "Ah, Mister Pennyworth . . . and friends." He extended his hand first to James, then to Elizabeth. "A pleasure to see you again, Inspector."

Bell next turned to Elizabeth. "And how shall I call you tonight, young sir? What *nom de guerre* are you using?"

She looked to me to translate. "Alias," I explained. "What name do you use in disguise?"

"Oh." She caught herself just as she started to curtsey and bowed instead. "James, like my father."

Bell nodded. "James the younger it is!"

Just then, Doctor Arthur Conan Doyle made his grand entrance. He was a bit thicker in the waist but still had an energetic step. I had seen an occasional notice in the papers of his sporting activity, and his personality was as large as his physical presence, filling the small room the moment he entered. I remembered a foggy night years ago when Doyle's quick wit engaged the Ripper while I prepared for my final act of defiance. And then there was the brief embrace we shared after. I shook my head. We—and time—had moved on.

I extended my hand, "Porthos, so good to see you again! Did you bring the cricket bat you owe me?"

"Porthos?" James the elder asked, looking to Doyle for signs of offense.

Doyle laughed deep within his large chest. "Mister Pennyworth! Splendid to see you again, my dear friend," he said, winking. "I'm afraid the matter of the cricket bat escaped my mind, and you may take me literally when I say that I shall always be in your debt."

His embrace this evening was chaste. Yes, time had moved on. He extended his hand to James: "And your name, sir?"

"James Ethington of Scotland Yard, Doctor." James followed up his own introduction by nodding toward his sometimes-son. "And this is my boy, also named James. He is a loyal fan of yours, Doctor, and wants to become a detective like Sherlock Holmes."

Doyle didn't offer his hand to Elizabeth but nodded amiably enough. "A loyal reader is always welcome, though I hope you've read other of my works as well."

"Yes, sir," our lad said in an acceptable tenor. "I quite enjoy your Brigadier Gerard tales."

"Excellent! My vain little French Brigadier provides the reader with a pleasant diversion while also instructing them in the important history of the Napoleonic era. I'm quite finished with Mister Holmes. It was either him or me there toward the end, and I'm well rid of him. But which of my stories is your favorite?"

"'A Scandal in Bohemia,' sir."

Doyle laughed, then nodded in my direction. "I think I know why. It might surprise you to learn that Mister Pennyworth was my inspiration for the character of Irene Adler, the only woman to ever get the better of Mister Holmes."

Her face lit up, and if she hadn't been restrained by her attire, I think she would have embraced me on the spot.

Bell's smile seemed innocent enough, though I detected a slight gleam in his eye as our comrade seemed taken in by Elizabeth's ruse.

Soon the professor and James were discussing the hunt for our assassin, with Doyle listening in. Doyle had little to add, but I could see in his eyes he was assessing our recent adventures as possible fodder for a story.

"From what you tell me of Peg Leg and his progeny," Bell said, "I doubt your assassin is still anywhere within the East End, and if he had a benefactor, he would have gone there first."

"So, what do you think his next move will be?" James asked.

"I suspect he'll find a mid-grade hotel on the outskirts of town in which to bide his time until the day of the ceremony. Anything of better quality or proximity to the center of London will already be full."

"Thank you, Professor. I believe you're correct. This close to the twenty-second, his options are limited. He might even be in a community within easy train travel of London."

"Oh, I doubt that, Inspector. On the day of the ceremony, the trains will be so crowded he would be in danger of arriving too late. I'd keep your hunt close."

I was happy to see James so engaged with Bell. The collegial exchange seemed to brighten his mood, and I was able to relax and start enjoying the evening.

Our meal did not disappoint, though it is an uncomfortable truth that the harder one tries not to think of something, the more prominent it becomes, and mid-meal I detected Elizabeth rearranging herself in her seat often enough to tell me the toilet was much on her mind.

I stood. "Excuse me, Professor, but could you direct me to the loo?"

Bell inclined his head, revealing nothing. "Just before you come to reception, on your right."

Elizabeth dabbed her lips and stood. "May I join you?"

"Of course, lad. Follow me."

Once outside the room, I whispered, "There will be individual stalls. If anyone is occupied at the urinal, pay them no heed. Men do not stare at other men's endowments. It's considered a serious breach of protocol."

"What's a 'urinal'?"

"Imagine a floor-level trough, similar to what horses drink from, but built for the opposite purpose."

She had no response to this bit of intelligence. I could tell I was expanding her world that night, and dessert hadn't even been served yet.

Thankfully, we had the place to ourselves. *No need to broaden her horizons too rapidly,* I thought.

We returned to the table in time to finish the main course before pastry was offered, though only Doyle partook. It was close onto seven-fifteen and it would take thirty minutes to travel to the theater, so the five of us crammed into another Clarence. After the evening's entertainment, we would go our own ways directly from the theater. But there was still one bit of business to tend to prior to moving on to the next phase of the evening.

I stood, glass in hand. "Gentlemen!" I said. "Charge your glasses!" My two old comrades knew what was coming next, while I motioned to James and Elizabeth to remain seated for what was to follow. "To the Three Musketeers!"

Doyle and Bell stood, glasses raised. Then I motioned to my new friends to rise and join us. "Now Five!" I exclaimed.

Then my comrades and I, both old and new, intoned—for what I was sure would be our final time together—"All for one, and one for all!"

43

Saturday, June 19, cont.

I was surprised when at the end of Mr. Twain's performance, the stage manager came up to our box and invited us backstage to the dressing room. The man said that he'd pointed Doctor Doyle out to the American just before the show began, and Twain had asked that Doyle and his companions be granted an audience.

Twain was as impressive as ever, with his silver hair, enormous eyebrows and trademark white linen suit. I regretted I could not reveal my true identity to him. I was soon to regret it even more.

"Doctor Doyle," he said, "you look familiar. Have we met before? In New York, perhaps?"

"We have met once before, Mister Clemens, and I'm flattered you remember, as I was still quite green as an author then. It was nine years ago, to be exact. I was with Professor Bell and our mutual friend, Miss Margaret Harkness. It was at the time of the Ripper murders, and you gave her an interview."

Twain's eyebrows rose slowly as he pondered Doyle's answer, and then they suddenly popped up. "Ah, yes! I remember now. She wore a black satin dress with a ruby pendant." He winked at Doyle. "Strategically placed."

Doyle laughed with him, while Bell tried to hide his smile, James looked down at the floor with sudden intensity, and Elizabeth grinned. I don't recall my reaction other than finding myself momentarily incapable of speech.

Twain was enough of a performer to know when a comment went

220

awry, so he waved his arm as though to sweep the statement away. "Please, Doctor Doyle, introduce me to your companions."

Doyle did the honors and smiled when he introduced me as "my dear friend, Mister Pennyworth." Elizabeth got a half-bow and a handshake from the great author, while the rest of us got nods.

"Well, lad," Twain asked as he shook Elizabeth's hand, "have you read any of my works?"

"Yes, sir. I especially enjoyed Tom Sawyer when he tried to pass himself off as a girl."

Twain laughed at that. "And a poor job he did of it, too. Well gentlemen, it's been a pleasure, but I need to retire shortly to prepare for tomorrow. I've two more days of readings, then Mister Randolph Hearst himself contracted for me to attend the Jubilee procession and write an article about it. No rest for the wicked, nor their close friends."

We were ushered out onto the street and as we headed out James whispered to me, "Apparently both Conan Doyle and Mark Twain number among your conquests." He smiled. "Well, at least I'm in good company."

Doyle was enjoying our private joke as to my identity, so to whittle his ego down a bit I whispered into his ear as our cab arrived, "The young lad is actually James's daughter. Bell and James had a small wager, I believe, as to whether she could fool you for the evening."

Doyle's mouth gaped as he understood the last laugh was on him. Good sportsman that he was, he gave Elizabeth a courtly bow, which she returned. We shook hands all around, Bell settled his debt of honor with James (five pounds, I believe), and then my two old comrades went their separate ways, while I returned to Soho with my new companions. Danger was ahead, so we savored this brief respite before the coming day's trials.

Herman oiled the rifle and ensured the air flasks were fully charged. The toilet flushed across the hall as he lay down to sleep, making him doubt he'd get much slumber that night.

Three days remaining.

44

Sunday, June 20

Herman knew he should lie low until the day of the ceremony, but his nervous energy wouldn't let him remain indoors for long. Inevitably, he was drawn to the steps of St. Paul's Cathedral. As it was the Sunday before the ceremony, the cathedral was packed with the devout and the curious from out of town, and Herman—in his more elegant attire—blended into the crowd quite easily. He was not devout, but on a sudden whim entered for a service. *Let's see if the damned catch fire when they walk on holy ground*, he thought. He was almost disappointed when he did not burst into flame upon entering.

After the service, he wandered back outside and surveyed the final preparations around the large plaza. A vendor was hawking tin buttons, each of which sported a red, white, and blue ribbon. In the center was a black-and-white image of Queen Victoria with the Diamond Jubilee's date underneath: *June 22, 1897.*

"Get your commemorative buttons here!" the vendor cried. "Get your souvenirs for a day you'll never forget."

Herman noted several within the crowd sporting buttons, and he purchased one for himself and affixed it to his coat. It would make him look all the more like he belonged there. He was certain he'd remember the day, button or no.

The sun was bright and when Herman noted another man selling glasses with smoked lenses, he purchased a pair. It seemed like a good investment, both to lessen the glare and to add to his disguise for later.

He glanced down the side street at the choir's boarding school.

Sunday was usually a busy day for them, but they'd been absent from the service today. The voices of the boys, interspersed with the exhortations of the choirmaster from the second floor of the school, made it clear how they were spending their day. Herman hoped none would get in his line of fire on Tuesday, but it was too late to be squeamish. He was already damned.

He stiffened suddenly when he recognized a woman standing at the bottom of the cathedral steps with a young girl and a man. They were all looking about curiously, and he felt a chill down his back when he recognized the woman: Margaret Harkness.

His hands clenched at the sight of her as he imagined them around her pale neck. *Remember Immanuel. Getting him back is more important than revenge.* He noticed she was looking down the side street toward the school. He cast about and saw a vendor selling lemonade from a pushcart beside them.

Herman strolled to the lemonade vendor and after purchasing a paper cup, turned and bumped into Miss Harkness, spilling the drink down her front.

"Dreadfully sorry!" he exclaimed. "How clumsy of me, madam." He pulled out a handkerchief and offered it to her. "Please, take it. I insist."

The moist, thin fabric of the summer frock now outlined her bosom to an immodest degree. She snatched the handkerchief, and after dabbing at the spill as best she could, returned it to the clumsy stranger and tied a scarf around her neck loosely enough to drape over the critical areas.

"A small matter, sir," she huffed. "I've suffered worse. I regret the loss of your lemonade."

He bowed. "Trifling in the extreme," he replied, in a strong Russian accent. They'd be looking for a mustachioed German, not a clean-shaven Russian. The addition of the glasses with the smoked lenses only augmented his disguise.

"May I buy the three of you a lemonade, as a way to express my apology?"

"I'd like one, please." The young girl said. "It's getting rather warm."

Margaret and her companion exchanged glances, then Margaret nodded. "Very well then," the man answered. "We accept, Mister . . ."

"Rodshenko, Boris Rodshenko. I hail from Minsk." Herman knew a fellow Russian would never believe his accent belonged to a native of Belarus, but it was the first city that came to mind. At least it was close enough to St. Petersburg; he could answer simple questions about it.

After introductions were given all around Margaret said. "You're a long way from home, Mister Rodshenko. By your button, I assume you're in town for the celebration?"

Herman bowed again. "Indeed, madam. I see now why Sherlock Holmes is an Englishman. Everyone wants to be a detective."

It's difficult to say who laughed the hardest at this remark, but James laughed the longest. Finally, after he caught his breath, he managed to mutter, "Quite so."

Herman swept his arm before them. "So, this is where the great ceremony will happen? With such an impressive cathedral, why is Her Majesty content to sit in her carriage beneath the sun?"

"The papers say it is to symbolize how the sun never sets upon the British Empire," James replied. "The truth is, Her Majesty, at seventy-eight, suffers from rheumatism and does not want to hobble from her coach before the multitude. I have also heard she will not be wearing her crown nor bearing her scepter, probably due to their weight. Whatever she wears, I'm sure it will become the latest fashion within the week."

Herman tipped his hat, his shaved scalp glistening in the sunlight. "I would never venture an opinion on women's fashion, but I thank you for your forgiveness and your courtesy to a stranger. I wish you a pleasant Sunday, and no more unexpected downpours."

Herman turned and walked to the north, directly away from the boarding school, in hopes of drawing their eyes in his direction. There was a small café in the courtyard about a hundred yards away.

He would be able to take a coffee and observe the trio. Having come into contact with them, he would have to proceed even more carefully. It was too late to make new plans, however. It was the boarding school or nothing.

"What a pleasant fellow," James said. He turned to me, "Except for the spill, of course."

I laughed. "I'll need a bath when we return to the flat, but no permanent harm done." I removed my scarf, as the fabric had dried enough that it was no longer needed to preserve my modesty. I replaced it in my bag and resumed my survey of the plaza. I wished I could recall the electricians' guild comment about a fraudulent bill, but it still eluded me. Something about the cathedral.

"We need to return and speak with the dean tomorrow," I told James. "I recall, as I was leaving the guild hall, there was some comment about some electrical work done there."

James shook his head. "The day before the Jubilee? Why would he agree to see me on the second-busiest day of his life?"

"Because," Elizabeth said, "you're the best detective at Scotland Yard, and you're protecting the queen."

I grinned. "I agree with Elizabeth. He needs to speak with you. You just need to explain why."

Some men on horseback were slowly riding across the plaza, led by an older, one-armed gentleman. They were followed by two police constables, another well-dressed man in civilian attire, and a uniformed military officer.

"Father, who are those gentlemen?" Elizabeth asked, pointing out the group.

"The man in front, my dear, is the finest leader I've ever known. Police Commissioner Sir Edward Bradford. That's his assistant behind him, and an officer of the household guards. They're probably reviewing the security preparations."

I grabbed his arm. "Speak with him, James! A note from him would be sure to get you an audience with the dean."

"Now? Here?"

"Yes, Father!" Elizabeth said. "If he's the leader you say he is, he'll understand why you need to see the dean. He's sure to help!"

"You're right," James said. "A note from him would not be ignored. Very well, but wait here, please. I don't want this to look like a family outing."

"That's only because he doesn't know your family," I said. "Go on!"

James approached the head of the police agency responsible for the safety of over six million people and one sovereign. The man, despite the loss of his arm, rode his horse comfortably, using his knees more than his reins to direct his mount, the mark of an accomplished rider. When James stood before his horse and doffed his hat, Bradford halted.

"Yes?" Sir Edward asked, his calm brown eyes studying the man before him. "What is it?"

James produced his badge. "James Ethington, sir. Special Branch."

"Ah yes, Inspector. I've heard your name mentioned regarding our anarchist visitor, and also that sordid little affair in the Municipal Utilities Department. You've been a very busy man these past few days. Any progress to report on our assassin?"

"I thought I had him cornered in the East End, sir. He killed one of our police constables before he escaped. I blame myself."

Bradford nodded. "I've ordered men to their death, Inspector. The man died in performance of his duty. His name was Williams, I believe?"

James was impressed that, despite commanding a force of over fourteen thousand men, Bradford was aware of the death of one of them so soon.

"Aye, sir. That's correct."

The commissioner sighed. "I know you will never forget the loss, but I need you to focus on the task at hand. Any other news?"

"Perhaps, Commissioner. I met with Professor Bell last night, and he recommended we look at moderately priced hotels within the city for our assassin, so I have shared this advisory with the force. Constables are making the rounds with his likeness."

"Excellent suggestion! Professor Bell comes highly recommended. How can I be of assistance?"

"I need a brief audience with the dean of the cathedral tomorrow. If you could give me a note, it might enable me to see him in time."

"Very well, Inspector," Bradford answered. He nodded to his assistant, and a note was quickly scribbled out and handed to him. Placing the reins into his teeth, the commissioner carefully signed the note on his left thigh and then handed it down. Taking the reins back, he said, "Please let me know what you find out, Inspector. You have my full support."

James saluted. It felt awkward yet appropriate at the same time. Bradford gave just a hint of a smile, to let James know his attempt at military protocol was somewhat lacking, but appreciated all the same.

"Now then, Inspector, if there's nothing else we have a queen to safeguard."

"God save the Queen!" James answered.

"God helps those who help themselves, Inspector." Without looking back, Bradford resumed his advance knowing the others would follow, with the confidence of one long accustomed to command.

Herman observed this exchange, unsure what to make of it. He didn't know who the one-armed man astride the black horse was, but he recognized a man in authority when he saw one. The conference was probably a report on the hunt for him. He sipped his coffee and picked up a *Times* left on the table by its last occupant. There was much about the ceremony and it wasn't until he got to page eight that he found a small notice about the bobby he'd killed the day before.

Herman wanted to go past the piece without reading it, but his eyes seemed to act of their own volition. Williams. Somehow giving the dead man a name made his crime more painful. Now he knew what name would be on the headstone, and he reflected that in a way he had engraved it with the squeeze of a trigger.

Further down the page, there was a mention of how the man's wife was due to have his first—and now only—child within the next few days. Herman put the paper down and looked across the plaza. He watched families strolling together. That's all he wanted. His experience in Russia proved one crowned head was easily replaced by another. It seemed there was never a shortage of those wanting to adorn themselves with symbols of power.

But families were real. Immanuel was real. In his effort to retrieve his son, he'd killed a father. He looked at the coffee grounds at the bottom of his cup. He'd heard the Turks could tell your fortune from them. He snorted. *I can tell my own fortune. My only hope of salvation now is to raise my son to be a good man. Better than his father.*

He watched a military contingent ride by, rehearsing for the procession, and wondered why it seemed to take so much time and effort to teach men to ride in a straight line. Then two men carrying some strange-looking equipment, one a tripod, the other shiny tin canisters and a box with a handle on top. They sat down beside him. The man with the box and canisters seemed overburdened. He wiped his forehead before ordering coffee from the waiter.

"Beg pardon," Herman asked, "but what sort of apparatus are you carrying?"

The tripod man appeared to be the leader, and it was he who answered.

"Moving pictures, sir." With his head, he indicated a small elevated platform at the north edge of the plaza. "We're here to photograph the royal procession. It will be quite popular, I'm sure. Just imagine," the man said, warming to his topic, "people throughout the empire will be able to see the queen's carriage pass by, just as though they were here themselves. The thought of young Australian lads seeing their sovereign move as though she were right in front of them . . . Well, it makes me proud to be a part of it all. We live in exciting times!"

Herman nodded without much enthusiasm, then an idea came to him. "Might I have your card, sir? Perhaps I could assist you in future. Your work sounds fascinating."

The man produced his card with a flourish.

"James McIntyre, sir. At your service. And your name?"

"Rodshenko, Boris Rodshenko. I am originally from Russia, obviously, but England is my home now. I wish you well on Tuesday. Perhaps we shall meet again." Herman bowed and departed after placing the card into his vest pocket. *People's fascination with moving pictures might prove useful.*

45

ommissioner Bradford sat astride his horse outside Buckingham Palace at the end of his six-mile ride. Though satisfied with the preparations for crowd control, he would never be satisfied as to Her Majesty's safety.

The household guards officer asked, "Shall we do the same tomorrow, Commissioner?" It was obvious which answer the man preferred as he cleared his throat.

He's naught to complain of, the old warrior thought. *He should try leading a hunt for thuggees.* Bradford's experience had taught him that the gaudier the uniform, the less capable the soldier. Shining buttons soon took priority over tactical proficiency.

"Yes for me, no for you," he said, irritated by the man's ill-disguised relief. "I've memorized the route and everything along it. If our assassin plants any bombs along the way, I should notice the change. You are dismissed." *Go get your plumes fluffed, or whatever it is you do with them.*

Herman returned to the hotel and paused when he saw a police constable talking with the clerk, Herman's mustachioed likeness in the bobby's hand. Herman sat down on a threadbare chair in the lobby, his *Times* in front of his face as he listened in.

"You seen a man what looks like this?" asked the constable.

There was a long pause. Herman, blinded by the paper, couldn't tell if the man was shrugging his shoulders or pointing at him. He tensed to run when the clerk answered, "Nay, Constable. No handlebar mustaches as fine as that. What's he done?"

"Killed one of ours, is what. Shot in the head. If I'm the one who nabs him, he'll have more than a few knots on his noggin before I give him up. Now, look again. Harder. Maybe he's shaved that lip brush off. I would, if every constable in London were after me. Think hard."

Herman had no weapon, and even if he did, the fight would only draw more people into the fray. He didn't dare lower the paper while he was facing the clerk. His life now depended on one man's poor memory and lack of imagination.

"Well . . . there is one man, now that I think on it. Foreign gentleman. I could take you to his room, see if he's in."

Herman heard a soft *smack* and imagined the bobby hitting the palm of his free hand with his club. His eyes stared at the paper inches from his face, an advertisement for women's support garments filling his field of view. He noticed his hands were still, and a sense of peace came over him. *So, this is how it ends*, he thought. He'd hang, no doubt as to that. He hoped Herr Grüber never told Immanuel of his father's end.

The sound of boots clambering up the stairs was soon replaced by the knocking on a door. Herman considered running, but without his rifle, he hadn't a chance of fulfilling his mission. Perhaps the constable would leave for reinforcements, and he could retrieve it before their return.

The knock was answered by a voice within. The door opened and was quickly followed by the sound of a scuffle as the bobby called out, "Police! You're coming with me!"

Curiosity overcame caution and when Herman lowered his paper, he saw a red-faced man tumble down the stairs, the constable rushing after him. The fall seemed to knock the wind out of him, and after the bobby snapped a set of manacles on him, he was jerked to his feet and the stunned man was quick-marched out the door.

The clerk returned to his station and seeing Herman's wide eyes, apologized: "Sorry, sir. Nothing to concern yourself with, I'm sure. Please, enjoy the rest of your Sunday afternoon."

Herman felt a wave of gratitude wash over him. He wanted to give a prayer of thanksgiving, then considered what deity would accept the prayer of an assassin. *Do the damned ever know peace again?*

James returned to Scotland Yard to learn if Ott had been apprehended. Police Commissioner Bradford had linked all the stations together by telegraph, so the inspector was spared the task of going to each one. Three suspects were in custody, and it took James until ten at night to establish none of them was his German assassin. He trudged home in the dark, knowing he was no closer to his quarry than when the day'd begun.

The custodian at the boarding school turned out the lights, though he knew the lads would be awake for some hours yet. They had rehearsed long that day and by rights should be exhausted, but at their age the excitement of the approaching ceremony was more potent than fatigue. They would have dark circles under their eyes tomorrow, but the buzzing of their whispers would fill the darkness until just before sunrise.

Ten-year-old Freddy Cummings's throat was sore and he felt warm, warmer than a summer night could explain, but he'd said nothing to the choirmaster. He wanted to see the queen.

In the basement, the short circuit Herman had fashioned was undiscovered, waiting in the darkness to be tripped.

Two days day until the Jubilee.

46

Monday, June 21

James, Elizabeth, and I were all appropriately attired for the occasion and waiting outside the dean's office when the Very Reverend Robert Gregory arrived. A robust man in his sixties, on the day before the most important day in his position he had no time for unannounced visitors.

"Who are you, what do you want, and why should I care?" he said. "I'm usually not an ogre, but I've no time for pleasantries today."

James produced his badge and note from the police commissioner. "Then I'll be blunt as well, Dean, and no offense to either side. I need to know if you've had any electrical work done in the cathedral recently."

The dean hesitated and began to speak, then caught himself and shook his head. "Sorry, Inspector, nothing affecting the cathedral in the last couple of years. If that's all, I've work to do." Without another word he entered his office and closed the door, the interview concluded.

I was grateful not to be in male attire at this moment, or my collar would have been too tight. "You'd think we were selling brushes door to door, not trying to save the queen!"

James shrugged and turned to Elizabeth. "Let this be an example. Not every clue leads to something. It was promising, and we were right to pursue it, but never pin your hopes on just one piece of information solving the case."

I suspected this lecture was as much for my benefit as Elizabeth's, and I suddenly understood one reason James attracted me so. He was kind, patient, and sensitive to the feelings of others. Perhaps that last quality made him not only a better man but a better detective. My anger faded as I looked at him. It was a dead end, but no matter. We would go forward ... together.

"What do we do now, Father?"

"Might as well go to the roof and see the view."

"Oh, let's!" Elizabeth said. "That would be wonderful, don't you think, Margaret?"

"I think you two intrepid detectives can do quite well without me as my knees are bothering me and the climb would be tiring. There is a café on the north side of the plaza. I can await you there and save you both a seat. You can wave at me if you like. Will that do?"

Elizabeth paused, "Yes, of course." She gave me a sympathetic glance, and I could see my secret fear of heights was safe with her.

"Now go off and climb mountains. You know where to find me when you return to a sensible height."

Elizabeth and James went off to find the stairs and as they turned to go, she slipped her hand into her father's for just a moment. I noticed he stood a little taller as they made their way off.

Elizabeth was stunned by the view. The roofs of the buildings facing the cathedral across the plaza were covered with wooden bleachers, the carpenters making final adjustments here and there. Vendors for the rental of cushions were setting up their booths, and another for the rental of opera glasses was putting the finishing touches on his kiosk. In the plaza below, officers and sergeants were going through their maneuvers, their troops dismissed. All troops had to do was obey orders. Those who gave them had to know their business, however.

Elizabeth suddenly understood, in a way she could not explain, how an empire that spread across the world would be completely focused on this small space for a moment. That moment would then pass, and that power and attention would diffuse back to the globe it inhabited. She was standing on the tip of a needle wielded by a giant that briefly knit the world together.

"Being a detective is the grandest thing in the world," she sighed. "Solving puzzles all day, stopping criminals. What fun!"

James shook his head. "There's satisfaction, yes, but you can't lose sight of why you're employed. Our assassin is from Germany. Relations between us are tense already due to the status of British citizens in South Africa. The Kaiser recently congratulated the Boers for putting down a rebellion by our people, and that did not sit well in the House of Commons, I can tell you. If Ott were to murder Queen Victoria literally before the eyes of the entire British Empire, the calls for war would be unstoppable. We aren't chasing this man merely for sport, but to save a life, and thereby potentially thousands of others."

"Sorry, Father. It's just so exciting to be with you and to help, in some small way."

James placed his hand on his daughter's shoulder and squeezed it gently. "It has been hard on you, hasn't it? You'll be grown soon enough. I promise to be the father you once knew, as long as you're mine to care for."

Elizabeth stood silent beside him, her head leaning against his shoulder, with only the pigeons of the cathedral as witnesses.

James's thoughts returned to the problem at hand. He looked left toward the boarding school, but the trees between the school and the plaza blocked his view of the second-floor window. He noted the roof was flat on the right, southern end, but would be in plain sight from the roofs of adjacent buildings. No hiding place for a sniper there. Plus, the statue of Queen Anne and its massive column would partially block the view. No. The roof was no threat. He considered. No harm in looking, though.

He started to turn for the stairs when he remembered Margaret. He looked off to his right, and there she was in her bright blue dress.

He waved, and she waved back. He reached for Elizabeth's hand and they headed for the stairs back down.

Freddy Cummings could no longer hide his condition. Even the choirmaster could not fail to note his flushed face and shivering. He was sent to his room with the school nurse, Mrs. Foster. Freddy bawled at not being able to see the queen, so the nurse moved him to the bed on the second floor, next to the window. "Tomorrow," she said, "If you're up for it, I can prop you up and you can watch the whole affair." Freddy sniffed, but allowed how that might be acceptable, under the circumstances.

His fever was one hundred and three, and his cough was deep and troubling. Mrs. Foster reached for the bottle with a cherubic little girl clutching a puppy on it: Doctor Seth's Cough Killer had never failed to stop a child's cough, and Freddy was soon fast asleep.

James decided to go directly to the school from the cathedral to save the walk to Margaret and doubling back. James knew Elizabeth would be denied entry as even female family members were not allowed inside.

"I'll go back to Margaret and wait for you there," she said. "Don't be long! Ladies don't like to be kept waiting."

James choked back a reply on the last bit of wisdom. As he trudged to the boarding school, his mind was fixed on the roof as a sniper's platform. As he drew near and walked beneath the tree limbs, he noted windows on the first and second floors on the corner. *Best see to those, too.*

The custodian was taking his ease at the reception area when he walked in. With the boys practicing at all hours, they weren't present long enough to generate much rubbish or general disorder. As far as he was concerned, the Jubilee should be an annual event, like Christmas.

"Inspector Ethington, Scotland Yard," James said. "I'd like a look at your roof as a security precaution for the ceremony."

The old man shrugged and pulled out a large ring of keys. "Very well, Inspector. I keep the door to the roof tightly locked, so my little hellions can't drop things on passersby."

They talked as they climbed the three flights up to the small steel door. "I imagine you'll be catching the view from here on the big day, eh?" James asked.

"Aye, me and the missus, and the rest of the staff. We'll have a view you'd pay twenty-five guineas for in the main square."

"How many people, all together?"

"Why do you ask, Inspector? Planning on joining us?"

"Please, just answer my question."

"Twenty folks, or thereabouts."

The old man had averted his eyes, and James understood. The custodian had entered into some free enterprise and had sold a few spaces on the roof.

"How many staff, and how many paying guests? I won't tell the dean. I just need to be assured there will be a goodly number of people here."

The custodian relaxed. "Then you've got naught to worry about, Inspector. I reckoned we'd have room for about forty people, all standing."

"Good. Let's see the space."

James was even more relieved when he saw the roof for himself. The door let out onto a small terrace with rails on two sides. There was a limited view through the trees between the school and the steps, but a sniper would have a difficult time of it. The other half of the roof would give a clearer shot but was steeply pitched and in plain view. No chance there.

"I'm satisfied, but to be sure, I'll leave a bobby at the entrance the day of the ceremony. Give your special guests a password, and my man will let them through. Fair enough?"

The custodian brightened. "Aye, fair enough. I was gonna lock the entrance, but if I did and the choirmaster sent a boy for something and couldn't get in, I'd never hear the end of it. One less thing for me to worry about."

"Just two more things, and I'll be off."

The custodian winced. "Yes, Inspector?"

"I noticed two windows, on the first and second floors, which also face the cathedral. I'd like a look at them." James could tell by the man's crestfallen state that he'd stumbled upon another source of income. "How many spaces did you sell for them?"

"You're a hard man, Inspector. Five spaces per window, but I've had to give five their money back. One lad's taken ill, and the nurse set him up by the window on the second floor. She'll be there with him the entire time."

"Very well, but I'll have a look all the same. Let's go."

The first-floor window was high, and James had to climb to the top bunk to see out. Given the crowd, the height of the carriage and the surrounding horsemen, a sniper would have a near-impossible shot. Still, it was the best opportunity he'd seen yet.

At the entrance to the room on the second floor, the barrel-shaped Mrs. Foster blocked his way. "Freddy just fell asleep, and I'll not have you waking him."

James noted the bottle beside the bed. "Madam, if you gave the child a dose of that syrup, given the amount of alcohol and morphine it contains, I am incapable of waking him. I will not step on him, but I must see if an assassin could take a potshot at Her Majesty from this vantage point. Surely you understand the need for precautions."

She glared but backed away. "Be gentle then, and quick."

James eased himself up the ladder to the top bunk until he was teetering on the next to top rung. He looked out the window. The angle was good. High enough to clear the crowd, low enough to be beneath the boughs of the trees, and far enough to the right so that the statue of Queen Anne didn't block the view. *If I were a sniper, this is where I'd be.*

James carefully clambered back down and was relieved Freddy didn't stir. Nurse Foster's protective instincts were fully aroused and given her dimensions, he didn't care to anger her further. "You'll be here the entire time of the ceremony, with the boy?" he asked.

"Aye. Freddy so wanted to see the queen, so I put him here. We'll watch the whole ceremony together."

"Very well, Miss, I'll leave you two alone. I hope your patient gets better soon."

"It's *Missus*, sir, thank you very much. He'll pull through. These rascals always do."

I'd best make that two bobbies at the entrance! James thought. *I'd rather catch him, but if I can scare him off, I've done my duty.* He wished the forbidding Mrs. Foster a good day and retreated from her lair. *If all else fails, she'll make an excellent guardian.*

James was deep in thought as he exited the building and failed to notice the clumsy Russian across the street. Herman had been doing his own surveillance. The Inspector's sudden interest in the boarding school worried him, but there was no place else to go. Whatever measures the man put in place, he'd have to deal with them. He shook his head. *How many lives must I take before I kill an old woman? Where does it end?* He ran his hand over his face. *When this is over, I'll never touch a weapon again. I pray Immanuel can someday forgive me.*

But he might need another weapon to deal with any security the inspector put in place, something small and silent. He remembered a reference in a penny dreadful about a cat burglar. Yes, that would do perfectly. The afternoon shadows were lengthening but he still had time if he hurried. Soon he was back at the Dog's Head. He wasn't sure how welcome he'd be, but it was the only place he knew where he might find a seller for what he wanted.

He saw two men at the end of the bar. One sported a black eye patch and the other wore a shabby topcoat, and Herman recognized them as some of Keys Malone's hangers-on. He took a deep breath and strode up. "Good evening, gentlemen. May I buy you two a drink?"

The two men sported a week's beard each, and likely at least that much filth, so they grinned at the title "gentlemen." Still, a drink was a drink.

"Howie!" one said as he motioned to the barman. "Three ales. This *gentleman* is buyin'."

The barman didn't stir until Herman laid a half crown on the scarred wooden surface. Only then did he pour three mugs full of ale and bring them over. Once the man retreated and Herman's two new friends downed a long pull of their ale, Herman got down to business.

"I need something I think you two may be able to help me find."

"What's that, eh?" said Eye Patch. "Keys warned us to keep away from you." Eye Patch leaned in closer, "he didn't say why."

"You took my ale readily enough," Herman pointed out. "I just need to know where I can buy a simple item. I'm in a hurry and willing to pay well for it."

"What is it, then?" Topcoat asked. "We ain't a bloody store now, are we?"

Herman laid down a five-pound note. "If you don't mind, I'll ask the questions."

James returned to his ladies awaiting him at the café. "I'd best report in. I want two men posted at the entrance to the school. I'll need to get that request in today, to ensure it happens, else I'll be trapped there myself. I'll see you two at home later."

At Scotland Yard, he shared his concerns regarding the boarding school with Murdock. "The roof's unlikely unless the custodian is an anarchist and can hold off a wave of sightseers on his own. The lower window would also be a poor choice, but the upper window might pose a risk. I'd like to post two men at the entrance to the school, if you'll allow."

Murdock frowned. "That'll mean two less for crowd control. I'll get some grief for that, but your two men will be there, though probably not too happy about it, given how they'll miss the spectacle. Well, can't be helped. Anything else?"

"Where do you want me tomorrow?"

The senior inspector leaned back to consider this. "Ott is our greatest threat. No one knows him like you do. I want you on the roof of the cathedral, looking for risks. Get some field glasses from the armory and scan the crowd, the windows, the rooftops. Look for anything out of the ordinary. I'll have a police sergeant on both the east and west sides of the plaza, and if you see something, signal to them and point to the threat. Understood?"

"Aye, sir. It seems like a sound plan to me. I'll be there."

In the tumult of the preparations, Herman walked into the boarding school unchallenged and slipped down the stairs to the basement. He found his auxiliary switch as he'd left it and tripped it, thus grounding the main power line to the water pipe, then walked back outside into the general bustle. He was confident that when the light switches were turned on that night, the entire building would go dark. He'd be ready.

Police Constables McFadden and O'Reilly were called out of the evening muster by their sergeant. "I've got a very important assignment for you lot," he said. "Coming direct from the Yard."

"What's that, sergeant?" McFadden asked. "Guard the queen's jewels while she's away?"

"Even better, lads. You're to guard the entrance to the boarding school for the choir. Can't be having anyone steal their sheet music while they're serenading Her Majesty. Report there at seven o'clock tomorrow morning. Clear?"

"Aye, sergeant." O'Reilly shrugged. "Pity, we'll be missing all the excitement."

Queen Victoria returned from Windsor Castle that afternoon and was impressed by the sea of Union Jacks and flowers covering the city. As she attended a state banquet that night, she chatted with the young man next to her, Archduke Franz Ferdinand.

"It is an honor to be included in your procession tomorrow, Your Highness," he said. "I am still unsure what is to occur at the cathedral, however."

"It shall be brief, sir. The entire procession shouldn't take much over an hour, save the twenty minutes or so for the ceremony itself." She noted his thick waist, "We shan't be late for luncheon."

The board was set, all the pieces in place. The opening move awaited nothing more than the pull of a switch.

47

Monday, June 21, cont.

A t sunset, the weary custodian went to the basement as always to throw the main power switch for the building. As before, he was greeted with light, but this time the light was provided by a brief cascade of sparks before full darkness returned.

"Bloody electricians!" He snarled. "The choirmaster'll have my 'ead if he can't 'ave a final run through tonight."

He stomped over to his desk in a corner of the basement and rummaged through the bills and invoices until he found the bill from the blasted man who'd said everything was fine. He grabbed the form, scribbled down the address, and headed off after leaving word with his wife where he'd be.

The streetlights were flickering on as the old man stormed down the street toward the electrician's shop. Herman had managed to loiter in an alley just around the corner. The shop had closed a half hour ago, so Herman had to time the next bit just right. As soon as he recognized the custodian approaching, Herman slipped to the entrance with the rifle's case and bent over the door as though locking it.

"Oy! You there! Mister Bloody Everything's Fine!"

Herman stood and looked around as though startled. "Ah, Mister Connery! I didn't expect to see you again so soon. What's wrong?"

"What's wrong? I was nearly glowing like a light bulb meself tonight, thanks to you! There ain't no light in the school, and I need you to come with me right now or I'm out of a job, all because of you!"

Herman sighed. "It's my son's birthday tonight. Can't I come round in the morning?"

"Are you listening to me, man? Tomorrow's the Jubilee. I need lights tonight. Now! If you don't come with me, I'll make sure your name is well known as an incompetent ass."

"All right, all right," Herman said. He hefted his case. "The sooner we start, the sooner it's done. Let's go."

The switch had performed perfectly. The custodian left Herman alone, grumbling as he left to see to the multitude of tasks awaiting him. The short was disconnected quickly, then Herman carefully constructed an elaborate coil of wires that appeared connected to the main switch but in reality had no purpose, nor any power flowing through it.

He finished just as the custodian came back down to check on his progress. Herman waited until the man was at the bottom of the stairs before throwing the switch. He wiped his hands on a greasy rag as the lights came on throughout the building.

"About bloody time!" the custodian thundered. "Don't expect to be paid for this. 'Twas your incompetence that caused this in the first place."

Herman shrugged. "Do as you like. This is a temporary fix. I'll need to come back in the morning to make it permanent."

"Why can't you do that now?"

"I need more wire and some tools I don't have with me. No charge. I've my reputation to uphold."

Mr. Connery's scowl faded away when Herman said, "No charge."

"Very well. Be here at seven tomorrow morning. Sharpish. Understand?"

"I do." Herman said. "Now, if there's nothing else, I'll be off."

"Good night, then. Don't forget!"

"Not for the world."

Herman felt bone weary as he approached the Underground station. As he passed the city parks, he noted families laying out blankets on the ground and preparing pallets for the night. Thousands of the Queen's loyal subjects would brave the weather that night, which threatened rain, to assure themselves a proper view of the following day's spectacle. Herman shook his head at the love these sensible-appearing people had for an old woman whom they would never meet in person. He had no affection for either the Tsar or the Kaiser, so their love for this aged symbol of their oppressors was beyond him.

Herman noted the moon becoming dimmer as clouds gathered outside. *Be my luck if a providence I don't believe in saved a monarch I came to kill.*

There was nothing he could do about it, however. He made the last train to Kensington and nodded to the clerk as he entered the lobby, careful to look for any signs of suspicion. The man returned his nod and went about his business. *One more night, and then I'll be the most hated man in the British Empire.* It struck Herman how much his life would change tomorrow. *What kind of life can I give Immanuel after this?* He trudged to his room, reached into his waistcoat, and stared at the picture of Astrid and their son long into the night.

48

Tuesday, June 22

I arose at dawn and looked out the window. People dressed in their best were already streaming toward the procession route.

"Where will you station yourself, James?" I asked as we ate breakfast. "The cathedral's roof? That seems to offer the best view."

"It's where Senior Inspector Murdock wants me, though it will slow down my response to any threat I see. The sergeants along the plaza have been told to keep an eye on me so as to respond to my signals. They'll be hard-pressed to do so while watching the crowd and their men, but it's the best we can do."

"And where would you like us, Father?" Elizabeth asked, between bites of poached egg and toast.

"I've just the place. Safe, yet it should give you a good view."

"Where, Father?"

James gulped down his coffee before answering. "In front of the boarding school. I've two constables there. You'll be able to see the ceremony well enough, and I can wave to you from the roof. You should be safely out of the way if our assassin does attempt some mischief."

Herman was up before dawn, having slept perhaps two hours. His eyes were bleary, but his mind was focused. The flasks were at full pressure. The magazine was full, though one shot should be enough. Having it full reduced any rattle as he carried it in its case. Herman dressed in his best clothes despite his upcoming role as an electrician. He had learned that good clothes could deflect suspicion almost as well as a badge. Time to start thinking about the moments after he fired.

He'd paid for one more night to prevent his having to take all his possessions with him. His earthly belongings had shrunk over the past six months. He left the room with only the clothes he wore and a weapon he despised. He felt chained to it and was looking forward to throwing it into the Thames even more than toppling a crown.

Today was a national holiday, and the Underground was crowded with those hoping to find a space along the route. Herman hoped those who chose a spot after the cathedral would be disappointed.

The extent of the British Empire was reflected in the faces of the hundreds of thousands of people crowding the sidewalks and the fortunate few heading for their reserved seating. Vendors loudly hawked Union Jacks, buttons with the date and a likeness of Queen Victoria on them, commemorative mugs, and programs listing the dignitaries in their order within the procession. The majority of the English-speaking world was holding its breath.

Police Commissioner Bradford took pride in the fact that he could still saddle his horse himself. He sat on it now and slowly made his way along the route. The proliferation of flags and bunting would make it easy for a sniper to hide, and his stomach burned as he looked for any suspicious new developments. He finished the route back at Buckingham Palace by eight in the morning and admitted he had done all he could. He wished heartily for the overcast sky to produce a downpour to cancel the entire procession, and for a bromide for his stomach.

Herman arrived at the school promptly at seven. The procession didn't begin until eleven-fifteen, and he didn't want to have to loiter too long beforehand. The longer he was there, the greater his chance of being found out. His palms began to sweat when he saw two sour-faced constables at the entrance.

"What business brings you here, then?" asked Constable O'Reilly. "None but those on official business or who are spoken for by the custodian may pass, and as 'e ain't given out any tickets, he'll have to say so himself."

Herman lifted the case. "Electrician, Constable. The custodian will vouch for me."

Mr. Connery popped out his head, saw Herman, and nodded to the two bobbies. "He's with me, more's the pity." The constables nodded and returned to their task of scowling at passersby.

The custodian was out of breath with his supplemental business, greeting his customers and conducting them to their places. The boys had left for a final rehearsal within the cathedral, leaving behind himself, the cook, his wife, and the nurse with her still-feverish charge. With all that empty space, he reckoned on making a tidy sum today.

"Oy! 'Bout time you got here!"

"Do the lights work or not?" Herman asked.

"They do," the custodian admitted, "But I don't like worrying they'll go out again with no notice. You fix it right and proper, or I'll see to it the cathedral never uses you again."

"I'll go right down."

The custodian gave Herman a quick up and down glance. "You're dressed fine to get your hands dirty."

Herman feigned embarrassment. "Well, I was hoping that once the wiring was fixed I might be able to watch from here. Surely you've got a spare window I can look out of?"

The man stuck his finger in Herman's face. "Now I see! You did this all a'purpose, to watch the ceremony. You bloody bastard! No, and hell no. I give you one hour, then you'd best be done and gone."

Herman shrugged. "Very well. I promise the lights will be

in perfect order before I leave. *An easy promise to make, since they already are.*

He went down to the basement and removed the false wiring. He considered placing another short, then decided against it. If he needed another subterfuge, he was already lost. Once complete, he went to the top of the stairs and listened through the door. He heard the custodian greet a family for the rooftop and counted to twenty to give them time to begin the long climb up.

He opened the door and ambled toward the stairs, careful to keep out of sight of the party above him. When he heard the roof door open, he sped to the second floor and went directly to the corner room. He opened the door and closed it silently behind him. He turned and found himself face-to-face with the formidable Mrs. Foster, standing guard between him and her charge, and the window.

James found Scotland Yard nearly deserted. Its staff was either out on duty or off to see the spectacle themselves. Murdock was in his office, however. It took no great detective to judge from the thick cloud of tobacco smoke that he'd been there for some time.

"A grand way to end your career with Special Branch, James." His initial smile faded, and his forehead wrinkled. "Any news?"

"None, Senior Inspector. I've done my best. It cost two men's lives—Peg Leg's son and Constable Williams—and I'll be glad to have this day behind me. I'll be on the roof to look for trouble. Those twenty minutes Her Majesty sits still in an open carriage will be the longest of my life. Any final words before I go?"

The older man extended his hand. "Only one thing, James. God save the Queen."

"Aye, sir. God save us all."

Elizabeth asked me what I was wearing to the ceremony and surprised me when she wore a blue dress similar to mine. She smiled shyly, twirled about and took my hand. We looked like family. I inspected my hair one last time, but as I turned to go, I paused. *Old habits die hard*, I thought. I reached into my suitcase and brought out an old, double-barreled .42 caliber friend. The derringer gave a comforting weight to my purse.

Then I reached into my small jewelry case and brought out my pendant made from an 1888 penny, slipping it around my neck. It wouldn't bring me luck but it might give me courage, which is better, as luck is a fickle companion while courage is your own to command.

The board is set, and the pawn advances.

49

Tuesday, June 22, cont.

"**W**ho are you, and what are you doing here?" Nurse Foster asked. "This child is seriously ill and needs his rest. If you don't leave this instant, I'll summon the constables downstairs to throw you out. I don't care what arrangement you've made with Mr. Connery."

Herman jumped back, nearly dropping his case. In his confusion, he reached into his vest pocket and felt something. A card.

Assuming a professional air, he handed it to the woman with a flourish. "My name is Boris Rodshenko, Madam. I work for this gentleman, Mister James McIntyre, as part of a team of moving picture photographers. We have been commissioned by the Home Office to record this moment for posterity. My colleagues are stationed along the route, and I am here to photograph the ceremony itself." He hefted the rifle's case. "Here is my camera. It is silent, so it shouldn't disturb the lad in the slightest. I trust we can watch the ceremony together without further animosity." He bowed. "Is that acceptable to you?"

"Then why wasn't I told?" she sniffed. "I'll have a word or two about this to the custodian." She glared for a moment more, and Herman slipped his hand into his right pants pocket, considering his other option.

"Oh, very well. Freddy's sleeping like the dead. Help me move his bed back a bit, and you should have enough space to set up."

Herman's hand slid out of his pocket and he tipped his hat.

"Thank you for your cooperation, Madam. I'll be sure to mention it to my superiors when I turn in the film."

The house guards would be the final contingent before the royal carriage, so they formed up outside the gates of Buckingham Palace. The representatives from various parts of the empire gathered in the square, and more than one sergeant expressed thanks no Indian elephants were included. Alone at the head of the gathering formation, in his shiny breastplate and plumed helmet, Captain Ames sat astride a magnificent black mare. At six feet eight inches, he was the tallest man in the British Army, and it was his honor to lead the procession, his sword drawn and held in the salute position the entire six miles. His opinion on this honor was his own secret to keep.

Several of the horses jerked their heads at the tight rein their riders kept them on. They had been trained not to react to gunfire, but the size and noise of the crowd made many of them skittish, and it took all of their riders' considerable skill to keep them in line.

Finally, all elements were ready save one. The royal carriage pulled up before the palace entrance, and several riders craned their heads to watch a small figure dressed in black creep down the stairs, leaning on her cane, while a lady-in-waiting held a parasol above her. The diminutive woman who ruled an empire was assisted by two liveried members of the royal household who tenderly half-lifted Her Majesty into place. Two burly soldiers from the guards sat behind her in elevated seats, two more ladies-in-waiting sat across from her, and then they waited.

The crowd had been noisy before, but at the appearance of Queen Victoria, loud cries of "God save the Queen!" rang out among cheers that resembled a waterfall's roar, as powerful and unceasing. The cannon fired on time, and as Captain Ames nudged his horse forward, the dark clouds parted. The sun never set on the British Empire, and on this auspicious occasion, it glowed.

The sound of the cannon was heard throughout the route and the crowd cheered along it, then paused, awaiting further spectacle. Even the old cynic Mark Twain was awed by the tall, proud figure of Captain Ames advancing toward him, his arrival prompting renewed fervor among the multitude.

The vast number of troops was such that the entire procession was never visible all at once. Soldiers in blue were followed by others in red, then buff, then yellow, then back to buff. Twain sighed and closed his notebook. It was too much, even for his seasoned eye. "This is a task for the Kodak, not the pen," he muttered to himself. "I know when I'm overmatched."

Herman heard the cannon. He had thirty minutes to prepare, then twenty minutes to take his shot. It was time for the next step.

"Don't you want to assemble your camera, Mr. Rodshenko?" Nurse Foster asked. "I imagine such devices are rather delicate and require frequent adjustment."

"You're right, madam. I also have the film inside the case, however, so I wanted to minimize the risk of its exposure. But it is time." He reached into his pocket. "Could you see if your patient is all right? I'd hate to prevent him from seeing the ceremony if he's awake. We could share the view, as it were."

The nurse nodded, and as she turned to check on her silent charge, Herman removed the leather bag from his pocket. It was about the size of the pouch boys kept for marbles, but this one was filled with lead shot. Herman swung it hard, hitting the woman just behind her right ear as described in the story he'd once read about a cat burglar.

The nurse staggered, then spun around and kicked him hard in the shins. "You bastard!"

Herman was stunned, both physically and emotionally. This had worked perfectly in the story, and he had never considered it wouldn't in real life. As he stood there hopping on one foot and rubbing his shin, his adversary followed up with a roundhouse to his nose, causing his eyes to water as blood spurted out. He staggered back, and Nurse Foster dashed for the door while Freddy sat up, rubbing his eyes. "Is the Queen here yet?" he asked, yawning.

James heard the cannon and turned to wave down to his two ladies in blue. They waved back. It would take half an hour for the procession to arrive, and he took several slow, deep breaths to steady his nerves before raising his glasses to resume scanning the crowd. He checked on his two bobbies in front of the school. They were in place, and they looked bored, which was excellent news on both counts. He moved his glass over to the rooftop, and he reckoned the custodian would have a very profitable reward for his illicit enterprise. He noticed five faces crowded together in the first-floor window, but there were none in the second. The nurse must be waiting until the royal carriage arrived before bringing her patient closer to the opening.

Herman made a blind grab at the nurse that spun her around. She stomped hard on his right foot with one stiff, leather-soled shoe. The edge of her heel smashed his toes like a dropped anvil. He was losing this fight, and he needed to put her down quickly.

He swung blind, but was rewarded with the woman falling to her knees. Down, but not out. He swung the leather bag at the back of her head, and this time she reacted as the story said she should and slumped unconscious to the floor.

Little Freddy sat wide-eyed in the bed, unable to make a sound. Herman turned to him as he pulled out a handkerchief to wipe the blood running out of his nose. Herman imagined how he must appear to the frightened child and wondered what Immanuel would look like at the boy's age. "Don't worry, my friend," he said as though to a skittish colt. "I'm not here to hurt you." He looked at his soiled handkerchief. "Sorry about the blood."

Between his fear and weakness from his illness, Freddy offered no resistance, and soon both he and the nurse were bound with strips of bed covers Herman had cut with his knife. Herman checked the nurse's pulse and was relieved to find it strong. *Now I understand why Dante had several levels in hell*, Herman thought, *for there are degrees of damnation. Every time I think I have reached the bottom of the pit, another abyss awaits.*

He opened the case and began assembling the rifle. *One final act and my small piece of Paradise awaits.*

Herman placed Freddy onto another bunk. "I'm sorry you won't get to see Her Majesty today, but you'll still have quite a story to tell when this is over." He tousled the bound boy's hair. *A useless gesture. He sees a monster. Perhaps he's right.*

He slid the bed to the window then placed three pillows on the end closest to it, climbed up, and assumed a prone position, resting the barrel on the small pile of pillows. The clotted blood in his nose forced him to breathe through his mouth, and his eyes were still teary from the pain. His throbbing right foot could not bear the weight of the leg, so he was forced to cross it over his left, splaying his right knee further out to compensate. He lay still and counted to four as he inhaled, six as he exhaled, and after several cycles his hands relaxed and the rifle felt comfortable in his grasp.

He looked out the window as a single tall man in a shiny breastplate rode by. It had begun. The parts were snug, the sights aligned. He looked through the scope and his view of the entrance to the cathedral was unobstructed. The choir and various dignitaries crowded the steps, but the place of honor at the foot was clear. Now all he had to do was wait.

James turned to wave to the ladies to indicate the procession was arriving when he saw a flash from the second-floor window. He looked through his field glasses and saw the bed was now pulled up to it. Perhaps the nurse wanted the child to get a better view? But where was he? The room was in shadow and James saw a dim figure lying on the bed. His breath caught when he saw something else. A black line extended from the figure toward the open window. A rifle barrel.

50

"Father seems very excited, doesn't he, Margaret?" said Elizabeth. "See how he's waving toward us."

I'd been standing on tiptoe to see why the crowd had become so animated and had just seen the plumed helmet of Captain Ames pass by when Elizabeth tugged at my sleeve and pointed to the roof. "Yes, he is." I smiled. "Just like a schoolboy on holiday."

Then I felt a cold hand on my heart. "Elizabeth! He's pointing to the top of the building. Someone's on the roof!"

I grabbed one of the constables. "Officer! Inspector Ethington sees something on the roof of the boarding school. You must investigate immediately!"

The bobby and his mate exchanged glances before he said in his most official tone, "We were told to stay 'ere, and 'ere's where we're staying! We'll not be running about the building unless we get a direct order from a superior officer, which you ain't."

His eyes narrowed. "As for that bloke on the roof, he might be an inspector, and he might be someone trying to make us leave our post so his mates (giving me a meaningful glance), can do some mischief. I'll need to see a badge before I leave my assigned post."

I spun toward Elizabeth. "Find one of the police sergeants along the plaza and get them to look up. I'll see what I can do in the meantime!"

Elizabeth turned pale and began working her way through the crowd in a very unladylike manner, earning glares from those she shoved past.

The two constables formed a solid barrier as they glowered at me. "You've no business inside the premises, Madam!" said the one I'd grabbed before. "Unless you've a pass of some kind, we'll not be letting you in!"

No time for diplomacy. I pulled my derringer from my purse. "I apologize, gentlemen, but I have my pass right here. Let me by, or I'll wound the both of you." I cleared my throat as the two bobbies shrank back against the door. "It's .42 caliber, by the way. It makes a large hole."

The two men slid to their right, leaving the door to the boarding school unblocked. "We'll get reinforcements, Madam! There'll be twenty men here before you can get out," one growled.

"Will they come sooner if I shoot one of you?" I asked, but the two constables were gone before I'd finished my question.

I took a deep breath, shoved open the door and made for the stairs.

James's hands tightened on his field glasses as he saw the two constables flee the building while Margaret rushed inside, hand held high holding her derringer. He dropped the glasses and ran for the stairs just as Captain Ames rode out of sight of the cathedral. The queen's carriage would arrive in less than ten minutes.

Herman heard the full-throated roar from Fleet Street erupt, and he knew what that meant. The rifle was ready. He felt rather than heard the safety click off. He watched the carriages pass by through the scope and smiled as Grand Duke Franz Ferdinand crossed his view. *He's an easy target,* Herman thought to himself as he noted the man's portly figure. He heard shouts on the roof above. At first, he assumed they were the enthusiastic hurrahs from the custodian's illicit customers. No. Something was different. A woman's voice was shouting, commanding. No matter. *Aristotle said that given a place to stand and a lever, he could move the world. Today I am in that place, and I am holding the lever.*

I stormed the stairs, but my knees grew stiffer as I climbed, and my lungs labored to keep up. After an eternity, I reached the door to the roof and leaned against the wall, gasping. I do not know what frightened me more at that moment, the thought of standing atop the building or facing an armed assassin, but after a final gulp of air I lurched through the door and out onto the roof, my pistol aloft.

My eyes were drawn to the edge of the veranda and down to the street far below with nothing but a vast space between. I felt it calling to me to fall forever, down into the emptiness and the brief illusion of flight. My head spun and my knees, stiff just moments ago, nearly buckled. I clenched my jaw. *No time for this, Margaret!*

I stood straight and grasped my pendant with my left hand, the solid shape of the penny bringing me back to the task at hand. "No one move!" I commanded, "There's an assassin among you!"

Some forty men and women stared at me with bulging eyes and open mouths, like fish out of water. My eyes darted about, seeking a rifle or weapon of any kind. Nothing, save a lady's parasol. I looked back to the cathedral roof. James was gone. I turned to look behind me to the pitched roof of the school. No one was there.

My head swiveled as the roar of the crowd grew to a fever pitch. Below me, a carriage bearing a small woman dressed in black halted at the cathedral steps.

James fought through the crowd toward the school. He felt as though he were in a dream where something evil pursued him while he dragged his feet through soft tar. The increasing roar of the crowds told him his time was running out. When he reached the schoolhouse door, it was unguarded, and he searched for any sign of Elizabeth. There was none.

James was gasping by now but had no time to catch his breath. No time at all. He drew his Webley as he dashed to the stairs and made for the corner room on the second floor.

My curse shocked everyone on the roof as I whirled around and ran back inside. *Fool! He must have meant the window!*

I saw James one floor below at the landing, bent over and panting. I hobbled down the stairs to his side as quickly as I could and helped him straighten. "Stay behind me," he gasped. He raised his pistol, but we both froze at the distinctive *thunk* we'd heard once before—the discharge of an air rifle.

51

Tuesday, June 22, cont.

Herman's finger barely made contact with the trigger as he sought to find a clear line between the two ladies-in-waiting sitting across from the old queen; they partially obscured his view. He considered shooting the one to his left. *I'd have time for a second clear shot before anyone could react,* he thought. Then he shook his head. *How much sin can one soul bear?*

The view of Victoria's seat was unobstructed on her right side—his left—as was a portion of her right shoulder. Perhaps a shot into the seat beside her would be enough to distract the queen and cause her to lean into view, much as one might fire into the air to flush out a pheasant. He sighted carefully and—as he let his breath ease out—the rifle coughed.

Her Majesty was deeply moved by the cheers of the crowd, and although the day was warm and moist, she savored sitting beneath her parasol as she took in the harmonious blending of the boys' singing above her.

She was lost in remembering other times when suddenly she felt the back of her seat shudder violently. She looked down and saw a trace of the cushion stuffing peeking out of a fresh hole. She looked up and saw a flash of light from the boys' boarding school. Her two household guards sitting above and behind her seemed oblivious in their boredom.

Her jaw set. "Ladies," she said in a calm voice, "please shift to your right. We wish to admire the colonel's fine horse." They did so and Her Majesty, empress of the British Empire, all four feet and ten inches of her, stared into the darkness of the window, and lifted her chin.

Herman lay poised, waiting for a panicked royal carriage to give him a second shot. He saw the small figure in black look down, then to his amazement the ladies-in-waiting shifted to their right and the queen stared straight at him. She neither moved nor looked away, as though daring him to fire.

Nothing could save her now. Herman's finger caressed the trigger, then it settled into place. She was still staring at him. She knew what was coming and wasn't afraid. *She put others out of harm's way.*

Herman knew no kaiser, no tsar, would ever do this, and he finally understood why she was loved while the other two were merely feared. She could be killed. She could not be cowed.

A pity, he thought, as the crosshairs were sliding down to align with her face. Then the door crashed open and on instinct he half-rolled to his left as he jerked the rifle to the right and fired.

"No!" James moaned and his jaw clenched. "We're too late!" His right hand fell to his side. "I've failed her." His hand came back up as he cocked the large bore pistol. "I'll make the bastard pay!"

He flew to the door and kicked it in as I followed right behind.

I saw the man with a rifle lying atop a bunk bed. I gasped. *The Russian. What a fool I was!*

The rifle spun toward us and coughed. The cheering of the crowd reached our ears as I looked down in horror and saw the bloodstain spreading across James's chest. The assassin stared at me as he reloaded his rifle. I was mesmerized as I heard the rattle of the lead balls in the magazine as he tilted the barrel and slid a bullet into the breech.

"Her name was Astrid," he said, as the barrel swung toward me.

The moment seemed frozen in time and I had an eternity to act. James's knees began to fold as he jerked his hand up and his Webley spat flame just as I fired my derringer.

The assassin released his rifle and sighed once, then lay still, a strange smile on his face.

Herman was back in Berlin, the warm spring sun shining between the branches of the trees. His head was on Astrid's stomach, and her voice was singing once more of the time of cherries.

"Je ne vivrai pas, sans souffrir un jour, J'aimerai toujours le temps des cerises, et le souvenir, que je garde au coeur."

"I do not live one day without grief, I'll always remember the time of cherries, and the memory I keep in my heart."

He closed his eyes, and the sound of the river flowing past grew louder. He let it carry him to a distant shore, where all were equal, and where Astrid awaited.

I stood beside James and as he wavered, helped him slide softly to the floor and onto his back. He labored to breathe, his face now a waxy white that told me he had but moments left. "The Queen?" he whispered.

The crowd had fallen silent, and I feared the worst when suddenly a strong voice called out, "Three cheers for the Queen!" and was awarded jubilantly by nearly half of London.

"Hear the crowd, James," I whispered. "She's fine. Our sniper missed. We saved her."

He managed a weak smile. "My final case solved. I ended better than average, after all."

I touched his face. "You were never average, James. Know that you are deeply loved and respected by Elizabeth . . . and me."

He coughed. "I'm sorry we end here. Margaret . . . take care of Elizabeth?"

"Like she was my own, James."

He started to say something more, then his chest slowly shrank in on itself and I breathed in the aroma of sandalwood and boot polish one last time. I put his hands in mine. Warm hands, and I held them, trying to preserve their warmth as long as I could.

They were just starting to go cold when the two angry constables returned with reinforcements and found me still holding those hands and cradling James's head in my lap, weeping for what might have been, regretting the second time in my life I'd been afraid to leap.

After the choir sang the final hymn, the Queen's carriage was supposed to move forward, but it didn't. There was a long pause of total silence from all, no one knowing what to do next. Then the Archbishop of Canterbury, in complete disregard for protocol, cried out, "Three cheers for the Queen!"

The Bishop of London recalled it thus: *"Never were cheers given with such startling unanimity and precision. All the horses threw up their heads at the same moment and gave a little quiver of surprise. When the cheers were over, the band and chorus, by an incredible impulse, broke into 'God Save the Queen.'"*

52

Tuesday, June 22, cont.

Herr Grüber had chosen a seat close to the Houses of Parliament, looking forward to the anguish soon to come, so when the royal procession rolled by to the adulation of the masses, he shook his head.

"Something wrong, mate?" The man to his right asked.

Grüber's smile was thin. "This isn't quite what I was expecting."

The man shrugged. "There's fireworks, bands, a grand parade, and Her Majesty herself. How could you possibly be disappointed?'

"I suppose it's a matter of perspective."

Police Commissioner Bradford had been among those granted a place of honor on the steps, so when he was notified about the sniper found in the school he arrived quickly. I watched, numb, as James's body was covered with a blanket from one of the beds. The boy and his groggy nurse were moved to other quarters. Between the commissioner's questioning of me and his examination of the scene, he quickly put together what had happened.

Elizabeth and I sat together on chairs placed outside the room, holding hands as we wept. Sir Edward leaned down to Elizabeth and placed his hand on her shoulder. "Your father died nobly. Never forget that. I, and an entire empire, are in his debt." Then Bradford turned to me. "The assassin's nationality puts us in an awkward position. If this gets out, war with Germany is almost certain. Things are heated enough with the Boer situation. I'll speak to the Home Secretary, but I think we'll want to keep this quiet. Can I count upon your discretion, Miss Harkness?"

I released my hold of Elizabeth and stood to be eye-to-eye with the man. I noted his empty left sleeve. *No coward*, I thought. *Now, let's see if he's a man of honor.*

I took a deep breath. "May we speak in private?"

53

Tuesday, June 22, to Thursday, June 24
The Ethington apartment

Sir Edward agreed to all my conditions without hesitation, proving he was indeed as honorable as he was brave. I felt more tired than I had my entire life. Time to discuss the future with Elizabeth and see what else I might lose this day.

I called her to the kitchen, and we sagged into our chairs to sip tea. I took a deep breath, then sat my cup down and began.

"Your father's last wish was for me to look after you but I have no legal standing to do so. However, if you agree to my being your guardian, we'll need to go to court. Commissioner Bradford has said he'll speak on my behalf, if you request it."

I took both of Elizabeth's hands in mine. "But if there is a relative, or someone else you'd prefer, I'll bow out. I am still bound for Australia the seventh of next month, so if you would rather stay here, I'll do all I can to expedite the process. Once we board the ship, there's no turning back."

Elizabeth sat silent for a moment, then she stood and extended her arms. "There's nothing for me here, Margaret. Let me be, if not your daughter, at least your friend and companion."

I thought about what it would be like to have someone across the table from me every day. To share a joke, or just to sit together in companionable silence. I knew that some handsome young Australian man who knew how to ride would all too soon take her away. *Time enough to mourn that day when it comes.*

"Aye," I answered, hugging her tightly. "For as long as may be."

The funeral service was well attended by James's colleagues in the force, and I sat beside Elizabeth to her left, Police Commissioner Bradford on her right. Senior Inspector Murdock surprised the attendees with his heartfelt eulogy, and more than a few of the stalwart constables and inspectors had need of their handkerchief before he'd finished.

As we were preparing to leave the gravesite, Sir Edward paid Elizabeth his parting respects and presented her with the senior inspector badge her father would have worn. A fine family heirloom to be sure, but a cold metal shield was a poor substitute for the kind and warm man it was intended for.

I never inquired as to who had fired the fatal shot into our assassin. Perhaps it was James, perhaps me, perhaps both. I understood why military firing squads had some rifles loaded with blank shots, so that the members of the firing party could find solace in their ignorance.

In much the same way I often wondered how things might have been different if I'd asked James to join me in Australia. Perhaps it was better not to know. The dreams we cling to in the dark often provide greater comfort than the truths we must confront at daybreak.

54

Wednesday, July 7
Aboard the HMS **Hampton**

When we boarded, the porters were amused that neither Elizabeth nor myself would entrust our hatboxes to them. I'm sure they assumed each contained some frilly woman's bonnet. They would have been surprised to know that both enclosed a man's black derby—Elizabeth's old but well-tended, save for a recently acquired bullet hole, a reminder of times past, and mine which was recently purchased, a reminder of what could have been.

We were pleased to learn we would share our table for eight with six members of a touring company of actors and musicians who were performing comic operas by Gilbert and Sullivan. Four of our table companions were bit players and understudies, and the other two the pianist and second violin.

"The director, conductor, and principal actors travel first-class," explained Mister Woolsey, the second violinist and music librarian, "as well as our young violin prodigy, Albert. The majority of our musicians we hire from the local area to reduce our traveling expenses. Employing local musicians also ensures that several of their friends and family will attend, so we usually make a profit from their hire."

He shrugged. "But a stodgy old war horse like me can't complain when I get to break bread with charming ladies like yourselves."

I looked up from my soup and put my spoon down. "Tell me, Mister Woolsey, will you be performing during our journey?"

"Of course, Madam. We must practice, and there's no better

rehearsal than before an audience. Is there a particular piece you'd like to hear?"

I looked across the table at Margaret chatting with a young actor and recalled my words to her that one's enemies could be your best teachers. Mine had taught me the value of friendship. I returned my gaze to the musician.

"Schubert's *Serenade* has recently become one of my favorites."

I could tell the old musician approved. "A beautiful piece, and a challenging one. I could speak with Albert to arrange a performance for you if you'd like."

I shook my head. "I'd much prefer you play it for me if you would. I was told by someone dear to me that only a mature artist like yourself can properly shape the silence."

EPILOGUE

Herr Grüber was in a foul mood when he boarded the overnight ferry from Stone Haven to Rotterdam and took scant notice of the two Italian gentlemen with a large steamer trunk in the adjacent cabin. The next morning as the steward made his rounds with hot tea, he noted Grüber's cabin was empty and suitcase gone, well before the ship entered harbor. As he surveyed the disarray of the bedding, he surmised the passenger hadn't slept very well. In that he was correct; Grüber had not slept at all.

AFTERWORD

This book is a work of fiction, though it was closely modeled on real events and people. Following, I list the various true personages in my story, and some of the facts I used to flesh out their character, as well as a few other odds and ends. I am a history geek, so I hope you find these details as interesting as I do.

PEOPLE

Archduke Franz Ferdinand

Fourteen years after Queen Victoria's death, her grandson would wage war with England, one caused by the assassination of the queen's tablemate the night prior to her royal procession. The portly Archduke Franz Ferdinand was felled by Gavrilo Princip, a member of the Black Hand, a secret Serbian military society dedicated to the unification of the Slavic people under one throne. He was not an anarchist, as several history books have erroneously reported.

As predicted by Herr Grüber, the war which followed brought the end of ruling aristocracies in Europe.

Queen Victoria

Queen Victoria insisted that no ruling
heads of state be invited to her Diamond
Jubilee celebration because she didn't
want to bother with protocol, nor with
having to house them during their visit.
(Lesser nobility were allowed.) From 1861
until her death in 1901, in mourning for
Prince Albert, she wore only black and
she refused to wear a crown or carry her
scepter during the royal procession. Her

one concession to her status was having gems sewn around the brim
of her bonnet, and this became quite the fashion for a short time
afterward.

In real life, she survived eight assassination attempts by seven
would-be assassins. John Francis tried to kill her on two successive
days (May 29 and 30, 1842) while she rode in her carriage through
a park. The Queen refused to alter her route the second day despite
the danger, though she forbade her ladies-in-waiting to accompany
her. The assassin's pistol misfired on the first attempt, but on day two
it functioned flawlessly. Fortunately, Prince Albert pulled his wife
down just as the bullet flew over her head. The Queen's concern for
the safety of others while disdaining the risk to herself inspired the
scene when she has her ladies-in-waiting shift to their right, out of
the assassin's line of fire, leaving her fully exposed.

A video segment of the Diamond Jubilee's procession can be
found on YouTube (https://www.youtube.com/watch?v=jnip
7RRc3Q4). Between the timestamps of 1:38 and 1:50, the Queen is
shown briefly in the carriage drawn by six cream-colored horses: She
is the small dark figure in the carriage that appears for perhaps three
seconds. At approximately four feet ten inches, this diminutive woman
was empress to the largest realm ever known.

Police Commissioner
Sir Edward Bradford

Sir Edward Bradford spent the majority of his military career in India, where he lost his left arm to a tigress, greatly impressing Indian royalty. He was appointed police commissioner after his tour of duty as Queen Victoria's aide-de-camp and served in that capacity from 1890 to 1903. He was responsible for the preservation of law and order in a city with over six million inhabitants, utilizing a force of only fourteen thousand men. He was active and well-respected by the men of his force. He insisted all stations be linked by telegraph, greatly enhancing the communications within the force, though in later years he refused to install telephones, preferring the brevity that telegraphs required.

His record of accomplishment as police commissioner is remarkable. When he assumed command, the Metropolitan Police were held in poor regard for their beatings of protestors during a public demonstration in 1887, and the police were actively striking. He settled the strike, established more stations, bettered the conditions in the older ones, established a summer uniform and insisted shifts be varied to prevent boredom. Easygoing by nature, at one time or another he visited every station, talked with the officers, and listened. In 1899 London recorded its lowest crime rate in the city's history, and the force was respected by all law-abiding citizens.

Luigi Parmeggiani

Signore Parmeggiani was a man of many talents, few of them legal. He was at one time an ardent anarchist and bomb-maker, but by the time we meet him in the story he had become the manager of two antiquity stores, one in Paris and the other in London. He often went by the name of Louis Macy. He founded the "Macy Collection," a line of minor art objects which wound up in private collections and smaller museums. Most of them turned out to be fakes.

Peter Kropotkin

Descendent of royalty (the Rurik Dynasty), as a young man he led geographic expeditions into Siberia and the Arctic, but his political activities led to his imprisonment in Russia. He escaped to Western Europe and lived in England, Switzerland, and France before returning shortly after the Bolshevik Revolution to Russia, where he died four years later.

Herman Ott/Viktor Zhelyabov

Andrei Zhelyabov, the lover of Sofia, was a leader of the anarchist group which successfully assassinated Tsar Alexander II on their third attempt. Sofia Perovskaya was also a real person and served as lookout for the assassination. She was reunited with her lover Andrei in prison after the assassination and they were hanged together shortly afterward. His younger brother, Viktor/Herman, is a fictional character.

Professor Joseph Bell

Fourth generation of a line of surgeons in Edinburgh, Bell was renowned both for his clinical skills (he was the Surgeon in Attendance to Her Majesty when she was in Scotland), and his keen powers of observation. He assisted the police in various cases. The two best known are the Jack the Ripper murders, in which he analyzed the handwriting of the notes signed Jack the Ripper, and the Monson murder case in Argyle, Scotland, this being the case that Oberst Adler mentions when first meeting Bell in my story.

Bell was Arthur Conan Doyle's professor of surgery while Doyle was a student in Edinburgh, and Doyle served briefly as his clerk of the surgery service. Years later Doyle would recall Bell's keen powers of observation and create the most famous fictional detective of all time, Sherlock Holmes.

Margaret Harkness

The image to the right is the only portrait of Margaret I could find. Despite spending some time in the company of George Bernard Shaw, an avid cameraman, no photograph of her is known to exist, which I believe only adds to her mystique.

I do not know if she was in the habit of wearing men's clothing or carrying a derringer, but everything else I have written in the book regarding her literary career and biography is accurate, except that in 1897 she was already residing in Australia.

Those interested in knowing more about Margaret can reference the excellent article about her on the Victorian Web (http://victorianweb.org/gender/harkness.html), a website for researchers into that era.

The Harkives is a fabulous website devoted entirely to Margaret's life and works (https://theharkives.wordpress.com).

ODDS AND ENDS

The Girandoni Air Rifle
I am indebted to Dr. Beeman and his excellent website (http://www.beemans.net/Austrian%20airguns.htm).

The air rifle I use in the story is closely modeled on one used by the Austrian army in the late eighteenth century. Capable of firing large-caliber lead balls at the astounding rate of one shot per second from a magazine holding up to twenty balls, it was greatly feared, and any soldier captured with one in their possession was executed on the spot as a sniper.

In my story, I make the butt-stock/air reservoir more fragile than it was in real life, though it wasn't as sturdy as a conventional firearm. Its principal weakness was the difficulty in pressurizing the flasks up to 800 psi, and the hand pump issued with it required over one thousand strokes. Typically, a sniper would be issued three flasks and they would be repressurized in the rear lines by a large rotating pump.

A Girandoni rifle, or one very similar to it, was carried by the Lewis and Clarke expedition but was used mainly for demonstrations to intimidate the tribes they encountered.

There's an excellent YouTube video demonstrating the operation and the actual sound of one firing (https://www.youtube.com/watch?v=VPjJ1Jcznzw).

St. Paul's Boys Choir Boarding School

I am indebted also to the staff of the Youth Hostel Association (YHA) London St. Paul's Youth Hostel (https://www.hihostels.com/hostels/yha-london-st-pauls).

Photo: Chere A Harper

The picture to the right was taken by my daring wife, Chere, from the (second floor European, third floor American), window of the old boarding school for the boys' choir as she lay on the top bunk. As you can see, it is on a side street ending at the plaza outside the cathedral. Together we measured eighty-eight paces from the inscription marking where the royal carriage sat to the wall directly beneath this window, well within the range of the model air rifle Herman carries in my story.

The Kruger Telegram

The Kruger Telegram was sent by Kaiser Wilhelm II to president Kruger of the Transvaal Republic, on January 3, 1896, congratulating the president on repelling the Jameson Raid, a sortie by six hundred British irregulars from Cape Colony into the Transvaal. The raid was a disaster for the British with sixty-five raiders killed to only one Boer, the rest surrendering. The telegram caused great indignation in Great Britain as it was taken as an endorsement by the Kaiser of the Transvaal's independence in what was seen by the British as their sphere of influence.

People in England were so angry that the windows of German shops were broken, and German sailors were attacked on the streets of London. A chastened Kaiser wrote a letter of apology to his grandmother and the anger died down somewhat, but was still a sore spot at the time of the Diamond Jubilee.

ACKNOWLEDGMENTS

I am indebted to the head concierge of the Hotel Rome in Berlin, for sharing with me the hotel's legend that it once provided the Kaiser with a bathtub on a weekly basis while the palace was undergoing renovation.

The tarot card sequence was due to the kindness of Sorin Lucien. He is a regular instructor in the practice, and I gave him a short biography of Margaret and asked him to construct a reading that would be sufficiently in tune with her later life. I was thrilled with the result.

I would like to thank my various beta readers who helped this aging man write from a woman's perspective. Any failings in that endeavor are entirely my own. Susan Putnam, Eleanore Brennan, Karen Chase, Vivian Makosky, Ted Petrocci, Milyn King, my agent, Jill Marr, and my freelance editors who helped make the manuscript a coherent document, Lourdes Venard, Derek McFadden, and Petra Winters. I was thrilled to work on the final version with Dan Mayer of Seventh Street Books, who was also my line editor for my first novel. Working with him is a joy and a true collaboration. I am especially grateful to my friend and mentor, John DeDakis, who read an early draft written entirely in third person, and it was he who suggested I write Margaret's parts in her own voice. My wife, Chere, was both beta reader and editor of last resort, as her eyes always make the final pass, before I hit "send."

The map of the cathedral and boarding school was created by Stephanie Caruso of Paste Creative, my social media assistant and all-around cyber-elf.

A special shout-out to Christopher Spencer. Christian was only seventeen years old when he read this and was helpful in giving me a young person's perspective. I am a professional Santa Claus and he was my elf in 2018 when we worked a Christmas party for children with cancer and their families. Later he told me how much that affected him, then told me wanted to do it again, next year. He reassures me that the world will be fine in his generation's hands.

Le Temps des Cerises, with lyrics in French, English, and Mandarin, as well as a brief history of the song's significance, can be found on YouTube (https://www.youtube.com/watch?v=E9bV8F6QLyo).

Much of my information regarding anarchists was found within the excellent reference book, *The World That Never Was*, by Alex Butterworth (Pantheon Books, New York, 2010).

ABOUT THE AUTHOR

Bradley Harper is a retired US Army Pathologist with over thirty-seven years of worldwide military/medical experience, ultimately serving as a Colonel/Physician in the Pentagon. During his Army career, Harper performed some two hundred autopsies, twenty of which were forensic.

Upon retiring from the Army, Harper earned an associate's degree in creative writing from Full Sail University. He has been published in *The Strand Magazine, Flash Fiction Magazine, The Sherlock Holmes Mystery Magazine* and a short story he wrote involving Professor Moriarty in the Holmes tale of "The Red-Headed League" (entitled "The Red Herring League") won Honorable Mention in an international short fiction contest. A member of the Mystery Writers of America, Authors Guild, and Sisters in Crime, Harper is a regular contributor to the Sisters in Crime bi-monthly newsletter.

Harper's first novel, *A Knife in the Fog*, involves a young Arthur Conan Doyle joining in the hunt for Jack the Ripper, and was a finalist for an 2019 Edgar Award by the Mystery Writers of America for Best First Novel by an American Author, and the audiobook version won Audiofile Magazine's 2019 Earphone Award in the category of Mystery and Suspense.